# THE MISCELLANEOUS WRITINGS OF
# CLARK ASHTON SMITH

# THE MISCELLANEOUS WRITINGS OF CLARK ASHTON SMITH

Edited by Scott Connors and Ron Hilger

With an Introduction by Donald Sidney-Fryer

Night Shade Books
San Francisco

Jacket design by Claudia Noble
Interior layout and design by Amy Popovich



**First Edition**

ISBN: 978-1-59780-297-0

**Night Shade Books**
Please visit us on the web at
http://www.nightshadebooks.com

# CONTENTS

Foreword by Scott Connors and Ron Hilger . . . . . . VII
Introduction: The Sorcerer Departs by Donald Sidney-Fryer 1

The Animated Sword . . . . . . . . . . . . . . . . . . . 45
The Red Turban . . . . . . . . . . . . . . . . . . . . . 51
Prince Alcouz and the Magician . . . . . . . . . . . . . 57
The Malay Krise . . . . . . . . . . . . . . . . . . . . 59
The Ghost of Mohammed Din . . . . . . . . . . . . . . . 63
The Mahout . . . . . . . . . . . . . . . . . . . . . . . 71
The Rajah and the Tiger . . . . . . . . . . . . . . . . 77
Something New . . . . . . . . . . . . . . . . . . . . . 83
The Flirt . . . . . . . . . . . . . . . . . . . . . . . 87
The Perfect Woman . . . . . . . . . . . . . . . . . . . 89
A Platonic Entanglement . . . . . . . . . . . . . . . . 91
The Expert Lover . . . . . . . . . . . . . . . . . . . 95
The Parrot . . . . . . . . . . . . . . . . . . . . . . 105
A Copy of Burns . . . . . . . . . . . . . . . . . . . . 109
Checkmate . . . . . . . . . . . . . . . . . . . . . . . 113
The Infernal Star . . . . . . . . . . . . . . . . . . . 119
Dawn of Discord . . . . . . . . . . . . . . . . . . . . 145
House of the Monoceros . . . . . . . . . . . . . . . . 163
The Dead Will Cuckold You . . . . . . . . . . . . . . . 179
The Hashish-Eater; or, The Apocalypse of Evil . . . . . 203

Appendix One: Bibliography . . . . . . . . . . . . . . 221
Appendix Two: O Amor Atque Realitas!
by Donald Sidney-Fryer . . . . . . . . . . . . . . . . 225

# Foreword

## by Scott Connors and Ron Hilger

With the completion of *The Collected Fantasies of Clark Ashton Smith*, all of Clark Ashton Smith's mature stories in the genre have been brought back into print. There remains a sizeable body of work, mostly juvenile stories (some of which were published professionally) and a number of experiments in ironic writing that he made in the early twenties, and again in the early 1930s. Many readers have requested these works, which can not even be called journeyman's pieces, so we bring them together here, where they are presented as not being more than what they are, the lesser works of a major fantasist, along with a few treats for the hardcore casophile.

Clark Ashton Smith was a lonely and precocious child who found comfort in books, and by the age of eleven he was writing fairy tales based upon those of Hans Christian Andersen and the Countess D'Aulnoy. The vistas of his writing were widened to encompass the *Arabian Nights*, William Beckford's gothic phantasmagoria *Vathek* (one of whose uncompleted episodes he would later complete in an early exercise in "posthumous collaboration"), and Rudyard Kipling's tales set in British colonial India. Stories told by his father, Timeus Ashton-Smith, who had traveled extensively in Asia and South America before settling in California, undoubtedly contributed to the young Smith's developing imagination. Curiously, although the discovery of the works of Edgar Allan Poe at the age of thirteen seemed "to have confirmed me in a more or less permanent slant" toward the weird and decadent, Smith's earliest stories fail to reveal much overt influence. Poe cast a more subtle, and profound, shadow on the fledgling writer in an unpublished document from this period, "Story-Writing":

> The first thing essential to a good short-story is clear and logical construction. Every incident should be in its place, and should tend to the climax. No incident or person unneccesary [*sic*] to the plot must be included. A good plot poorly developed or illy-constructed [sic] is inferior to a poor or commonplace plot well developed and constructed.
>
> Clearness and terseness of style is the second requisite. Express your thoughts as clearly as possible and as tersely as is compatible with clearness—omit every unessential word, phrase, or sentence. The shorter the story the better—but nothing neccessary [*sic*] must be left out. The idea is to tell the tale in the fewest words possible without sacrificing clearness and force, or omitting any essential detail. Avoid all padding. Repetition of ideas in the same words is unbearable. A thorough knowledge of synonyms is invaluable to the story-writer.
>
> Most stories are spoiled by lack of finish. A commonplace idea when well told is more acceptable than a brilliant thought poorly expressed.
>
> Always revise your stories. Close and vigorous scrutiny will often reveal some hitherto unobserved crudity, and a crudity, no matter how small, spoils the story. All errors of grammar, spelling, and punctuation must be corrected, for tho [*sic*] the tale is otherwise good, an editor has no time to correct such mistakes—and punctuation will save you many postage stamps. It is desirable that you should have some talent to begin with but talent without perseverance is of little use. Success in literature, as in other things, is largely a matter of hard work.[1]

Several points are apparent in this document. First, Smith had grasped the principle of "unity of effect" outlined by Poe in "The Philosophy of Composition." Second, even at this early age he had a sense for the nuances of language. He had by this time read *Webster's Unabridged Dictionary*, making a thorough study of both the meanings and etymologies of its contents and would develop a knack for distinguishing the subtle variations between words of nearly (but not quite!) identical meaning. Third, the technique of composition which Sidney-Fryer describes in *Emperor of Dreams*[2] and elsewhere, involving several re-writings and revisions, complete with reading aloud on strolls with a sense as to the musicality of the prose, originated early in Smith's career. This is an altogether remarkable and not unsophisticated aesthetic theory for one not yet past the middle of his teenage years.

When dealing with the juvenilia of any given author, many factors are involved in the decision regarding whether or not to publish this material, assuming that the author is deceased or otherwise unable to grant his or her permission. The author's wishes, insofar as they can be discerned, must still be considered, along with the actual literary quality of this material, the author's reputation and popularity, what the writings contribute to our understanding of the author's life and work, and the amount of such material already available to interested readers.

In the specific case of Clark Ashton Smith, we can surmise something of his intent regarding his juvenilia even though he left no direct instructions regarding it. The very fact that Smith saved his juvenilia for some fifty years before distributing it among his friends and family during his last years tells us that he obviously did not want it destroyed, and believed (or hoped) that his first literary endeavors would be of interest to someone, someday. This is in contrast to the destruction of much of his writings between the publication of his first two collections of poetry, *The Star-Treader and Other Poems* and *Odes and Sonnets*, in 1912 and 1918, respectively.

In recent years much of Smith's juvenile writing has seen publication, beginning with *The Black Diamonds*, a long (over 90,000 words) and involved adventure story written before his fifteenth year, followed by another shorter novel, *The Sword of Zagan*, written a few years later. In addition to these substantial works, a number of short stories have also been published, but more remain unpublished among the Smith Papers deposited at the John Hay Library of Brown University, where they may be found alongside the manuscripts of Smith's great friend H. P. Lovecraft. One story which has not previously been collected is a brief vignette entitled "Prince Alcouz and the Magician," which was first published as a chapbook thirteen years after his death. (An earlier draft, "Prince Alcorez and the Magician," was among the papers that Smith gave to a young friend, William C. Farmer, who published it along with *The Sword of Zagan* and other early works in 2004.) While not much more than a vignette, this brief story displays one of Smith's principal themes, irony, in a manner that he would display to greater advantage in such stories as "The Weird of Avoosl Wuthoqquan," while also displaying a contempt for self-important autocrats that would come to fruition in such stories as "The Seven Geases" and "The Voyage of King Euvoran."

Also published in *The Sword of Zagan* was an untitled fragment which concerned a stolen sapphire and a lost turban. While researching the index of the Clark Ashton Smith Papers at Brown University, it became apparent that a two page fragment titled "The Red Turban" might well be the lost beginning to this untitled piece. A subsequent examination of the pages in question confirmed that the two fragments fit together seamlessly, and detail the investigation by the chief of police in Delhi into the theft of a large and valuable sapphire. This hand-written piece is apparently influenced by the Indian tales of Rudyard Kipling, and closely resembles "The Bronze Image" in style and format. Written over one hundred years ago and separated shortly before Smith's death in 1961, we proudly include this recently re-assembled tale as yet another example of the hard-working young Clark Ashton Smith.

And what of the quality of CAS' juvenilia? If "The Animated Sword" (which dates from around 1905–06 when Smith was twelve or thirteen) is any indication it is obvious that the young Smith was light-years ahead of even the most precocious of his peers. Smith exhibits a natural talent for story telling even in his earliest works, a talent that he developed constantly throughout his lifetime. We are pleased to present this gem to Smith's readers as a harbinger of future glories.

Smith's first known appearance in print was with a poem, "The Sierras," in the September 1910 issue of *Munsey's*. The next month saw the appearance of his first published short story, "The Malay Krise," in *The Overland Monthly*, a prominent West Coast magazine founded by Bret Harte. This is a reworking of a story called "The Afghan Knife" that may be found in a notebook bearing the title of *Tales of India*.

The November 1910 issue of the same magazine contained a second story, "The Ghost of Mohammed Din," which is notable for being his first published story with a supernatural theme. As is evident from the title, the most apparent influence is that of Kipling, with perhaps some of Robert Louis Stevenson, but these stories also reveal a taste for exoticism and irony, as well as a surprising competence for plot. Some critics would charge that in his later stories Smith failed to handle plot well. If we follow the definition of Smith's friend E. Hoffmann Price, that a story is a narrative in which something happens, then these early stories demonstrate Smith's mastery of this aspect of the short story at a very early stage of his career. What these critics fail to grasp is that as Smith's aesthetic evolved, he would advance the story less by action and more by atmosphere.

Two of Smith's stories were also published in *The Black Cat*: "The Mahout" in August 1911 (later reworked for *Oriental Stories* in 1931 as "The Justice of the Elephant"), and "The Tiger" appeared in the February 1912 (as "The Raja and the Tiger.") Smith was paid thirty dollars for the last story, which was not a bad sum for a lad still shy of his twentieth birthday.[3] L. Sprague de Camp offered the opinion that they were "undistinguished tales of popular adventure but up to the professional standards of the popular fiction of the time",[4] but failed to see in them signs and portents of one who would become pre-eminent among American poets and fantasists of the twentieth century.

Despite these early successes, Smith wrote no more short stories for many years. This is due to a great extent to the influence of the uncrowned King of Bohemia, George Sterling, with whom Smith began a correspondence and a friendship in 1911. Under Sterling's tutelage, Smith devoted his energies to mastering pure poetry, resulting in several fine collections beginning with 1912's *The Star-Treader and Other Poems*. A close reading of the letters exchanged between Smith and Sterling reveals that Sterling regarded prose as an inferior form of expression to poetry. This attitude was not peculiar to Sterling, but was a part of the Romantic aesthetic that went back to John Milton and his "Essay on Education." (Put succinctly, poetry was regarded as the product of imagination and emotion, while prose [also called "history," "philosophy" and "science," depending upon the commentator] was the product of reason and depicts what is "real.") For example, shortly after writing what may well be the most remarkable poem in *The Star-Treader*, the dramatic monologue "Nero," Smith half-apologized to Sterling, describing it as "four-fifths [...] prose, and not particularly good prose at that".[5] When Sterling attempted to write some short stories for sale to magazines, he sheepishly referred to his efforts "to earn a dishonest living".[6] As late as 1927 Smith would commiserate with Sterling: "Too bad you have to write prose. It's a beastly occupation" (*SL* 91). And "I don't blame you for writing prose, if you can make money by it. But it's a hateful task, for a poet, and wouldn't be necessary [sic], in any true civilization" (*SU* 292).

Despite these reservations, Smith would attempt some short stories before 1925. CAS wrote Sterling on September 9, 1915 that he had "a few short-story plots" (*SU* 132). Sterling had some influence with a romance magazine called *Snappy Stories*, and he encouraged Smith to submit some of his work, such as the prose poem "In Cocaigne." CAS reported that "*Snappy Stories* has accepted a little prose-sketch of mine, entitled 'The Flirt.' They pay 2 cents a word for prose. Maybe I'll do some more whore-mongering, at that price" (*SL* 65). For many years the only clue to the publication of "The Flirt" was a tear sheet or galley proof of the story found among the papers of Smith's friend Genevieve K. Sully. In 2007 Phil Stephensen-Payne announced on Fictionmags ( a Yahoo newsgroup) that he had located "The Flirt" in the March 1, 1923 issue of *Live Stories*, a companion magazine to *Snappy Stories.*

Another sketch, "Something New," appeared in the August 1924 issue of *10 Story Book*, for which CAS received the munificent sum of $6. He told Sterling that "the story was rotten, anyhow—except for the spanking—which was what I **ought** to have administered, some time back, to a certain badly spoiled female person." (*SU* 242)

After completing (on February 28, 1923), and failing to sell, "The Perfect Woman," Smith would not write another short story until early 1925, when he wrote his first true weird tale, "The Abominations of Yondo." When he began the composition of short stories for commercial markets in late 1929, CAS directed most of his efforts to markets such as *Weird Tales* and *Wonder Stories*, but he apparently still harbored hopes that he might expand upon his prior beachhead in the realm of "sophisticated" adult irony by writing "The Parrot" (also "The Pawnbroker's Parrot" and "The Parrot in the Pawn-Shop" [written January 5, 1930]), "A Copy of Burns" (February 27, 1930), "Checkmate" (November 7, 1930). It does not appear that Clark ever submitted these to any markets. All of these stories, along with "A Platonic Entanglement" and "The Expert Lover," are discussed in more detail by Donald Sidney-Fryer in his essay "O Amor Atque Realitas!" elsewhere in this volume.

Although we have generally decided not to include fragmentary stories in this edition (these are available in *Strange Shadows*, edited by Steve Behrends, and published by Greenwood Press in 1989), it was decided that "The Infernal Star", which is even in its unfinished state still one of Clark Ashton Smith's longest chunks of prose, deserves inclusion. Smith recorded its germ in his notebook of story ideas, the fabled *Black Book*, thus: "An extra-galactic world from which an influence of stupendous evil emanates, seeping through the farthest reaches of the cosmos".[7] This theme, which would appear to be an expansion of the core idea of "The Devotee of Evil," also appears in the famous lines from "Nyctalops," "We have seen the black suns/ Pouring forth the night." He described it in a letter to August Derleth as

> a weird-interstellar novelette de luxe. The tale involves a harmless bibliophile in a series of wild mysterious happenings, ending in his translation to Yamil Zacra, a star which is the fountain-head of all the evil and bale and sorcery in the universe. It mixes wizardry and necromancy with the latest scientific theory of "radiogens," or atoms of sun-fire, burning at a temperature of 1500 Centigrade in the human body. I am using the innocuousness of the hero's normal personality as a foil to that which he temporarily assumes beneath the influence of an amulet that stimulates those particles in his body which have come from Yamil Zacra. (*SL* 199)

As Smith worked on "The Infernal Star" he realized that it was rapidly becoming a novel. *Weird Tales* ran one or two serials per issue during this period. While Farnsworth Wright was willing to publish stories that he perhaps thought might be too good for his readership (the list of tales that the fickle Farnsworth originally rejected includes H. P. Lovecraft's "The Call of Cthulhu," Donald Wandrei's "The Red Brain," Carl Jacobi's "Revelations in Black," Robert E. Howard's "The Phoenix on the Sword" [the first adventure of Conan of Cimmeria], Smith's "The Tale of Satampra Zeiros" and "The Seven Geases," among many others), he was much more conservative in his choice of serials; of all the serials that ran in *Weird Tales*, only those by Robert E. Howard, as well as Jack Williamson's "Golden Blood" (April to September 1933) are generally well-regarded today. One reason why "The Infernal Star" (which according to a fragmentary holograph first draft was originally to be titled "The Dark Star") grew was that it seemed that CAS wanted to use it in the same manner that Lovecraft did "The Whisperer in Darkness," tying together elements of his own invented mythologies (Hyperborea, Averoigne, Poseidonis, Zothique) along with those of Lovecraft and Ambrose Bierce. Smith eventually bowed to reality and put "The Infernal Star" aside "since there is no prospect of landing it as a serial even if completed. Wright is so heavily loaded down with long tales (all of them tripe, I dare say) that he can't even consider anything over 15,000 words till next year" (*SL* 203).

After a brief spurt of productivity in the early fifties, Smith began to exhibit a reluctance to write anything, even letters. He had toyed with the idea of completing "The Infernal Star", and August Derleth encouraged him with an offer of Arkham House publication despite his own lack of enthusiasm for the work itself.

"Dawn of Discord" and "House of Monoceros" appear on Smith's completed stories log after "Double Cosmos" (originally "Secondary Cosmos"), which was completed on March 25, 1940 although he had been working on it intermittently since 1934.

Late in 1938 *Weird Tales* was purchased by a New York businessman, William J. Delaney, who already published the highly successful pulp *Short Stories*. Delaney relocated the operation to New York City. Wright was kept on as editor and made the move, but was let go with the March 1940 issue. An interview with Delaney appeared in a fanzine at the time of Wright's dismissal that boded ill for Smith. After promising that *Weird Tales* would continue to publish "all types of weird and fantasy fiction," the interview went on to add:

> There is one rule, however: *Weird Tales* does not want stories which center about sheer repulsiveness, stories which leave an impression not to be described by any other word than "nasty". This is not to imply that the "grim" story, or the tale which leaves the reader gasping at the verge of the unknown, is eliminated. Mr. Delaney believes that the story which leaves a sickish feeling in the reader is not truly weird and has no place in *Weird Tales*. . . . And, finally, stories wherein the characters are continually talking in French, German, Latin, etc. will be frowned upon, as well as stories wherein the reader must constantly consult an unabridged dictionary.[8]

The interviewer was Robert A. W. Lowndes, who shed some light on this in a letter published years later:

> Delaney, who was a pleasant and cultured man, was very fond of weird stories, but he was also a strict Catholic. . . . He also found some of the Clark Ashton Smith stories on the 'disgusting' side and told me that he had returned one that Wright had in his inventory when he left. It was about a monstrous worm which, when attacked and pierced, shed forth rivers of slime. Later in 1940, when Donald A. Wollheim was starting *Stirring Science Stories*, Smith sent him 'The Coming of the White Worm' and Don used it. When I read it, there was no doubt that this was the story Delaney had been talking about. . . . Concerned about the magazine's slipping circulation, he felt that the "more esoteric" type of story was a handicap, so this was mostly cut out.[9]

The memoirs of E. Hoffmann Price illustrate just how frustrated and upset Smith was with this development and with magazine publishing in general. When Price visited Smith later that year, Smith presented him with the typescripts of "House of the Monoceros" and "Dawn of Discord." Smith told Price to do what he wanted to do with them: "Scrap the goddamn things if after all you don't like them. The less I hear of them—." Price's take on this was that Smith realized "his stories did not fit into the publisher's new pattern. Clark, fed up with adverse criticism or outright rejection, rejected the rejector, and gave me the scripts."[10]

The *Spicy* line of pulps that were published by Culture Publications (a subsidiary imprint of Harry Donenfeld's Trojan Publications) were one of Price's main markets, and he pared Smith's prose to fit their formula, which he, according to fellow writer Henry Kuttner, described as "sex, sadism, and destruction of valuable property."[11] (Kuttner also observed that "words over three syllables seem to be out, definitely.") "Dawn of Discord" appeared in the October 1940 issue of *Spicy Mystery Stories*, while "House of the Monoceros" was published (as "The Old Gods Eat") in the February 1941 issue. According to Price's records, the proceeds were split 33-67 in CAS' favor,[12] although both stories appeared under Price's byline alone. Smith did acknowledge his authorship to friends, writing in a letter that "My latest yarn is a filthy mixture of sex and pseudo science...which won't appear under my own name but under that of a friend, a very successful pulp-writer, who had more commissions on hand than he could get through with." (*SL* 330) "House of the Monoceros" was reprinted, under its original title, in Price's collection *Far Lands, Other Days* (Carcosa, 1975), without credit to Smith, but "Dawn of Discord" has not been reprinted until now.

When Price was asked about the whereabouts of CAS' original versions many years later, Price claimed that he destroyed them, stating that "Scripts were not sacred relics." In the absence of Smith's original manuscript it is impossible to determine just where Smith ends and Price begins, but it is still possible to wager a guess. "Dawn of Discord" resembles the science fiction stories that CAS had written for Hugo Gernsback, especially "The Letter from Mohaun Los" and "The Dark Age," but the misanthropy that had long embued Smith's work had taken center stage. Smith's letters make it clear that he was observing the deteriorating world situation with alarm. Writing shortly after Lovecraft's death to R. H. Barlow, who was at that time advocating communism as a panacea to contemporary social-economic problems, Smith observed bitterly that:

> I have no faith in *any* political or economic isms, schisms, and panaceas. Theoretically, almost any kind of a system might serve well enough, if human beings were not the stupidest and greediest and most cruel of the fauna on this particular planet. No matter what system you have—capitalism, Fascism, Bolshevism—the greed and power-lust of men will produce the same widespread injustice, the same evils and abuses: or, will merely force them to take slightly different forms.

He concluded "In my opinion, the whole fabric of western civilization is nearly due for a grand debacle" (*SL* 300). A few letters later, he told Barlow that "the word 'civilization' would make a jackal vomit in view of the general situation" (*SL* 313) We speculate that the conclusion of Smith's version of "Dawn of Discord" ended with the discovery that John King's temporal excursion itself was responsible for introducing warfare into history, but unless the original typescript should turn up in the late Mr. Price's papers, it remains mere conjecture.

We suspect that "House of the Monoceros" originally was similar to Smith's contemporary horror stories such as "The Nameless Offspring," but where bits of Smith occasionally flash through in "Dawn of Discord," little remains outside of the name Treganneth and the word "monoceros" itself. There may be little of Smith's original concepts left in these two stories, but the Smith afficionado may find something of interest in them.

"The Dead Will Cuckold You" was described by Smith as one of his "few unpublished masterpieces" (*SL* 373). While the author's omnipresent touch of irony was almost certainly not entirely absent from this evaluation, this play in blank verse (written during the winter of 1951 and revised in 1956) his penultimate story set in Zothique (the last continent of earth under a dying red sun) contains some of his most vivid, and most macabre, writing. Although it remained unpublished until after Smith's death, he and his friends enjoyed acting out or reading aloud its sonorous, rhythmic lines.[13]

"The Hashish-Eater; or, The Apocalypse of Evil" is Clark Ashton Smith's longest and most well-known poem; and was described by his friend H.P. Lovecraft as "the greatest imaginative orgy in English literature."[4] Written in early 1922 and published later that same year in *Ebony and Crystal,* this epic poem owes at least some of its inspiration to George Sterling and "A Wine of Wizardry," which the young Smith discovered in the pages of *Cosmopolitan* in 1907. Smith would later describe his intentions and rationale behind his cosmic masterpiece in a letter to S.J. Sackett: (*SL* 259)

> . . . *The Hashish-Eater*, a much misunderstood poem, which was intended as a study in cosmic consciousness, drawing heavily on myth and fable for much of its imagery. It is my own theory that, if the infinite worlds of the cosmos were opened to human vision, the visionary would be overwhelmed by horror in the end, like the hero of the poem.

During the preparation of his *Selected Poems,* Smith would slightly revise the poem, removing many commas and asterisks and adding a few lines and word-changes. He would also replace such British spellings as *colour, harbour*, and *rigour*, with standard American. More significantly, Smith increased the number of episodes from ten to twelve, perhaps to impart more of a classic aesthetic structure. Although this revised version has superseded the original as Smith's own preferred text, the editors felt it important to keep the *Ebony and Crystal* version in print as well for the sake of the CAS scholar who may wish to compare texts or, perhaps, who wish to experience Smith's *magnum opus* exactly as it appeared in 1922.

Unlike the other works that we have included in the Night Shade Books edition of Clark Ashton Smith, "The Hashish-Eater" is not prose, yet it contains so many germs and ideas that would find maturation in his short stories that its inclusion is warranted. This may also be said of the other pieces included in this collection: they do not represent his best work, but for the devout acolyte at the altar of Klarkash-Ton they provide glimpses of ideas that failed to come together for some reason, as well as signs and portents of wonders yet to come.

## Notes

1. Clark Ashton Smith, "Story-Writing Hints" (Ms, Clark Ashton Smith Papers, John Hay Library, Brown University).
2. Donald Sidney-Fryer, *Emperor of Dreams: A Clark Ashton Smith Bibliography* (West Kingston, RI: Donald M. Grant, 1978): 19.
3. F. E. Dyer (President, The Shortstory Publishing Co.), letter to Clark Ashton Smith, April 13, 1910 (TLS, Clark Ashton Smith Papers, John Hay Library, Brown University).
4. L. Sprague de Camp, "Sierra Shaman." *Literary Swordsmen and Sorcerers: The Makers of Heroic Fantasy* (Sauk City, WI: Arkham House, 1976): 198.
5. *Selected Letters of Clark Ashton Smith*, ed. David E. Schultz and Scott Connors (Sauk City, WI: Arkham House, 2003): 11 (hence *SL*).
6. *The Shadow of the Unattained: The Letters of George Sterling and Clark Ashton Smith*, ed. David E. Schultz and S. T. Joshi (New York: Hippocampus Press, 2005): 86.
7. *The Black Book of Clark Ashton Smith*, ed. Donald Sidney-Fryer and Rah Hoffman (Sauk City, WI: Arkham House, 1979), item 65.
8. "*Weird Tales* Stays Weird." *Science Fiction Weekly* (March 24, 1940): 1.
9. Robert A. W. Lowndes, "Letters." *Weird Tales Collector* no. 5 (1979): 31.
10. Henry Kuttner, letter to Clark Ashton Smith, September 5, 1937 (TLS, private collection).
11. See Don Herron, "Notes on Clark Ashton Smith," *Hyperborian League* mailing 12 (July 1978).
12. See William C. Farmer, "Clark Ashton Smith: A Memoir," in Smith's *The Sword of Zagan and Other Writing*, ed. W. C. Farmer (New York: Hippocampus Press, 2004): 178.
13. Quoted in George Haas, "Memories of Klarkash-Ton." In *The Black Book of Clark Ashton Smith*. Ed. Donald Sidney-Fryer and Rah Hoffman (Sauk City, WI: Arkham House, 1979): 137.

# The Sorcerer Departs

## Donald Sidney-Fryer

I pass… but in this lone and crumbling tower,
Builded against the burrowing seas of chaos,
My volumes and my philtres shall abide:
Poisons more dear than any mithridate,
And spells far sweeter than the speech of love…
Half-shapen dooms shall slumber in my vaults
And in my volumes cryptic runes that shall
Outblast the pestilence, outgnaw the worm
When loosed by alien wizards on strange years
Under the blackened moon and paling sun.

"The Sorcerer Departs"
Clark Ashton Smith
Fragment of unfinished poem (*The Acolyte*, Spring 1944).

## A Biography of Clark Ashton Smith

For those of us who recognize in the late Clark Ashton Smith a poet and a poet in prose as remarkable as the French genius Baudelaire, the preceding "fragment"—actually far more complete than many a longer poem—cannot but possess certain poignant autobiographical associations. The eventuality stated symbolically in the last lines is devoutly to be wished: that *connoisseurs* of fantasy, whether in the immediate or the far future, shall indeed come to know the canon of Smith's works and appreciate his quite considerable achievement, and that Smith shall thus come to realize the only type of immortality any human being may reasonably expect, at least as far as such is known.

When Clark Ashton Smith died on August 14th, 1961, his death passed almost completely unnoticed, apart from a few local newspapers in his native state of California. No *Saturday Review of Literature*, no *Atlantic Monthly* devoted an entire memorial issue to the man and his writings. To the knowledge of the present writer, not a single science fiction or fantasy magazine even mentioned the fact of his death. Smith's connections with the main literary river of his own time were at best tenuous, if not just about non-existent; his connections with the tributary or sub-tributary of the science fiction and fantasy magazines, proved only a little less gossamer. The echoes of his earlier poetic fame in the Bohemian circles of San Francisco and Monterey had long since died away, and thus he died, little better than unknown to his own time.

The biography of Smith's external life is relatively uneventful, although still significant; but this relative uneventfulness places a greater importance on the life of the inner man, on the inner life of the literary creator, where such is known to us and where it is revealed in his works. However, it will still be to some purpose to review the more salient facts of biography with particular emphasis on those details which strongly relate to his creative life.

Smith was born of Yankee and English parentage on January 13th, 1893, in Long Valley, California, about six miles south of Auburn, in the house of his maternal grandparents (the Gaylords) located along the old road leading south of Folsom out of Auburn, and about five miles from the northern reaches of Boulder Ridge where Smith was to spend the major portion of his life. In 1902, his parents, Fanny and Timeus Smith, moved to Boulder Ridge, to a spot about a mile south of Auburn and about one-fourth of a mile east of the Folsom Road. Here his father with the help of the then nine-year-old boy, built a cabin and dug a well, and here Smith lived almost continuously until 1954, apart from visits to Sacramento, San Francisco, Monterey, the neighboring state of Nevada, and a few other places. He almost visited New York City sometime in 1942 under the ægis of his friends Benjamin and Bio De Casseres.

One can easily imagine the effect that the surrounding countryside had on the sensitive and imaginative boy; a countryside that was and still is a veritable garden of fruit trees—pear, plum, peach, cherry, apple—located on the rolling foothills of the Sierras and alternating with copses of evergreen and deciduous trees and with broad park-like areas; the foothills filled with deserted mines, some of them still containing gold; and arching overhead, the diurnal or nocturnal immensitudes of the heavens rendered remarkably clear in the clean smog-free country air.

He attended the equivalent of the first three grades of grammar school (in Smith's own words) "at the little red schoolhouse of the precinct." He completed the five remaining grades of grammar school in Auburn. Smith wrote later that "As a schoolboy, I believe that I was distinguished more for devilment than scholarship. Much of my childhood was spent in the neighborhood of an alleged gold mine; which may be the reason why the romance of California gold mining failed to get under my skin." However, in spite of his disclaimer, this neighboring gold mine—the "Old Gaylord Mine" close to his grandparents' property—evidently had some influence on the young Smith because his mature literary work, both poetry and prose, abounds in mining and geological terms. Without realizing it, he had succumbed to the greater romance of telluric splendor, as numerous references to precious and semi-precious metals and stones attest in his poems and in his tales.

Smith did not go on to either high school or college; he preferred to conduct his own education and later, when he turned down the opportunity for a Guggenheim scholarship, it was for the same reason. Thus early in his life he manifested what was to be his lifelong independence. To judge by his creative work, we may be sure that Smith—always an omnivorous but discerning reader—proved to be his own best teacher.

From the very first Smith seems to have been attracted to the exotic, the far away, and the literally astronomically far away. The gold mine near his grandparents' home, with its hints of precious, untold wealth, may account to some minor degree for Smith's predilection for the exotic. The fact that his father Timeus Smith had travelled extensively as a young man, and that he would often reminisce to his son about those travels, may also explain Smith's early attraction to the far away and the fabled, to the Orient and to those mysterious lands of the imagination so beloved by visionary youth.

The last receives ample confirmation when Smith would later report that his "first literary efforts at the age of eleven, took the form of fairy tales and imitations of *The Arabian Nights*. Later, I wrote long adventure novels dealing with Oriental life, and much mediocre verse." These "long adventure novels dealing with Oriental life" culminated in Smith's first professional short-story appearances in magazines: "The Malay Krise" and "The Ghost of Mohammed Din" in the then well-known West Coast literary magazine *The Overland Monthly*, in the issues for October and November 1910, respectively; and "The Mahout" and "The Raja and the Tiger" in *The Black Cat*, in the issues for August 1911 and February 1912, respectively. Significantly enough, all these tales are laid in the Orient, the first-named in the area of Singapore and the last three in India. "The Ghost of Mohammed Din" is important as being Smith's first professional story in which he features the element of the supernatural (handled with considerable skill, it may be added). In "The Raja and the Tiger" the climactic action of the story takes place in the Jain cave temple where "Huge stone pillars, elaborately sculptured, supported the roof, and around the sides great gods and goddesses of the Jain mythology, called Arhats, glared downward. The torch illuminated dimly, leaving much in shadow, *and in the shadow imagination created strange fantasies*." (The present writer's italics.) Smith later re-used the theme of "The Mahout," of a mahout who trains and uses an elephant to wreak his revenge upon a hated Oriental despot. When Farnsworth Wright, the editor of *Weird Tales*, came to found in 1930 a companion magazine called *Oriental Stories* (later changed to *The Magic Carpet Magazine*), Smith contributed two tales: "The Justice of the Elephant" in the Autumn 1931 issue of *Oriental Stories*, and "The Kiss of Zoraida" in the July 1933 issue of *The Magic Carpet Magazine*. In the former laid in India, Smith used again, in slightly altered form, the theme of "The Mahout." In the latter laid in Damascus, appears one of Smith's principal inspirations, the manifestation of death. The Oriental background continued in "The Kingdom of the Worm," a tale of the mediæval adventurer Sir John Maundeville, published in *The Fantasy Fan* for October 1933; and it continued in "The Ghoul," published in the same amateur magazine for January 1934; this last is a tale laid in Bagdad during the reign of the Caliph Vathek, William Beckford's fictional "grandson" of Haroun al Raschid.

The four earlier tales of 1910–1912 are written with a control, a sense of selection that would have done credit to a mature writer. If it were not for the evidence to the contrary, a reader might very easily mistake the four later Oriental tales as being of the same period as his four earlier ones; or vice versa. These four early stories serve as testimony to the care with which Smith has schooled himself for one of his self-appointed spheres of creation.

Besides witnessing the appearance of the very first of Smith's professional short stories, 1910 was also the very first year that saw Smith professionally in print, whether in verse or in prose. Then, for some reason Smith lost interest in writing short stories, and devoted himself almost wholly to poetry from 1911, from the time he was eighteen, until 1925, when he was thirty-two. Smith's parents proved fortunately sympathetic to their son's creativity all during this time, and indeed up until the time of their death in the 1930s.

In 1906, when he was thirteen, Smith had made an important literary discovery for himself, one which profoundly influenced his own writing. Let Smith tell this in his own words: "Unique, and never to be forgotten, was the thrill with which, at the age of thirteen, I discovered for myself the poems of Poe in a grammar-school library; and, despite the objurgations of the librarian, who considered Poe 'unwholesome,' carried the priceless volume home to revel for enchanted days in its undreamt-of melodies. Here, indeed, was 'balm in Gilead,' here was a 'kind nepenthe.'" Later, and equally important, Smith discovered Poe's short stories. Then, when Smith was almost fifteen, he made yet another important discovery: "Likewise memorable, and touched with more than the glamour of childhood dreams, was my first reading, two years later, of "A Wine of Wizardry" [by George Sterling], in the pages of the old *Cosmopolitan*. The poem, with its necromantic music, and splendours as of sunset on jewels and cathedral windows, was veritably all that its title implied..." Meanwhile and after, Smith was writing the "much mediocre poetry" which served as the practice prerequisite to the creation of his mature verse. Also it was probably during this period of poetic apprenticeship that Smith worked out of his system any and all desire to create slavish imitations of such poems by Poe as "The Raven," "The Bells," and company. The cosmic-astronomic poetry of Sterling, "The Testimony of the Suns" above all, may have suggested to Smith to try his hand at the same theme; that, together with the beauty of the Auburn countryside with its immense blue skies at day and its black profundities of heaven ablaze with stars and planets at night.

Through the suggestion of Emily J. Hamilton, a teacher at the Auburn high school (officially Placer Union High School), Smith came into personal contact with Sterling, at that time the unofficial poet laureate of the West Coast and very much the social lion. In Smith's own words: "Several years later—when I was eighteen, to be precise—a few of my verses were submitted to Sterling for criticism, through the office of a mutual friend; and his favorable verdict led to a correspondence, and, later, an invitation to visit him in Carmel, where I spent a most idle and most happy month. I like to remember him, pounding abalones on a boulder in the back yard, or mixing pineapple punch (for which I was allowed to purvey the mint from a nearby meadow), or paying a round of matutinal visits among his assorted friends." This personal friendship and correspondence with Sterling lasted for sixteen years, until Sterling's death in November 1926.

It was during these years, 1911–1912, when he was eighteen and nineteen, respectively, that Smith wrote his first mature poetry—the bulk of his first volume *The Star-Treader and Other Poems*. Evidently with some taste for art and literature, Boutwell Dunlap, a well-known property-owner in Placer County (in which both Auburn and Long Valley are located) and an acquaintance of Smith's, assisted the young poet in securing publication for his book. The San Francisco publisher A.M. Robertson, owner of a much-frequented bookshop and publisher of much of Sterling's poetry, agreed to bring the volume out. Sterling himself helped Smith with the reading of the proofs, and otherwise advised him; and in November of 1912 *The Star-Treader* appeared. The leading San Francisco newspapers proclaimed Smith "the Keats of the Pacific Coast," and discerning critics hailed him as a prodigy and a genius. Sterling later wrote that "the story of… [Smith's] triumph with his neighbors, when hundreds of copies of his first book of verses were promptly bought up in a small California hill town, is a romance in itself."

Thus, Smith made his début into the Bohemian literary and artistic life of the West Coast, centered in San Francisco and the surrounding area, a life that included and had included such notables as Bret Harte, Frank Norris, Jack London, George Sterling, Ambrose Bierce, Joaquin Miller, Edwin Markham, Ella Sterling Mighels, Charles Warren Stoddard, Nora May French, Ina Coolbrith, Gertrude Atherton, and many, many others. As the "discovery," protégé, and friend of Sterling, Smith may have had access into the charmed circle of San Francisco's haut ton. However, it is important to remember that, for all the éclat of his introduction to this

San Francisco literary and artistic life, Smith continued to live with his parents at their cabin on Boulder Ridge. It is fascinating to learn that Smith in fact almost met "Bitter" Bierce, who with Poe and a few others ranks as one of the greatest masters of the macabre. Before he departed in 1913 for Mexico where he later disappeared, Bierce had been living and working in Washington, D.C. Just before his departure for Mexico, he returned to California for a few months to renew old acquaintances. He did see Sterling again (even though Bierce had broken with both Sterling and Jack London when they had taken up Socialism), since Sterling had been one of the chief protégés of the older writer, who had once enthusiastically championed the younger man and his poetry. On one occasion Smith and Bierce almost met in San Francisco by means of Sterling, but the young Auburn poet was unable to travel to the city at that time. One cannot help but wonder what Bierce might have said in person to Sterling of the young Smith's poems.

Between 1912 and 1922, the year that Smith's second major poetry collection appeared, we hear relatively little of the poet. Sometime during this decade Smith first came to know both *Les Fleurs du Mal* and the *Petits Poèmes en prose* of Baudelaire, possibly in 1912, but not however in the original French but in some English translation, probably that of Arthur Symons. Smith was not to learn French and come to know Baudelaire in his original language until the middle 1920s. Smith later acknowledged that Baudelaire's poems as well as his poems in prose had exercised a considerable influence on Smith's work, especially on the latter's poems in prose. However, the Baudelairian influence manifests itself perhaps more in the technique of the *poème en prose* rather than in the subject matter. Also during this decade Smith began to contribute to a wide variety of magazines.

Violet Nelson Heyer, a long-time resident of Auburn as well as a long-term friend of the Smiths, recalls Clark's family during this period in the following words: "our family home adjoined Clark's family acres from the years 1908 until 1919, and the three personalities (Clark and his parents) are well-remembered by us,—the dark, reticent father and the happy, light-hearted soul who was Clark's mother… a lady of beautiful spirit and intense dedication to her family."

Sometime after the publication of *The Star-Treader*, Smith suffered a nervous breakdown and an attack of tuberculosis; from the former he fortunately recovered but the latter, while arrested, continued to bother him intermittently the rest of his life. Smith had endured terrific nightmares from his early boyhood onward—he based at least one of his later stories on a nightmare experienced in his early youth (see "The Primal City")—and the terrible nightmares that he suffered during this difficult period left a profound impression on his memory: he later recalled for friends that many of his later horror tales he founded on these frightful dreams. Vivid dreams and nightmares often accompany the occurrence of fever; and the victim of tuberculosis, alternating as he does between bouts of raging fever and periods when the body temperature falls below normal, experiences dreams and nightmares of even greater intensity. The student of Smith's works may well wonder as to the white-hot intensity of the nightmares endured at this particular time by Smith, always a highly sensitive and imaginative person. All of this—the nervous breakdown, the attack of tuberculosis, the terrible nightmares, and the dreadful uncertainty of whether he would or would not be cured, whether he would live or die—all of this must have had a shattering effect on Smith: he must have lived an eternity of lives during this period. It would serve to explain the rich and varied emotional background which undoubtedly inspired much of the work in Smith's next major poetry collection, *Ebony and Crystal*.

That he had been putting his inner life to excellent poetic advantage, he demonstrated beyond a doubt when in 1918 the Book Club of California issued fifteen of Smith's poems in an *édition de luxe* of 300 copies, under the title of *Odes and Sonnets*, with decorations by Florence Lundberg of New York City and with a preface by George Sterling. The first four poems were reprinted from *The Star-Treader*; the remaining eleven reappeared in *Ebony and Crystal*. The preface contained not only a discerning appreciation of Smith's genius but also an incidental prophecy that, alas, sadly came to eventualize, that Smith was "unlikely to be afflicted with present-day popularity." Distinguished recognition, however, was immediate. Edwin Markham, a poet now most famous for the poem "The Man with the Hoe," wrote: "These poems have lines of unusual beauty, glints and gleams of true genius. There is something terrific in Smith, as there was in John Martin, the illustrator of Milton's *Paradise Lost*. It cheers me to know that you Californians have honoured yourselves in your honouring of this distinguished poet." Grace Atherton Dennon, editor of the West-Coast poetry magazine *The Lyric West*, wrote: "Your poems are rich in feeling and expression. I regard you as a genuine poet, one whose name will endure." And from across the Atlantic the distinguished English poet and essayist Alice Meynell Smith wrote: "I think the imagination in your poems very remarkable, and wonderfully original. They are poems of true genius." In recognition of his services to literature the Book Club of California presented Smith with a bronze plaque designed by the noted San Francisco sculptor Edgar Walter, an honor bestowed only on such literary notables as Sterling and Edwin Markham.

About this time Smith began a number of important correspondences, one with the poet Samuel Loveman, a close friend of Ambrose Bierce and the author of *The Hermaphrodite and Other Poems*; and, in 1922, through the offices of Loveman, with H.P. Lovecraft. This last was the beginning of what emerged as a wonderfully rewarding friendship through letters for both men, as it is evident that they held many views, opinions, and tastes in common—in archæology, astronomy, astrology, languages ancient and modern (and a consequent interest in the systematic invention of personal and place names for fictional purposes), demonology, sorcery, mythology, legendry, folklore, and only Cunthamosi, the Cosmic Mother (in Smith's tale "The Monster of the Prophecy"), knows what else!

As an example of how much Smith and Lovecraft had in common, it is of interest to compare their respective lists of "favorite weird stories." In *The Fantasy Fan*, December 1934, appeared (through the "Courtesy of H. Koenig") the following list of Smith's ten favorite weird stories: "The Yellow Sign," by Robert W. Chambers; "The House of Sounds," by M. P. Shiel; "The Willows," by Algernon Blackwood; "A View from a Hill," by M. R. James; "The Death of Halpin Frayser," by Ambrose Bierce; "The Fall of the House of Usher," by Edgar Allan Poe; "The Masque of the Red Death," by Edgar Allan Poe; "The Novel of the White Powder," by Arthur Machen; "The Call of Cthulhu," by H.P. Lovecraft; and "The Colour Out of Space," by H.P. Lovecraft. In the preceding issue for October of the same amateur magazine, had appeared (also through the "Courtesy of H. Koenig") Lovecraft's list of ten favorite weird stories. Six of them duplicate Smith's choices, with only four titles different: "The Novel of the Black Seal," by Arthur Machen; "The White People," by Arthur Machen; "Count Magnus," by M.R. James; and "The Moon Pool" (original novelette), by A. Merritt. Yet for all such similarities in taste and opinion, the creative work of each man is strikingly different from that of the other; and each fully appreciated the other's genius.

In 1922, Smith selected and arranged into book form the best from the work of the years following the appearance of his first volume, and in December 1922, he published in Auburn his second major poetry collection *Ebony and Crystal: Poems in Verse and Prose*, with a preface by George Sterling and dedicated to Samuel Loveman. Again distinguished recognition was immediate. Henry Anderson Lafler wrote: "I wonder that you speak so slightingly of these poems. It seems to me that nothing being written today overtops them. You and George Sterling are two eagles in 'strong level flight,' winging sunward above flocks of sparrows."

The novelist and poet Frank L. Pollock wrote: "I must make you all possible compliments on your magnificent piece of blank verse, 'The Hashish-Eater.' The technique is superb, the verse hard-spun and close-woven. It would be difficult to conceive of greater power and variety of imagination, or a greater splendour of vocabulary. Almost every episode has the material for a long poem in itself—in fact you have used up enough poetical material to make half a dozen volumes of modern poets. As a decorative poem, it seems to me that this is one of the finest things I have ever read. I do not think there are six men living who could have done it—certainly no one else in America. Continually one comes cross absolutely right and infallible lines, giving the joy of a thing perfectly said; or some burst of metaphor that is like a flash of lightning; or some violent and vivid feat of imagination. I could pick examples by scores; there is only an *embarras des richesses*."

The secretary of the Book Club of California, Alfred M. Bender, wrote: "Thank you for your wonderful poem, 'The Hashish-Eater.' The subject may seem unappealing to many, but it has such richness of imagination, sustained thought, and stately beauty of expression that I am sure it will enhance your reputation and bring you new laurels. It should be an inward satisfaction to add another star to the firmament of California literature. Your place is growing firmer with each new effort." Smith's great friend and mentor George Sterling wrote: "'The Hashish-Eater' is indeed a most amazing production. It contains more imagination than anything else I have ever read." In the poetry journal *L'Alouette* for January 1924, appeared a highly favorable review of *Ebony and Crystal* by Smith's correspondent living across the continent, H.P. Lovecraft, who gave unstinted and eloquent praise to the volume, especially to its crowning achievement "The

Hashish-Eater."

Unfortunately, the fact that Smith himself privately published *Ebony and Crystal* in a limited edition (as he did the following volume *Sandalwood*), prevented it from reaching a nationwide audience, with the consequent larger critical recognition. To what extent its poetic originality and excellence, its oftentimes extraordinary cosmic vision, would have found appreciation is a moot question, since the year 1922 saw the beginning of the apotheosis of that modernist poet par excellence, T.S. Eliot, who had won the $2000 Dial Award for his 434-line poem "The Waste Land" (1922). It would be interesting and amusing (if nothing else) to compare Eliot's extended ode on sterility and desiccation to Smith's longest poem, the 576-line "The Hashish-Eater." One had summed up in a thoroughly modernist manner the disillusionment, the disenchantment of a postwar generation of the first half of the twentieth century of the Christian Era. The other, who rarely bothered himself in the least with his own age, without the manifest gesture of even turning his back on his own times, celebrated in a highly original and inventive manner the eternal, ever-renewing, even if perverse, splendors of the cosmos.

Acclaim of his own age or not, Smith continued on his own supremely independent way, letting no external clamors or censures interfere with the voice of his own personal *dæmon*. During the 1920s Smith was contributing to a wide range of magazines, from those of national or international circulation to the "little" magazines. The poetry journal *The Step-Ladder* honored Smith by devoting its entire issue of May 1927 to his poems (principally from *Ebony and Crystal* and *Sandalwood*). Among this wide range of magazines was one whose founding in 1923 and existence up until 1954, was to play a pivotal role when Smith later came to write short stories. This was *Weird Tales* "The Unique Magazine" (as the subtitle ran), in which Smith first appeared in the issue for January 1924 with the poems "The Red Moon" and "The Garden of Evil" (later collected into *Sandalwood* as "Moon-Dawn" and "Duality," respectively).

During the first half of the 1920s, to repay part of his indebtedness to the owner-editor of *The Auburn Journal* for printing *Ebony and Crystal,* Smith became a "journalist" and thus contributed to the town's chief newspaper 101 installments of a column entitled "Clark Ashton Smith's Column": the first column is dated April 5, 1923, the last is dated January 7, 1926. To this column Smith contributed both poetry and epigrams, largely the former:

in all, 81 poems (59 original poems and 22 translations from Baudelaire) and 329 original, and 17 selected, epigrams and pensées. (To the *Journal* overall, Smith contributed 84 poems.) The majority of the poems in *Sandalwood*—that is, 49 of the total 61 poems in that collection (37 of the 42 original poems and 12 of the 19 translations from Baudelaire)—appeared in this column of Smith's, most of them previously to their publication in *Sandalwood.* While most of the poems first published in the *Journal* have since appeared elsewhere, virtually all of the 329, or 346, epigrams and pensées have not, although publication of a selection of them (made by Smith) was tentatively considered by an eastern publisher in the early 1940s. The epigrams and pensées appeared in the *Journal* under the following titles: *Epigrams* (once), *Cocktails and Crème de Menthe*, *Points for the Pious*, *Unpopular Sayings* (once), *New Teeth For Old Saws* (once), *The Devil's Notebook* (which title has its obvious analogy with that of *The Devil's Dictionary* by Ambrose Bierce, originally entitled *The Cynic's Word-Book*), and *Paradox and Persiflage.* In 1990, Starmont House brought out a complete edition—or as complete as then possible—of Smith's epigrams and pensées under the title *The Devil's Notebook*, edited by Don Herron.

In October 1925, again in Auburn, Smith published his third major poetry collection *Sandalwood*, dedicated to George Sterling: a volume distinguished not only for its many beautiful love poems but also for nineteen translations from the French of Charles Pierre Baudelaire. The translations are indeed a remarkable accomplishment in view of the fact that Smith knew virtually nothing of the French language a year prior to October 1925, and hence had learned the language in something less than a year, beginning his study of it and subsequently of Baudelaire in November or December 1924, or during the very first part of 1925. This volume, because of its private printing in a limited edition, has shared the fate of *Ebony and Crystal* of being little better than unknown. In addition to the recognition given Smith's poetry of 1911–1925 by divers distinguished literary persons, the newspapers of the San Francisco area accorded long, elaborate, and overall excellent reviews to at least the first two of Smith's three major early poetry collections. As the result of *Ebony and Crystal*, one critic wrote apropos of Smith that "Among the living [poets] he stands alone."

The year 1925 also saw a new development in Smith's creative evolution: in this same year he had written two short stories, "The Abominations of

Yondo" and "Sadastor," stylistically and thematically growing out of his earlier poems in prose as well as out of his poems in verse. He submitted them to Farnsworth Wright, the editor of *Weird Tales*. The latter, always wary as to negative reader reaction to something overly new, rejected both stories, which he very well may have considered a little bit of too much, since both tales are essentially extended poems in prose. Later Wright did accept "Sadastor," printed in *Weird Tales* for July 1930; and *The Overland Monthly* accepted "The Abominations of Yondo," printed in the issue for April 1926, with the following note on Smith in the section entitled "April Contributors": "Clark Ashton Smith is a California poet and he proves something else in his 'Abominations of Yondo.'" Indeed, he had proven himself a unique poet in prose—that is, a practitioner of the poem in prose—and had proven the possibility of writing an extended poem in prose, in the manner of Poe's "The Masque of the Red Death," that unique creation in the canon of the elder writer's works. In fact, it is not too much to say that technically Smith had almost created—or at least re-created—the genre of the extended poem in prose.

In November 1926, at the Bohemian Club in San Francisco, occurred the death of George Sterling, Smith's great friend and mentor, ostensibly by suicide, a theory with which Smith never agreed: "...As Smith points out in his article [of personal reminiscences of Sterling written in 1941], the evidence indicating suicide was largely circumstantial. At the time of his death, Sterling had in his possession not only the fatal poison (cyanide) but also a morphine derivative that he had sometimes taken against sleeplessness. He was ill and perhaps suffering the profound mental confusion that often accompanies illness. What could have been more probable than a mistake? Sterling's last letter, written to Smith less than a week before his death, gave no evidence of mental depression or a failing of his vital interests." (From *The Auburn Journal*, Dec. 15, 1941: see article "Notes on Clark Ashton Smith.") Moreover, Sterling had been eagerly awaiting a visit from H. L. Mencken.

His death was a source of great bereavement to Smith, who paid a beautiful and moving tribute to his friend in the memorable poem "A Valediction to George Sterling," published in *The Overland Monthly* for November 1927. Earlier in the same year had appeared in the same magazine, in the issue for March, an article of reminiscences by Smith of Sterling entitled "George Sterling—An Appreciation." In it Smith recalled Sterling in the following words: "Always to me, as to others, he was a very gentle and faithful friend, and the kindest of mentors. Perhaps we did not always agree in matters of literary taste; but it is good to remember that our occasional arguments or differences of opinion were never in the least acrimonious. Indeed, how could they have been?—one might quarrel with others, but never with him: which, perhaps, is not the poorest tribute that I can pay to George Sterling.... But words are doubly inadequate, when one tries to speak of such a friend; and the best must abide in silence." Later (in 1941), Smith recalled Sterling in these words: "He was essentially lovable, gave himself without stint and assisted scores of young poets." Smith remained devoted the rest of his life to Sterling's memory and to his poetry.

A few weeks before his death, Sterling had said to David Warren Ryder: "Clark Ashton Smith is undoubtedly our finest living poet. He is in the great tradition of Shakespeare, Keats and Shelley; and yet, to our everlasting shame, he is entirely neglected and almost completely unknown." Also shortly before his death, Sterling had advised Smith, apropos of the latter's poems in prose of death and similar subject-matter, to give up "this macabre prose," a piece of advice Smith fortunately ignored. One of the very last services which Sterling performed for Smith and the cause of his poetry occurred when the elder poet brought an article for publication into the editorial offices of *The Overland Monthly* in San Francisco. This article was a highly enthusiastic, almost ecstatic essay on Smith's poetry entitled "The Emperor of Dreams" and written by the then eighteen-year-old Donald A. Wandrei. The monthly subsequently published the essay in its issue for December 1926.

Sometime after the publication of *The Star-Treader*, Vachel Lindsay had read some of Smith's poetry and had begun a correspondence with him. This correspondence-friendship lasted until Lindsay's death in 1931.

After *Sandalwood*, Smith had evidently given up the creation in quantity of poetry. He had now turned his attention once more to the writing of fiction. Earlier, in 1924, in the August issue of *10 Story Book*—a magazine which featured a piquant combination of short stories with what are now known as "girly pictures"—had appeared Smith's first professional short story since his contributions to *The Overland Monthly* and *The Black Cat* in 1910–1912: this is an amusing, deft, and very brief short story entitled "Something New," in which Smith incidentally mocks the extraordinarily rich style of imagery characteristic of *Ebony and Crystal*. In 1925 he had written the two extended poems in prose "The Abomination of Yondo" and "Sadastor." As we have seen, Farnsworth Wright rejected them. However, Smith continued to contribute to *Weird Tales* his own original poems in verse as well as translations from Baudelaire, all of an expectedly high quality. The issue for August 1928 included Smith's first appearance in prose in *Weird Tales*; this was in the form of translations in prose of three poems originally in verse by Baudelaire—"L'Irréparable," "Les Sept Vieillards," and "Une Charogne"—presented to the readers as *Three Poems in Prose, by Charles Pierre Baudelaire and Translated by Clark Ashton Smith from the French*. Smith had translated the verse originals of the poet into a supple and idiomatic English prose. In the succeeding issue for September 1928 appeared Smith's first short story in *Weird Tales*—a strange parable of love and death entitled "The Ninth Skeleton," but giving relatively little indication of the shape of things to come. The tale is significant, however, in that it is one of the very few laid by Smith in his general natal area: the action takes place on Boulder Ridge not far from the narrator's cabin; and the description of the area in the story is a poetic but exact one of the area around Smith's own cabin during his lifetime.

However, Smith did not begin the writing of fiction in any quantity until the beginning of the Depression in 1929. We may postulate the years 1926 to 1929/1930 as the period in which Smith was carefully preparing in his imagination the divers backgrounds for his stories. In the poem in prose entitled "To the Dæmon" and dated December 16th, 1929, Smith wrote: "Tell me many tales, O benign maleficent dæmon.... Tell me tales of inconceivable fear and unimaginable love...." And tell him many tales the *dæmon* veritably did. Between summer 1928 and summer 1938 Smith wrote something less than 140 short stories and novelettes.

His next story to appear in *Weird Tales* was "The End of the Story," laid in Smith's imaginary province of mediæval France, Averoigne; this was in the issue for May 1930. The tale proved immediately popular with the readers of "The Unique Magazine," and the distinguished writer and critic Benjamin De Casseres, in "The Eyrie" for July ("The Eyrie" was the readers' letter department in *Weird Tales*), commended Smith's tale as a story "which is not only a philosophic thriller but possesses real literary quality, which is not lost (quite the contrary) on readers, such as you have, of imaginative tales." The majority of Smith's tales appeared in either *Weird Tales* under Farnsworth Wright or *Wonder Stories* under Hugo Gernsback.

To the latter Smith contributed a highly imaginative, not to say unique, type of science-fiction story. To the former he contributed all manner of tales, many of them laid in Smith's carefully constructed backgrounds: the primeval continent Hyperborea; "the last isle of foundering Atlantis," Poseidonis; mediæval Averoigne; the last continent Zothique; the planet Xiccarph; and many other worlds. Although these stories may have become known only to a specialized audience, they introduced a new dimension in the art of the short story: many of the more characteristic tales are actually extended poems in prose in which Smith has united the singleness of purpose and mood of the modern short story (as first established by one of Smith's literary idols, Edgar Allan Poe) together with the flexibility of the *conte* or tale; an entire short story being unified and, in part, given its powerful centralization of effect, mood, atmosphere, etc., by a more or less related system or systems of poetic imagery and language (simile, metaphor, archetype or allegory). This ranks as a technical achievement of the first order, although it has received relatively little or no recognition.

It is indeed fortunate that both *Weird Tales* and *Wonder Stories* existed during this period of intense creation in Smith's life: by providing a more or less ready market for Smith's stories, they served as the necessary commercial incentive which Smith, genius or not, financially needed. Smith paid tribute to the needed existence of such magazines for writer and reader alike in a letter published in "The Eyrie" in the December 1930 issue of *Weird Tales*: "Speaking as a reader, I should like to say that *Weird Tales* is the one magazine that gives its writers ample imaginative leeway. Next to it comes three or four magazines in which fancy can take flight under the egis of science; and after these, one is lost in a Bœotian desert. All the others, without exception, from the long-established reviews down to the Wild West thrillers, are hide-bound and hog-tied with traditions of unutterable dullness." Hugo Gernsback, the editor of *Wonder Stories*, appears to have welcomed Smith's stories quite enthusiastically. However much Farnsworth Wright may have appreciated their literary excellence (Wright himself was a considerable scholar who professionally edited, among other things, a very fine version of Shakespeare's play *A Midsummer Night's Dream*), the editor of *Weird Tales* appears always to have been rather anxious as to how his readers would react to Smith's extended poems in prose. Undoubtedly this is what caused Smith to publish privately six of his finest tales in his first collection of short stories *The Double Shadow and Other Fantasies*, in February 1933, at Auburn.

Outwardly during this period Smith led a quiet, uneventful life. However, in August 1934, Smith successfully fought a severe wood and grass fire on his ranch. All during this time (1929–1937) Smith continued to write verse but necessarily in a much smaller quantity. In 1933, George Work, the author of *White Man's Harvest*, and one of the then best-known writers in the country, declared Smith "the greatest American poet of today" whose "poems do not compare unfavorably with those of Byron, Shelley, Keats or Swinburne." In *Controversy* for November 1934 appeared the article *The Price of Poetry*, by David Warren Ryder. In this article Ryder acclaimed Smith as "a great poet" and as being "in our generation… the fittest to wear the mantle of Shakespeare and Keats," thus adding his considered opinion to the similar one of George Sterling, George Work, and the well-known and respected educator and man-of-letters, Dr. David Starr Jordan, one-time president of the University of Indiana and the first president and "the builder" of Stanford University. Ryder's article was reprinted in June 1937 to accompany the slender collection *Nero and Other Poems*, published in the preceding month of May by The Futile Press, Lakeport, California: this volume included ten reprints (somewhat altered from their original versions) from *The Star-Treader*. Just as the poetry magazine *The Step-Ladder* had devoted its entire issue of May 1927 to his poems, the California poetry journal *Westward* in the issue for January 1935 honored Smith by making numerous quotations from poems in *The Star-Treader* and *Ebony and Crystal*. This magazine featured in its early issues, at the bottom of the pages carrying poems, quotations from the works of the established poets of the past, including the great names in the poetry of the English language.

In 1936 the output of Smith's tales started to drop off, and by the latter 30s, during the 40s and the 50s, Smith had virtually stopped writing fiction. However, he continued writing verse until his death in 1961. The reasons for this cessation of Smith's writing fiction are not clear: it could have been that he had exhausted even his seemingly inexhaustible fancy; or perhaps the *dæmon* no longer told him "tales of inconceivable fear and unimaginable love"; or Smith may have found the production of his small sculptures more interesting. This last seems likely as Smith once wrote, in a brief autobiography published in *The Science Fiction Fan* for August 1936, that he found "the making of these [small sculptures] far easier and more pleasurable than writing." He had begun the carving of these small sculptures possibly in the early 1930s, and it may have been that this was now the new step in Smith's further creative evolution; he made besides hundreds of paintings and drawings, starting in the early 1920s or earlier. Also, the death of his parents as well as that of his correspondent and friend Lovecraft, may have removed some of Smith's incentive for creating fiction. His mother, Fanny Smith, died in 1935; his father, Timeus Smith, died in 1937; and in March of this same year Lovecraft died, and death thus robbed Smith of one of his greatest, most sympathetic and understanding friends. H.P.L. had always proved an enthusiastic and perceptive audience for Smith's short stories: both Smith and Lovecraft had been in the habit of exchanging manuscripts of stories before their publication, and mutually commenting on them.

Smith paid homage to H.P.L. in the lovely and moving memorial poem "To Howard Phillips Lovecraft" and in a letter in "The Eyrie" in *Weird Tales*, both published in the issue for July 1937. Two tributes in prose had also appeared earlier: "In Memoriam—H.P. Lovecraft," in *Tesseract* for April 1937; and in a letter published in *The Science-Fiction Critic* for May 1937, in "A Note From The Editor." His last tribute appeared in 1959, the sonnet "H.P.L.," published in *The Shuttered Room and Other Pieces* (Arkham House) and dated July 17th, 1959.

Lovecraft, before he died had paid his homage to Smith in the sonnet "To Clark Ashton Smith" (published posthumously in *Weird Tales* for April 1938), which concludes with the lines: "Dark Lord of Averoigne—whose windows stare / On pits of dream no other gaze could bear!" In Lovecraft's essay "Supernatural Horror in Literature" H.P.L. concludes the section "The Weird Tradition in America" with a paragraph of high and perceptive praise of Smith's fictional art.

During the late 1930s Smith began another of his notable correspondences, this one with Lilith Lorraine, the founder and principal poet of the Avalon Poetry Foundation. In Lilith Lorraine's volume of science-fiction poetry *Wine of Wonder*, she pays Smith a lovely and worthy tribute in the poem "The Cup-Bearer". Also during the late 1930s Universal Studios considered the possibility of filming two of Smith's most extraordinary tales "The Dark Eidolon" and "The Colossus of Ylourgne." This project never materialized, and this may have been a blessing rather than a misfortune, however much Smith could have used the money from the movie rights.

To have adapted either of these tales would have required not the typically conventional treatment of Universal Studios but such combined talents as those of Vincent, Alexander, and Zoltán Korda as demonstrated in their classic fantasy film *The Thief of Bagdad* with its excellent score by Miklós Rózsa. Conrad Veidt, the evil Vizir and archimage in this film, would have been superb as the archimage Namirrha in "The Dark Eidolon" or as the mediæval sorcerer Nathaire in "The Colossus of Ylourgne." Alas, the might-have-been....

Whatever may have been the reasons for the cessation of his writing fiction—the continued production of his quintessential sculptures or the loss of his parents and of his literary *frère et semblable* H.P.L.—Smith only wrote little more than a dozen stories between the late 1930s and his death in 1961. Increasingly, it has now turned out that the real or chief reason for his apparent abandonment of writing fiction was his ever-growing disgust with the arbitrary capriciousness of magazine editors, a not inconsiderable factor for a sensitive artist in words as Ashton Smith. Also, he had returned to his first love, the creation of poetry in verse: by late 1941 Smith had three collections or cycles of verse in preparation: *Incantations*, *The Jasmine Girdle*, and *Wizard's Love and Other Poems* (later retitled *The Hill of Dionysus*). Thus, it was during the penultimate decade of his life that Smith composed and/or assembled his final poem-cycles. *Incantations* contains mainly poems composed during the 1920s and 1930s, hitherto largely uncollected, as well as many unpublished poems. *The Hill of Dionysus* and especially *The Jasmine Girdle* both contain many poems never-before published; both are cycles of love poems. And if all the preceding mass of poetry, much of it new, were not already quite enough for a man in his fifties—a man who had moreover in the early part of his career created three major collections of poetry—Smith also experimented with such miniature forms as the quintrain and the haiku, the last surely the quintessence of quintessential forms. All-told, he now created over one hundred miniature poems, a small sampling of which is presented in *Spells and Philtres* (Arkham House, 1958). These divers collections are included in the *Selected Poems* that Smith was concurrently engaged in assembling during the 1940s. In addition, Smith learned Spanish during this decade, made translations from Spanish poets, and even wrote a small number of poems in Spanish. Such productivity, much of it in new forms and in new directions and some of it even in a new language for Smith, must be considered remarkable indeed for a man in age already past the half-century mark. Phoenix-like, the poet had been reborn out of the ashes of the fiction-writer.

The founding of Arkham House in 1939 by August Derleth assured the publication of six collections of Smith's short stories in book form: *Out of Space and Time* (1942), *Lost Worlds* (1944), *Genius Loci and Other Tales* (1948), *The Abominations of Yondo* (1960), *Tales of Science and Sorcery* (1964), and *Other Dimensions* (1970). Upon publication of *Out of Space and Time*, the well-known writer and man-of-letters Benjamin De Casseres in his syndicated column "The March of Events" dated Sep. 23, 1942 (this column appeared on the editorial page of the Hearst newspapers), commented briefly on Smith's first major prose collection and hailed Smith not only as a great poet and a great story-teller but as "a great prose writer" as well.

Only to the encouragement of his publisher do we owe the existence of the omnibus volume of Smith's first Arkham House poetry, the *Selected Poems*. This volume was originally entitled *The Hashish-Eater and Other Poems* and was intended by Smith's publisher to be a complete collection of all of Smith's poetry. Subsequently Smith decided instead to make it a selective volume. Produced during the period 1944–1949, it contains about 500 poems, virtually two-thirds of the 800 poems or so extant at the time of Smith's death. Delivered to his publisher in December 1949, this collection of collections contains the following sections: *The Star-Treader and Other Poems*, *Ebony and Crystal* (minus the twenty-nine poems in prose), *Sandalwood*, *Translations and Paraphrases* (from Baudelaire, Verlaine, Victor Hugo and other poets both French and Spanish), *Incantations*, *Quintrains*, *Sestets*, *Experiments in Haiku* (*Strange Miniatures*, *Distillations*, *Childhood*, *Mortal Essences*), *Satires and Travesties*, *The Jasmine Girdle*, *The Hill of Dionysus*. (*Incantations* and *The Jasmine Girdle* between them contain some ten examples of the small body of poetry Smith composed in French.) This omnibus poetry collection had to wait until November 1971 to see publication. During that long wait of twenty-two years a large sampling of the *Selected Poems* appeared in Smith's first published Arkham House poetry collection *The Dark Chateau* (1951), which Smith dedicated significantly "To the Memory of Edgar Allan Poe" and which contains many remarkable poems: eighteen of its forty poems are taken from the omnibus volume. A further and still larger sampling of the *Selected Poems* appeared in Smith's second published Arkham House poetry collection

*Spells and Philtres* (1958): fifty-one of the sixty poems in this last collection are taken from the same volume.

About the end of August 1953, Smith received a personal visit from his publisher, correspondent, and friend August Derleth, in company with his then wife, the former Sandra Evelyn Winters. Before his death in June 1971, Derleth managed to bring out under his Arkham House imprint three more volumes by Smith: the two final collections of short stories *Tales of Science and Sorcery* (1964) and *Other Dimensions* (1970), and an almost complete collection of his unique prose-poems under the title *Poems in Prose* (1965).

A near lifetime of celibacy, brightened here and there by the bowers of divers "enchantresses" (as Smith was wont to call them), came to an end in 1954 when Smith married Carol Jones Dorman, the last and "The Best Beloved" of Klarkash-Ton's enchantresses. To his wife he pays a delicate and a gallant tribute in the sonnet which opens "From this my heart, a haunted Elsinore, / I send the phantoms packing for thy sake:" This sonnet, originally entitled "The Best Beloved," was used by Smith under the title "Dedication/to Carol" to preface *Spells and Philtres*, which in its entirety is dedicated to his wife. Between 1954 and his death in 1961 Smith maintained his residence alternately in Pacific Grove and near Auburn. The old cabin of the Smiths, in which Clark had lived for over half a century, from 1902 to 1954, burned down to the ground in August 1957. This was understandably a source of deep distress to Smith, even though he had sold the major portion of the Smith ranch, about forty acres, in 1937 (to a local contractor for the purposes of a private airport), sometime after the death of Smith's father. This left about two and a half acres, including the land upon which stood the cabin.

Smith still chopped wood and did gardening during the last decade of his life, in addition to working on his quintessential sculptures. However, these last years saw relatively little literary activity on Smith's part, although he did continue to write poetry, even if sparingly. During the 1910s, the 20s, the 30s, and the 40s, in addition to his literary work, Smith had done much hard manual labor. Among other things, he had been a fruit-picker, a fruit-packer, a cement-mixer, and a hard-rock miner, mucker and windlasser, as well as a wood-chopper and a gardener. Smith did this work primarily in order to earn enough money to support himself while writing his poetry and his prose. However, his literary output shows no or very little reflection of this manual labor.

It was toward the latter part of these last years in Smith's life that the present writer—on two different occasions—had the pleasure of meeting Smith and his wife Carol at their home in Pacific Grove: in August of 1958 and in September of 1959. I recall with warmth and gratitude the unstinted way in which the Smiths gave of their hospitality to me, and made me feel perfectly at home. I had become so accustomed to the strong statement characteristic of much of Smith's poetry in verse and prose that, prior to meeting Smith, I am afraid that I somewhat naively anticipated the poet to speak in a voice of brass and in a manner as sententious and orotund as that of a sorcerer in one of Smith's tales. To my considerable surprise Smith spoke in a deep, quiet, pleasant voice that put me instantly at my ease. With his trim mustache and his handsome, distinguished features, he seemed a perfect gentleman, affable but not unctuously so, civilized and tolerant, about whom there hovered a certain aura of individuality that would have set him apart anywhere but not in any blatant, affected manner: that true individuality which comes from within and has nothing of the theatrical in it.

Of that first visit I recall in particular a delightful picnic we held on the beach about a block and a half east of their home. It was literally a "golden afternoon" with but a few fleecy clouds high overhead, with the gulls crying about us and the waves lisping among the rocks. Smith wore his beret and Mrs. Smith an immense straw hat which gave her the piquant appearance of a twentieth-century enchantress. With Mrs. Smith generously purveying the food from a straw hamper, we ate a simple but tasty repast of good, crumbly wheaten bread piled with miniature slabs of a sharp cheddar cheese, all washed down with one of the good red wines of California poured into paper cups: a wine of pomegranates from Hyperborea held in goblets of crystal and orichalch could not have tasted any better. Our conversation was informal and covered a wide range of topics, occasionally spiced by some wise, witty, and often ironic comment from Smith on the contemporary political and international scene.

Of my second visit I recall, among other things, a lengthy discussion Smith and I had apropos divers literary figures, especially Poe and Baudelaire. The discussion reached its climax when Smith, with an unforgettable intensity, read aloud in French one of the powerful sonnets of Baudelaire. Smith commented afterwards: "That's terrific stuff!" I nodded my head in agreement and said, "Well, it certainly wasn't written by Alfred Lord Tennyson!" Then we both laughed, breaking the tension. Earlier, upon my noticing and commenting upon a "complete works" of Poe in some eight or ten volumes on a bookshelf in the dining room, Smith had confided to me that he had read virtually everything written by Poe that he had been able to obtain. However, it was during my first visit that Smith showed me his portfolio of drawings and paintings. I must confess myself somewhat taken aback by their deliberately primitive technique, having become somewhat spoiled by the technical excellence of Smith's verse and prose; but there were a number of demonic heads which struck me as powerful and original. Smith's sculptures, on the other hand, as deliberately primitive as the paintings, impressed me far more favorably and suggested something Egyptian or Mayan or Peruvian of the Inca period, without being quite the same as those. These carvings of Smith's possess a quality rare in sculpture, which generally surrenders its essence at once to the beholder, especially sculpture of a conventionally technical perfection. Smith's carvings grow gradually in the onlooker's appreciation: the more one sees them, the more fascinating they become, adumbrating an essence never fully revealed but extending itself infinitely.

Smith was as generous and fine a friend as Sterling must have been. I happened to lack only one of Smith's volumes of poetry, the slender reprint collection *Nero and Other Poems*, published by The Futile Press. Smith took a copy he had given and inscribed to his wife, cut out the inscription page, wrote in a new inscription to me and then gave me the book gratis. I protested—somewhat feebly, I admit—but Clark and Carol insisted I keep it. I can still recall the thrill that I felt when Smith gave me out of his own hands that copy of *Nero and Other Poems* or, in the words of Smith's inscription, "this relic from an ironically named printing press."

Smith died on the 14th of August 1961, and in the latter part of the same year Arkham House published its second anthology of macabre poems, *Fire and Sleet and Candlelight* (the first had been *Dark of the Moon*). This included six largely hitherto-unpublished poems by Smith, in many respects the equal of much of his earlier verse, as all or most of them were evidently composed during the years 1911–1925. Smith demonstrates his admiration for Baudelaire and his works to the very last, as witness the title of the last poem in this group of posthumously published verse: "The Horologe," which title is the English equivalent of the French "L'Horloge," which Baudelaire uses as the title for the last poem in the first section *Spleen et Idéal* of *Les Fleurs du Mal*.

Thus, death finally came to him who had been, in part, one of death's most lyrical celebrators. As stated earlier, no *Saturday Review* or *Atlantic Monthly* devoted an entire memorial issue to him and his works; and while Smith was alive, no *New Yorker* had ever allowed him into the charmed and perilous circle of its "profiles." Neither the science-fiction nor fantasy magazines even mentioned Smith's death. He died as he had lived, as an outsider for the most part.

As far as the present writer has been able to determine, Smith left comparatively little unpublished material at his death. Apart from his juvenile fiction, only some two dozen stories, including "The Face by the River," "Like Mohammed's Tomb," "Double Cosmos," "Told in the Desert," "The Red World of Polaris," "A Good Embalmer," "Strange Shadows," "Nemesis of the Unfinished," and "The Dart of Rasasfa." An unfinished novel, *The Infernal Star*, begun about 1936 with about 10,000 words written. Some incidental poetry. A play in blank verse (written before 1951), *The Dead Will Cuckold You*, telling in six tableaux a tale of necromancy in Zothique. Most important of all, *The Black Book*, the notebook used by Smith from about 1930 to 1961. Although some of this material appears irretrievably lost, much of it has appeared in published form, whether in collected form or individually between 1961 and the present day.

To judge by *The Hill of Dionysus—A Selection* (published in November 1962), and by the more abundant presentation in the *Selected Poems* (published in November 1971), the section with the title *The Hill of Dionysus*, this penultimate poem-cycle of Smith's must be pronounced the equal of the earlier *Sandalwood*, if not perhaps in some respects the superior of the two collections.

Smith was by no means a prolific writer, except in the sense of creating many writings of a high literary merit. Over-all, there are about 140 tales extant, about 40 poems in prose, and indeed about 1000 original poems in verse, with about 500 thus not collected in the *Selected Poems* (this estimate includes the juvenilia, together with the original poems in French and Spanish, but excludes the almost 400 translations, almost all of them from French, with only about a dozen from Spanish).

For a person who dedicated most of his life to poetry, Smith issued comparatively few volumes. He maintained only about ten or fifteen correspondences of any importance or length. Smith, with his relatively small output of art in various form, provides a striking contrast to those authors whose complete collected works fill one, two, or three full library shelves, or sometimes even more. But if the quantity of his over-all output is negligible, the quality is the reverse.

## SOME GENERAL REMARKS ON SMITH'S POETRY AND PROSE

When Smith died at the age of sixty-eight, he left behind him a unique body of work; a body of work remarkable for its consistency in theme and quality from the very first to the very last. It serves as a notable example of an artist who, in his mature creative work, has remained faithful to the ideals, the dreams, and even the creations of his childhood. Fortunately, Smith never betrayed his enchantments.

His poems in verse and prose and his tales and/or extended poems in prose form the integral complement of each other. It is impossible fully to understand or appreciate the tales without some knowledge and understanding of the poems. Conversely, a knowledge of the stories aids toward a richer, a fuller understanding of the poems. Stylistically and thematically the tales grow out of the rich and varied emotiono-imaginative life of the poems.

If Smith had written nothing else but his first volume of poems, *The Star-Treader*, he would still take rank as an unique poet. The very title of the title poem forms a quintessential poem all in itself, a poem filled with amazing imaginative overtones. It seems incredible that such a poem as "Medusa" could have been written by a youth of only eighteen, or even more incredible, that such a hymn to death, destruction and night as "Nero," so mature and controlled in concept and composition, could have been written by Smith *before* his eighteenth year. In "Nero," the very first poem of his very first volume, Smith gives expression, for the very first time, to one of the principal concepts uniting his entire output, the concept or theme of the Man-God, first given crystallized expression by Baudelaire in his study *Les Paradis artificiels*, although it is actually a very ancient concept.

In other poems Smith celebrates the astronomic splendors of the cosmos, or hymns the gods of antiquity, or combines the cosmic-astronomic with the mythological in striking and original fashion. The divination or evocation of past epochs, places and peoples appears for the first time, later to reappear in Smith's unforgettable tales of necromancy. The theme of lost continents appears for the first time in the sonnet "Atlantis." The sonnets are all of a uniformly high quality. Some of the sonnets as well as some of the other poems manifest powerfully Smith's early and continuing preoccupation with death, destiny and doom. In the extraordinary sonnet "Retrospect and Forecast," Smith strikes for the first time the superb baroque antithesis of life feeding on death, and death feeding on life: a concept that, along with metamorphosis, continues throughout a goodly proportion of Smith's entire output. At the opposite pole there are charming nature vignettes, in addition to poems celebrating ideal beauty. Marked by an astonishing technical command and assurance, and by an immense vocabulary used with unerring and creative precision, *The Star-Treader* is as remarkable an achievement today as it was not quite one hundred years ago when it was published in 1912.

While it may have obvious affinities with *Les Fleurs du Mal* of Baudelaire as well as with the work of the Symbolists on the one hand and on the other with that of the Parnassians; yet *Ebony and Crystal*, published in 1922, remains an unique collection, quite unlike any other body of poetry whether in French or in English or in any other language. All the themes and ambiances in *The Star-Treader*—the cosmic-astronomic, the mythological, the implicitly necromantic, and those of splendor, death, beauty, nature, and of lost continents—reappear in the present volume. But, with what a wealth of difference. For not only have the poet's technical and metrical skills attained their perfection, but a new and undeniably universal theme manifests itself—that of love. The poet uses an even larger vocabulary than in *The Star-Treader*, and with the same extraordinary precision. He has mastered the Baudelairian technique of treating a perverse or unpleasant subject (i.e., from a conventional viewpoint) with the utmost lyricism of imagery and language: such sonnets as "Love Malevolent" and "Laus Mortis" form worthy companion-pieces to Baudelaire's "Une Charogne". Over-all the sonnets reach a high-water mark of classical perfection and romantic fervor and, sometimes, baroque intensity and complexity. Smith's handling of blank verse—especially in "The Hashish-

Eater" and in the dramatic dialogue "The Ghoul and the Seraph"—is nothing less than supreme. The final speech of the ghoul Necromalor in the last-named piece provides a quintessential example of Smith's unique literary baroque both as to subject and as to style, besides brilliantly illuminating his highly baroque philosophies of death and change, of life feeding on death, and death feeding on life; with everything informed by a burning romantic fervor, and controlled by a classic sense of tone and form. Much of the fascination of Smith's poems (as well as of his poems in prose and of his extended poems in prose) stems from their baroque, shifting and kaleidoscopic imagery; such imagery as appears in the sonnets "Eidolon," "Ave Atque Vale," "Mirrors," "The Orchid," and others. An important technical innovation is Smith's revival of that unjustly neglected and deprecated metre in English, the alexandrine. The most outstanding poem employing this metre, appositely entitled "Alexandrines," is perhaps one of the single most perfect poems Smith ever penned; although it is admittedly difficult to point out even a few outstanding poems amid the plethora of excellent ones.

Standing apart from the volume and Smith's over-all output of poetry, the compressed epic "The Hashish-Eater; or, The Apocalypse of Evil" remains an unparalleled masterpiece of cosmic invention and imagination. It stands as the unique example of the seemingly impossible combination of the epical with the lyrical. Its apparently endless pageant of wonders and episodes forms a veritable catalogue of things to come in Smith's tales of 1929/1930 and 1936/1937. Even more than that sovereign poem "Nero," it exemplifies in an unique manner the all-important concept of the Man-God in the person of the hashish-eater, "the emperor of dreams," empanoplied with demiurgic powers. Arranged into ten clearly-defined sections, the epic, with an apocalyptic splendor of imagery and language, plunges *in medias res* and relates the already-begun "supreme ascendance" of the Man-God (through the supreme drug or liberating agent of the imagination) to his arch-sublime throne of "culminant omniscience manifold," wherefrom in a series of visions or "memories" and "dreams" he surveys the divers pageantries of the cosmos; the epic then relates the muffled threat to the Man-God's omnipotence by some innominate evil; then the brief but evil-omened respite enjoyed or endured by the Man-God; then the first full-scale apocalypse of evil in the form of the monsters of classical mythology cosmically extrapolated; then, ever pursued by "the dragon-rout," the flight of the Man-God to the utmost edge of the cosmos beyond which plunges the arch-abyss of the void or of chaos; then, rising up from the very depths, the ultimate revelation or realization of evil: the "huge white eyeless Face" "With lips of flame that open," which involves into it (but logically without destroying either) both the Man-God and the rout of now rather childish monsters however macrocosmic. "The Apocalypse of Evil," the subtitle of this epic (for such it is in everything but length—it satisfies all the desiderata of an epic), has a considerable significance since it indicates for the poem a literary tradition stemming in part directly from *The Flowers of Evil* by Baudelaire. Whatever this compressed epic may owe apropos of general structure and style of imagery to its ultimate model, "A Wine of Wizardry" by George Sterling (which is essentially a brief travelogue of imaginary wonders, a literal "flight of fancy," which Smith first read in late 1907 when he was almost fifteen—the poem was first published in *The Cosmopolitan* for September 1907), yet "The Hashish-Eater" has no true parallel in cosmic concept or in sustained power of imagination. It stands alone. Perhaps the closest thing to Smith's compressed epic is that highly poetic prose-piece in semi-dramatic form by Gustave Flaubert, *La Tentation de Saint Antoine*,—with its saintly anchorite-hero Anthony who undergoes a series of fantasmagoric visions instigated by the Devil to tempt him. Ignoring the over-all differences in narrative-purpose of the two pieces as well as the differences in symbolic intent of the endings of both, yet these endings outwardly do have a considerable resemblance.

The *Poems in Prose* which conclude *Ebony and Crystal* possess a paramount significance in terms of the over-all canon of Smith's work, for these twenty-nine poems in prose—representing a logical continuation of the thematic material in the preceding poems in verse—lead directly to Smith's two extended poems in prose of 1925, "Sadastor" and "The Abominations of Yondo," and on through them to the tales and/or extended poems in prose of 1929–1937. Many of these poems in prose are essentially condensed or implied tales, and two of them, "The Flower-Devil" and "From the Crypts of Memory," served as the inspiration or nuclei (in regard to the over-all plot, atmosphere and even as to actual phrases) for the later extended poems in prose, "The Demon of the Flower" and "The Planet of the Dead," respectively. Smith is one of the very, very few poets in English who have fully understood the technique of this difficult and eminently French genre (the *poème en prose*) more or less created by Baudelaire (under the dual influence and/or suggestion of that unique collection of prose ballads *Gaspard de la Nuit* by Aloysius Bertrand, published in 1842, and of such poems in prose by Poe as "Shadow - A Parable," "Silence - A Fable," "Eleanora," and "The Masque of the Red Death"). Indeed, it is not too much to say that as a practitioner of the poem in prose Smith has no peer in English, and that, considering his achievement in this genre from a universal literary viewpoint, he takes equal rank with Baudelaire, the technique of whose *Petits Poèmes en prose* influenced Smith in the technique of his own. These poems in prose clearly pave the way toward the highly baroque prose of Smith's later tales and/or extended poems in prose, as of where the latter designation applies. Even if little recognized or heralded, the publication of Smith's over-all more than forty poems in prose in one volume (the total is now known to be only a little less than sixty) has helped to establish his pre-eminence in the literature of this genre.

The remarkable love poems in *Ebony and Crystal* find their complement on an extended scale in the even more remarkable love poems that make up most of *Sandalwood*, published in 1925, and concluding with nineteen translations from *Les Fleurs du Mal* of Baudelaire. After the cosmic and exotic splendors of *The Star-Treader* and *Ebony and Crystal*, and the oftentimes monumental tone of those two volumes, the tender, muted, vertumnal or gently autumnal tone of this third major poetry collection by Smith, comes as a surprise, almost—paradoxically—as a quiet shock. Many of the love poems, as well as some of the non-love poems, Smith has cast into many beautiful forms of his own invention that suggest the old French forms of the rondeau, the triolet, the ballade, and the villanelle, without actually being the same. The poems in *Sandalwood* are above all remarkable for haunting song-like effects, with all manner of refrain and echo-like devices. Smith's successful experimentation with lines of differing lengths and metres suggests on the one hand the similar experimentation by the poets of the Pléïade and on the other the same by the most eminent Elizabethan poet influenced by the Pléïade, Edmund Spenser. Perhaps the single most beautiful and artistic poem in the entire volume is the incomparable "We Shall Meet." But the entire collection is rife with excellent poems, haunting, unforgettable, of a rare poignance, charting as many of them do the course of love that runs disastrously and ultimately perishes. Like *Ebony and Crystal*, *Sandalwood* is a talismanic, touchstone volume. The nineteen poems from Baudelaire, as well as

Smith's Baudelairian translations elsewhere, establish Smith as a sovereign translator of the French genius, far superior to Edna St. Vincent Millay or even Arthur Symons.

Of Smith's tales and/or extended poems in prose there is little that one can say in this brief space save that they are prodigies of invention whose style is integrally one with their themes. They synthesize and extrapolate the themes, backgrounds, concepts and stylistic elements of Smith's three major early poetry collections. Smith's unique type of science fiction (contributed mostly in the 1930s to *Wonder Stories*) represents a return to the cosmic-astronomic material of his very first volume of some twenty years earlier. As a perfectly logical consequence Smith's tales employ the same immense vocabulary to be found in his poetry; a vocabulary used with a precision fully as creative and as masterly as that evident in his poems. Not only does the same vocabulary used in his poetry reappear but even the same or similar phrase-patterns and mannerisms. Such tales as "The Dark Eidolon," "The Empire of the Necromancers," "The Last Hieroglyph," "The Isle of the Torturers," "Xeethra," "The White Sybil," "The City of the Singing Flame," and so many, many others, have no parallel in the creations of any other writer. They are unique like the genius that created them. They form in their entirety a worthy congener to "The Hashish-Eater." In them Smith again gives striking embodiment to the concept of the Man-God, whether personified in such archimages as Malygris, Maal Dweb, Avyctes and Namirrha or in such necromancers as Mmatmuor, Sodosma, and Vacharn or in such kings as Adompha, Euvoran and Xeethra. Such protagonists of Smith's, like true heroes Baudelairian, despite their frequent sovereignty of temporal and/or necromantic power, are yet paradoxically often impotent to escape that ultimate bane of godhood or of the Man-God, to wit, *ennui* or spleen. (This last is, of course, one of the central Baudelairian themes, both in *Les Fleurs du Mal* and in the *Petits Poèmes en prose*, the alternate title of which is *Le Spleen de Paris*.) The poet-author himself may be seen in an ideal sense as a literary Man-God creating and peopling many worlds of his imagination; the tales and/or extended poems in prose may be seen as the complement and fulfillment of the seemingly endless procession of visions or episodes that make up the compressed epic "The Hashish-Eater."

Smith's tales, because of their efflorescent richness and their baroque combination of seemingly contradictory and incongruous elements, become very difficult to characterize. The love poems in *Ebony and Crystal* and *Sandalwood* find their fictional counterparts in the love interest in a great many of Smith's so-called "tales of horror." But the label of "tales of love" is also inadequate. What should one call them? Tales of death? Tales of splendor? Tales of beauty? Tales of deathly beauty? Tales of necromancy? Tales of demonology? Tales of magic? Tales of the supernatural? Tales of sorcery? Tales of metamorphosis? Tales of wonder? Tales of cosmic irony? Tales of deity, destiny and nemesis? Perhaps, after all, the label "weird tales" serves as well as any. Smith's weird tales were certainly among the most ineffably weird ever to appear in the magazine of that same name.

And then there is the "magic" of Smith's style. One seems to be reading some sort of incantation or litany with measured invocations and responses. Just as Smith's subject-matter, his symbolism and his philosophies, so may his style be defined as baroque—a literary baroque quite unlike any other. By literary baroque we intend a style wherein certain Gothic elements—such as savageness, grotesqueness, antithesis, changefulness or metamorphosis, redundance or, in Smith's case, largely pseudo-redundance—have evolved from an ultimately classic matrix. To these we might also add the preoccupation with illusion, sometimes manifested in the use of the mirror, the mirage, the mask, and the maze; the fascination and obsession with death and gruesome physical detail; the love of paradox; the use of symbolic ambiguity; the emphasis on extravagance of color and an often outrageous efflorescence of vegetation and décor; the preference for objects and words and imageries of splendor; the element of the theatrical, often manifested in a kind of theatrical spotlighting on crucial objects or persons at critical moments; and a delight in what Leon Edel once termed "the familiar symptoms of decadence" but which are equally as well those of literature in its primal stages—a delight in the wonderful, the marvellous, the strange, the exotic, the bizarre, the hypernatural, and we might add, the unknown and the unknowable. For all the poetic denseness of his prose style—a style which makes heavy and deliberate use of the technique of poetic compression—Smith's syntax remains remarkably clear, and with striking rhythmical effects.

In his poems in prose and in his tales and/or extended poems in prose, there are prose rhythms that challenge comparison with those of the finest stylists in the language, including those of Sir Thomas Browne; whom, in sheer sustained stateliness and sombre splendor of style and subject, Smith surpasses in many instances, or at the very least fully equals. Smith's genius for creating and sustaining a powerful mood—partly through a more or less related system of imagery and through a lucid, even if elaborate, syntax—simplifies the baroque antitheses and complications inherent in his tales, and thereby succeeds in giving his tales their characteristic tense unity. The prose of Clark Ashton Smith features, as does the prose of Sir Thomas Browne (and as does, of course, Smith's own poetry), a skillful, often uncanny juxtaposition of Anglo-Saxon words with those of Græco-Latinate polysyllables—this creates an effect approximating the incantatory effect of poetry. The prose of Smith's tales is as studied and deliberate as the prose of his poems in prose and as the language of verse. It goes without saying that such a prose demands an unusual and a careful quality of reading to be fully grasped and appreciated. While Smith's style is based in part on Poe, and suggestive in certain respects of Sir Thomas Browne, yet the result is wholly original, quite unlike the style of any other writer. And despite its elaboration and seeming excess, it is essentially a highly compressed, compact, and economical prose. Without such a prose style it would have been impossible for Smith to have created the illusion of reality so characteristic of his tales of superficial unreality.

As poetic and mythical considerations of death and mortality, such poems in prose as "The Memnons of the Night," "From the Crypts of Memory," and "The Shadows," together with such extended poems in prose as "The Planet of the Dead," "The Empire of the Necromancers," or "The Death of Malygris," form worthy twentieth-century companion-pieces to the last chapter of Sir Thomas Browne's *Urne-Buriall*, i.e., *Hydriotaphia*.

Merely regarded as short stories told in a heavily poetic style, Smith's fictions would appear extraordinary. Regarded more exactly as extended poems in prose, which is what many of them are in all actuality, his tales are nothing less than astonishing. To sustain a poem in prose for one or two pages is not an impossible feat; but to sustain one for ten, fifteen, even twenty pages, as Smith has undeniably done on many occasions, must be accounted a technical achievement of genius.

Smith's finest tales are in the nature of condensations, distillations, quintessences. They have all the richness of element usually associated with the novel; indeed, many of them could well have been told as novels; in fact, at least one of them (to wit, "The Chain of Aforgomon") Smith did first project as a novel; but the poet-author preferred to condense his stories into as small a space as possible. A few of Smith's tales are allegories; but many are parables of emotional truth, although often allegorical in part. Regarded as strange parables of love and death, or as quintessences of beauty, fear, love, wonder, ineffable strangeness, and much, much else; the tales of Clark Ashton Smith must in all truth take rank as something unique in the annals of prose fiction.

## The Sorcerer Departs

Smith remained the poet to the very end. He composed his last poem, the sonnet "Cycles," (to quote his own words) "in the midst of the Sabbath pandemonium of dogs, brats and autoes" of June 4th, 1961. A little more than two months later, on the 14th of August, Monday night, at the age of sixty-eight, Clark Ashton Smith died quietly in his sleep at his home in Pacific Grove, attended to the last by his devoted wife Carol.

Smith's true literary affinities have been given little serious recognition. The affinity with Poe manifests itself primarily in a certain weirdness, in certain phrase mannerisms, and in the extreme musicality of much of Smith's verse and of his prose. Indeed, for sheer gorgeousness of sound the student of poetry must go back to the lyrical beauty of Edmund Spenser's strikingly baroque epic *The Fœrie Queene* for a just comparison. In the cosmic range of their fancy Spenser and Smith have much in common, as well as in an inexhaustible sense of wonder. Smith's tale "The Garden of Adompha," with its infernal and sentient vegetation, seems like a curious amalgam and extrapolation of "The Garden of Proserpina" (Book II: Canto VII) and of "The Garden of Adonis" (Book III: Canto XII) in *The Fœrie Queene*. There is an interesting evolution from the idyllic mediæval dream-garden in *Le Roman de la Rose* to such examples of the Spenserian garden as "The Garden of Proserpina," "The Garden of Adonis," and "The Bowre of Blisse" (Book II: Canto XII) and then the garden of venomous flowers in Hawthorne's tale "Rappaccini's Daughter" and then to "The Garden of Adompha."

Smith's affinities with Baudelaire are so obvious as to pass almost without mention. However, we must allude to one fundamental affinity between Smith and Baudelaire. The French poet sought to create beauty out of the filth, the squalor, the disease, the evil and the horror of a great metropolis (Paris). Similarly, Smith sought to create beauty not so much out of the filth, the evil, the implicit or actual horror of one great city as he did out of the ugliness of death and decay and destruction, out of the horror of an irrevocable doom, out of the terror of an ultimate nothingness beyond death (what Sir Thomas Browne terms "the uncomfortable night of nothingness"), or paradoxically out of the possibility that there is no death, that all animate things whether in life or in death as well as all things inanimate—in short, absolutely all things—by virtue of their theoretically indestructible atoms are part and parcel of an inconceivably monstrous and perverse arch-life-form without beginning and without end whether in space or in time that involves not only the cosmos but also the void beyond the cosmos. (This last is given its most powerful symbolic embodiment in the "huge eyeless Face, / That fills the void and fills the universe, / And bloats against the limits of the world / With lips of flame that open," in the tenth and final section of "The Hashish-Eater.") If, as averred by Victor Hugo, Baudelaire did introduce into the literature of poetry "un frisson nouveau," then Smith has in his own turn introduced "le frisson cosmique."

Smith also has a certain similarity with such Jacobean dramatists of death and the perverse as Cyril Tourneur and John Webster and their arch-imitator of the early nineteenth century, Thomas Lovell Beddoes. However, Smith has far more than the single string of death on his harp; there are also, among others, the strings of love and beauty. His love poems alone would rank Smith as a poet of unique attainments. For form, for originality of imagery, for originality of created poetic forms, for choice of line length, and for depth of emotion, such collections or cycles of love poems as *Sandalwood* and *The Hill of Dionysus* compare favorably with the best of the series of love poems and sonnets by such English poets as Sir Philip Sidney, William Shakespeare, or Ernest Dowson or by such poets of the French Renaissance as Pierre de Ronsard and Louise Labé.

There is besides an unmistakable resemblance between Smith and the French Protestant, eminently baroque poet Agrippa d'Aubigné, in their love of antithesis and their preoccupation with death and destruction. For example, d'Aubigné devotes at least two, *Les Feux* and *Les Fers*, of the seven principal divisions of his epic *Les Tragiques*, to catalogues of people meeting violent deaths through civil war and the tortures of martyrdom. Such a poem by Smith as "The City of Destruction," published in *The Arkham Sampler*, winter 1948, seems especially d'Aubignesque: its long lines, strong rhythms, relentless piling-up of images, all suggest the forceful alexandrines of d'Aubigné, with their realization of emotional intensity through the steady accumulation of synonyms and phrases of a similar nature.

The much "quaint and curious... forgotten lore" to be found in the canon of Smith's works, especially of his tales, has extended parallels in the works of Sir Thomas Browne, particularly in the latter's *Pseudodoxia Epidemica* or *Vulgar Errors* (1646)—with its inquiry into and consideration of the basilisk, of griffins, of the phoenix, of the salamander living in fire, of the chameleon living only upon air, of the unicorn's horn, of the ostrich digesting iron, of "the musical note of swans before their death", of "the pictures of mermaids, unicorns, and some others," etc., etc. That which Lytton Strachey once cited as the peculiarities of Browne's style—"the studied pomp of its latinisms, its wealth of allusion, its tendency toward sonorous antithesis"—could be cited just as well as being the peculiarities of Smith's own style. However, there are far more than stylistic affinities between these two highly baroque literary creators. Browne's works demonstrate a sense of wonder and a taste for wonders real or imaginary equal to the same demonstrated by Spenser or by Smith. Browne was a great student of Dante's theological fantasy in epic verse *La Divina Commedia.* Just as *Hydriotaphia* (1658) with its theme of death and of implicit hell connotes with Dante's *Inferno*; and just as *The Garden of Cyrus* (1658) with its implicit theme of life eternal and ever-renewing connotes with the Italian poet's *Paradiso*; so does *Hydriotaphia* connote with the emphasis in Smith on death, on funereal monuments and paraphernalia, on deserts, on desolation, on an ultimate nothingness; and so does *The Garden of Cyrus* connote with the emphasis in Smith on verdure, on the vernal, on extravagance of color, on an ultimately outrageous efflorescence, or on the green fire of "the singing flame." In Smith's compressed epic "The Apocalypse of Evil" the ultimate conclusion, that immortality is part of an infinite and eternal arch-life-form of the cosmos and of the void, is similar to but yet distinct from—due to Browne's over-all Christian perspective—the sentiments implicit in some of the concluding pensées in *Urne-Buriall*, such as: "Life is a pure flame, and we live by an invisible Sun within us," and "Ready to be anything in the extasie of being ever..." Such a phrase by Browne as "The night of time far surpasseth the day..." could serve as the motto or moral of Smith's poem in prose "The Memnons of the Night." Such a phrase by Browne as "The number of the dead long exceedeth all that shall live," finds an unexpected similarity to the phrase "...the dead had come to outnumber infinitely the living," in Smith's poem in prose "From the Crypts of Memory," and to the phrase "...its immemorial dead, who had come to outnumber infinitely the living," in Smith's extended poem in prose "The Planet of the Dead." And the following selection from Browne's posthumously published *Christian Morals* (1716), Part the Third, Section XIV, is amazingly similar to the spirit animating so much of Smith's verse and prose, and could easily have been written by Smith himself: "Let thy Thoughts be of things which have not entered into the Hearts of Beasts: Think of things long past, and long to come: Acquaint thyself with the *choragium* of the Stars, and consider the vast expansion beyond them. Let Intellectual Tubes give thee a glance of things, which visive Organs reach not. Have a glimpse of incomprehensibles, and Thoughts of things, which Thoughts but tenderly touch."

The extended short story by William Beckford, *The History of the Caliph Vathek*, and much of Oriental fiction as exemplified in *The Arabian Nights*, connote with the extravagance of color, incident, and décor or background in many of Smith's tales. For sheer color and bizarrerie the extended poem in prose "The Dark Eidolon" out-Vatheks *Vathek*. If Poe did create the extended poem in prose in such masterpieces as "The Masque of the Red Death," it remained for Smith to re-create the genre and create extensively within it. Stylistically the tales of Clark Ashton Smith are, in part, a continuation and a fulfillment on the one hand of the work of Edgar Allan Poe (the Poe of "Shadow - A Parable," "Silence - A Fable," and of course "The Masque of the Red Death") and on the other of the *Petits Poèmes en prose* of Baudelaire, as well as of Smith's own earlier Poems in Prose in *Ebony and Crystal*.

The critical pontiffs of the twentieth century have so far passed over the work of Smith in verse and prose through a peculiar series of circumstances. Smith's poetry, because it was published mainly in private and limited editions, has become the property of only a fortunate few. His prose has been known principally to a specialized audience. The reviews of *Out of Space and Time* and *Lost Worlds* in *The New York*

*Times Book Review* proved almost completely inadequate: one cannot help but wonder as to the reception that would be given to Sir Thomas Browne if he lived today, with its distaste for an elaborate style and for anything that might seem a little bit of too much. And there is much else in Smith's work to make an adequate larger critical recognition difficult, at least during the present century with its frequent and tasteless emphasis on creative literature primarily as autobiographical revelation or as a happy hunting ground for "specialists" in critico-psychoanalysis or for "professors with a system" (to quote in part an early epigram of Smith's). It is, alas, the age of "the brave hunters of fly-specks on Art's cathedral windows" (to use George Sterling's phrase). But, like the ones antecedent, this convention as well as its fostering age will in their own turn pass on to the special nirvana reserved for such, leaving the way clear mayhap for better, more generous ones to take their place.

In an admirable and perceptive essay on Baudelaire first published in 1875, the great English critic George Saintsbury once stated: "It is not merely admiration of Baudelaire which is to be persuaded to English readers, but also imitation of him which is with at least equal earnestness to be urged upon English writers." He then states further, rather ruefully, that "we have always lacked more or less the class of *écrivains artistes*—writers who have recognized the fact that writing is an art, and who have applied themselves with the patient energy of sculptors, painters, and musicians to the discovery of its secrets," and that if the sense of a distinguished prose style has been lost in English, nothing could be more effective for its rediscovery than a study of Baudelaire's prose as a model and a stimulant to writers in English. Less than half a century later, in 1922, as if in answer to this earnest exhortation, appeared *Ebony and Crystal* with its twenty-nine *Poems in Prose*. Alas, Saintsbury is dead, and critics of his stature, of his broad culture and perspective, are rare indeed in this present day and age. Perhaps somewhere in the long circle of eternity there will come a people who will take unhesitatingly to their hearts Smith's brilliant creations in verse and in prose. As the barriers of space and time are steadily removed through the white magic of modern science, Smith with his emphasis on the cosmic and the astronomic could easily become "the poet of the space age."

The poetry and the prose of Clark Ashton Smith represent, in part, a continuation of the humanities of the Renaissance and of classical antiquity. But by giving them a cosmic framework, that is, by emphasizing the surrounding cosmos, Smith has indicated a new avenue of approach to those old, old, old human values and relations. And at the same time, for a literature tending toward an over-anthropocentrism, he has indicated an avenue toward the stars, toward the outer cosmos, and toward possible other universes. He thus avoids the greatest pitfall, the greatest handicap of so much of the serious creative literature of the twentieth century, as well as of the attendant serious literary criticism,—"that introversion and introspection, that morbidly exaggerated prying into one's own vitals—and the vitals of others—which Robinson Jeffers has so aptly symbolized as 'incest.'" (From Smith's letter to the editor, *Wonder Stories*, August 1932.) Curiously, much of Smith's literary work certainly satisfies the thesis put forth by Arthur Machen in his study *Hieroglyphics* (1902) "that great writing is the result of an ecstatic experience akin to divine revelation." Much of Smith's works also satisfies the present writer's contention that great writing should give the reader a sense of cosmic universality and, above all, a sense of unlimitedness.

The first major poet in English to be influenced by Poe and very likely to remain the last as well, Smith certainly does not belong to any *Weird Tales* "school"—nor yet does he belong to any Gothic or neo-Gothic tradition except, in part, that of his own synthesis and creation. He is essentially *sui generis*. In the words of his own epigram: "The true poet is not created by an epoch; he creates his own epoch." Never lived a poet more than Smith of whom this could be said: Smith, the creator par excellence not only of one epoch or of one world but the creator of many epochs, of many worlds. A deliberate independent and outsider, he belongs to no particular time nor literary period or school: only to that mystical mainstream of literature and art which is one with all cultures and all ages. His tales and/or extended poems in prose are far more than mere exotic "divertissements." They represent a return to the fantastic fictions of serious intent of the Renaissance—to the *Utopia* of Sir Thomas More, to the *Gargantua et Pantagruel* of Rabelais, to *The Færie Queene* of Spenser. They are informed with the seriousness of theme and concept and with the wealth of artistry, of technique, of invention that distinguish Smith's finest poems or that distinguish any great poetry. His finest poems, poems in prose and extended poems in prose are deliberate gestures toward the infinite and the eternal, toward those legendary eternal verities which ultimately can be neither proven nor disproven, and which in that sense are indeed timeless. He uses fantasy both in his poems and in his tales deliberately and manifestly in order to transcend the prosaic and unstable reality of a mere ephemeral contemporariness, and to attain to a greater and eternal reality beyond. He searches not only the ultimate meaning of man and his principal emotions of love and fear but, far more than those, the very significance of life and of the cosmos itself.

Smith, in translating himself and his readers to the elaborate worlds created of his imagination, seems to be fulfilling the Baudelairian aspiration to be transported "Anywhere! Anywhere! as long as it be out of this world!" In Baudelaire's poem in prose "Anywhere Out of This World," the poet asks his soul where they should go: to an idealized and picturesque Lisbon, Rotterdam, Batavia, Torneo, the Baltic, or the North Pole with its splendors of the aurora borealis. After the poet has finished his inquiry, the soul shouts in answer: "Anywhere! Anywhere! as long as it be out of this world!" This aspiration Smith embodies in one of his own poems, the sonnet "To the Chimera," wherein the poet cries out: "Unknown chimera, take us, for we tire / Amid the known monotony of things!" and then entreats the chimera not to pause "Till on thy horns of planished silver flows / The sanguine light of Edens lost to God." The first complete publication of Baudelaire's *Petits Poèmes en prose* (the French poet's last work, one which in many respects he regarded as his most important) took place posthumously, in 1869, two years after his death in 1867. The third poem in prose from the end of the book is the one entitled "Anywhere Out of This World". This fact has considerable significance as three has been, from primal times down to the present, the mystical number of creation, re-creation, and of life eternal. Thus, in one sense, Smith takes up where Baudelaire has left off. Nor can we over-emphasize here—in regard to this inspired aspiration toward the unknown and the otherworldly—the essential trinity of souls formed by Poe, Baudelaire and Smith; for the title of this *poème en prose* is a quotation by Baudelaire out of the canon of the works of the elder American poet.

There are certain things in the works of a literary creator of which the industrious and systematic student can cite catalogues of examples, in which he can discern principal themes and concepts, of which he can analyze the style, of which he can trace the evolution, and in which he can trace or discern the influence of other writers. But there is something which cannot be treated or understood in this way; and that something is the genius which in Smith manifests itself as the "sheer dæmonic strangeness and fertility of conception" (to use Lovecraft's happy and perceptive phrase). It is almost as if Smith were literally from another sphere than our own, or at least were literally inspired by some cosmic or otherworldly *genius* or *dæmon*; and ultimately these two words have meanings remarkably alike: *genius*, a tutelary spirit; and *dæmon*, a tutelary spirit or divinity.

In the crystal of his mind's eye Smith beheld strange, ineffable things. His consummate art was the arch-magician's mirror through which he permitted others to view and share his visions: those curious pageantries of doom, of death, of beauty, of love, of wonder, of destiny, of stars and planets, and of the cosmos. Let us therefore be grateful to him for the enchantment and ecstasy and revelation that he created for kindred souls. And let us salute the passing of a generous and a noble spirit whose like we shall not see again.

*Quotations from Smith used in this essay, unless otherwise noted, are principally from "George Sterling—An Appreciation" in* The Overland Monthly *for March 1927, and from "An Autobiography of Clark Ashton Smith" in* The Science Fiction Fan *for August 1936. Quotations from Sir Thomas Browne, unless otherwise noted, are all from Chapter V of* Urne-Buriall.

## CYCLES

The sorcerer departs... and his high tower is drowned
Slowly by low flat communal seas that level all...
While crowding centuries retreat, return and fall
Into the cyclic gulf that girds the cosmos round,
Widening, deepening ever outward without bound...
Till the oft-rerisen bells from young Atlantis call;
And again the wizard-mortised tower upbuilds its wall
Above a re-beginning cycle, turret-crowned.

New-born, the mage re-summons stronger spells, and spirits
With dazzling darkness clad about, and fierier flame
Renewed by æon-curtained slumber. All the powers

Of genii and Solomon the sage inherits;
And there, to blaze with blinding glory the bored hours,
He calls upon Shem-hamphorash, the nameless Name.

Clark Ashton Smith
June 4th, 1961.

## AFTERWORD

Reading again after many years this biographico-critical essay that I wrote in the early 1960s, I discover that there is very little about it that needs correction or other changes except the purely statistical data (mostly found at the end of the first and longest of the essay's three major sections) and other material of a similar nature. These few corrections and changes (some of them still involving an educated guess) I have accordingly made, but for the most part the essay remains more or less as it was when it made its first appearance in August of 1963. Other tributes and memorial publications in honor of Clark Ashton Smith have since presented themselves to the interested reader. However, the Klarkash-Tonophiles (that solid core of Smith's admirers both inside and outside the U.S.A.) remain indebted to Jack L. Chalker and his associates, then centered at Baltimore, Maryland, for sponsoring and publishing their chapbook *In Memoriam: Clark Ashton Smith*, that initial and large-scale tribute, during that long-ago summer of 1963. Apart from the few corrections and changes deemed fundamentally needed, the opinions and evaluations expressed in this essay by me concerning Smith's output in verse and prose remain the same. I formulated these in my latter twenties, and albeit I am in my early seventies now, I have not changed my mind in regard to the general or specific uniqueness, beauty, and worth of his poetry and fiction. At least on this one subject I still hold the same opinions now that I held back then, and (if such is possible) even more obdurately.

Looking back on the person that I was then—in that era just before the arrival of the Beatles in the U.S.A.—I note how concerned I was, and with very good reason, to give Smith his just critical due. Apart from those articles and reviews (1911–1927) resulting from his early poetic career (beginning in 1910 and ending in the latter 1920s), there existed in the early 1960s very little critical writing on C.A.S., especially material that interrelated the poetry with the later fiction. That Smith like H.P. Lovecraft had become by the time that he died one of the great outsiders of his over-all period, seemed obvious enough, and I made this condition the solid basis for my critical evaluation. If he did, or does, not quite compare with anyone else born in the latter 1800s, and expiring sometime in the 1900s whether early or late—except perhaps his poetic mentor and progenitor George Sterling, as well as his counterpart in fiction, H.P. Lovecraft—then that fundamental condition freed me completely. I could thus roam through the literary history of the Western World—from the Middle Ages and the Renaissance on through the nineteenth and twentieth centuries—to find those writers and poets with whom I sincerely felt that Smith could honestly compare.

As a poet in verse and in prose Klarkash-Ton (as H.P.L. playfully dubbed him) ranks as a great and unique artist, particularly in view of all the profound changes that have happened just in the art or science of verse technique, that is, of prosody, in the English language. Smith remained true to the poetic tradition to which he was born, and which he learned, painstakingly, with genius and originality, to use from the time of his early adolescence until his death. Such a poet does not change his practice to suit the latest fad or fashion of the passing moment—a poetic tradition, moreover, inherited from hundreds of years of experimentation as well as of genuine achievement. At this late date in time one is constrained to admire such rare integrity, no less than the solid belief that he maintained in the poetic tradition that he received and that he mastered. As he was in life, so is Smith in death: *sui generis*.

Tsathoggua Press rendered a real service by republishing this essay in January of 1997 as a separate booklet, thirty-three years after its first appearance, just as Silver Key Press, the English-language imprint of the French nonprofit small press La Clef d'Argent, renders a no less valuable service by republishing it again today. On behalf of Klarkash-Ton I personally give the successive publishers of this essay—Mirage Press, Tsathoggua Press, and Silver Key Press, and now Night Shade Books—all possible credit and gratitude.

*Donald Sidney-Fryer*
*Westchester, Los Angeles, February 2007.*

# The Animated Sword

"The blade is not for sale, sahib, nay, not for ten times a hundred rupees."

Of Benares workmanship, sharply curved, razor-edged, with a jewel-studded hilt, and grooves down the blade containing those little pearls which are known as "the tears of the enemy," the sword was one that a king might have been proud to own. But the price I had offered Pir Mohammed, a hundred rupees, was a high one even for such and I was greatly surprised when he refused to sell it. It was in his stock, with a number of other blades, of all kinds, from Hussaini scimitars to khitars and Malay krises and I had naturally assumed that it was for sale. I am an inveterate collector of curios, and certainly the sword would have been a valuable addition to my collection.

"Why?" I queried.

The old sword-dealer did not answer at once. A faraway look had come over his face at my question, as though something past and far distant had suddenly been called to mind. At last he spoke.

"The tale is a strange one, sahib, and haply thou wilt not believe it. But if it is thy wish, then will I unfold it and thou shalt know why I will not sell the blade."

I begged him to tell it, and in his thin, quavering voice, with his hands caressing the hilt of the sword, he spoke:

"Long ago, sahib, long ere the great earthquake in Kashmir, even before the Sepoy Mutiny, I dwelt in a large city of the Deccan, under the rule of one of its most powerful chieftains. I was but twenty at the time, but my father was dead and I had succeeded to a considerable fortune. I was a merchant, a dealer in rugs, as was my father before me and his father before him. I had no family and but one man whom I might call friend. This was a young Moslem of about my own age, a native of the same town. We had played together, learned the Koran under the same moolah, and, in short, had grown up together.

His name was Ahmed Ali. His father, Shere Ali, was a horse-trader, and as he was, so was the son after him. When Shere Ali died we concluded to live together, and though we conducted our respective trades apart, we broke bread on the same table. No two men were ever truer to each other, sharing each other's secrets and allowing no woman to come between us.

One evening when Ahmed came home he brought with him a sword, the very same that you see before you. He said he had bought it of a Hindu in the bazaar, paying him much money for it.

"He asked more," said Ahmed, "but I refused to pay it and he gave in readily enough when he saw that I was in earnest. Indeed, he seemed very eager to get rid of the sword. After I had laid down the money he told me that it had been stolen from a great Rajah, a man engaged in a war with the Feringhees.

"And beware," he went on, "for the cursed thing is possessed of a devil. Thinkest thou I should have sold it thee for but a tithe of its real worth had it not been for that?"

"With that he went away, nor would he tell me more when I followed him to ask further about the sword."

"What did he mean by saying that it was possessed of a devil?" I asked.

"I know not," replied my friend gaily. "I have not yet seen it. Doubtless it is only a Hindu devil, anyway, and not a true son of Iblees. Such can only harm infidels, like the man of whom I bought it. But it is a good blade and the possession of a devil or two can but increase its effectiveness."

"Beware," said I, "lest the fiend leave it for thee."

Ahmed laughed and went to his room. He wore the sword when he went out the next morning, and for several days thereafter.

One morning, as I was arranging the folds of my turban, I heard a crash in his room, as of something falling to the floor, and a moment later Ahmed rushed in half-clothed, pale with terror and shivering all over. There was a wild stare in his eyes, as though he had just looked upon some awful and unaccountable thing.

With chattering teeth he managed to pour out something incoherent, in which all I could distinguish was:

"The sword! The sword!"

"Meanest thou the Hindu blade?" I asked.

His agitation had now subsided somewhat, and he was able to speak more clearly.

"Truly, the Hindu uttered no falsehood. I swear that the sword is haunted not only by one but by many devils—so many that the doubly-cursed weapon of shame leaped from the rack and fell in the centre of the room."

"Surely this is madness," said I. "Did man ever see before a sword imbued with power to move of itself?"

"I have told thee the truth. There is a devil in the blade—and a most lively imp it is—an orthodox, well educated son of Iblees."

"Not even Dulhan, who dwells in the slippers of the Faithful, is so mischievous. And as a sword is to a slipper so is this most lively and accomplished devil to Dulhan.

"Come thou and see for thyself!"

We went into his apartment, and surely enough, there lay the glittering blade, full on a Punjaub rug in the centre. A shield of rhinoceros hide, behind which it had hung, lay on the divan and the scabbard was some distance from it on the floor.

Ahmed picked up the sword gingerly, lest the devil that he supposed to be in it should scorch his fingers. He handed it to me and I examined it closely, but could see nothing unusual about it. I told him that he must have been dreaming.

"But how came the sword here? Nay, it was a devil that made it jump from the wall."

Naught that I might say could shake his faith. However, I persuaded him to hang the blade up again and see if its strange actions were repeated. So he put it back on the rack with the scabbard and the shield.

The afternoon of the next day we were seated on the divan opposite, talking over our affairs. Both of us had been engaged in important business transactions that morning, and we had temporarily forgotten the sword and its strange actions.

Suddenly I heard a slight sound, and glancing up saw the rhinoceros hide shield begin to move and then spring from the rack and crash on the floor. The scabbard followed, and then the sword, with a flash and a hiss, flew vengefully down, and striking the floor point-first, stuck there glittering in the sunshine that streamed through the open window, while we stared with eyes starting from our heads with astonishment.

"Art thou satisfied now, Pir Mohammed?" asked Ahmed.

"Truly, " I answered, "the weapon's behaviour is strange."

"I shall fling the blade into the deepest part of the Nerbudda river." said my friend.

"Nay, give it to me. It is too fine a sword to throw away, and I warrant thee that I can brave a dozen devils such as the one thou believest possesses it."

"Take it then. But if thou dost not like the gift, do with it as I would have done. And remember the evil spirit thou hast seen spring to life in it, so that if evil befall thee, thou mayst not say that thou wast not warned in time. Surely no good can come from association with the malignant son of Iblees who hath taken it into his head to animate the accursed Kafir blade."

I took the weapon to my room and hung it on a rack with my other arms. For two weeks the strange performance was not repeated, and I began to think that the evil spirit, or whatever it was, had departed, and would trouble the blade no more. But Ahmed was not so sanguine, and seemed to be possessed of a fixed idea that harm would yet come of it. He was wrapped in gloom, and although he made repeated efforts to rid himself of his forebodings, could never entirely do so. Several times he implored me to throw the sword away, but I was obstinate, and ridiculed his premonitions of evil, telling him that they were but vapours of the mind. The devil, if such it were, was a Hindu one and should not daunt a true believer.

Early one evening we were seated in my room. The date, the fifteenth of Saphar, is fixed indelibly in my mind. Ahmed, strangely enough, had for once succeeded in shaking off his forebodings. He had made a very good sale that day, and was in high feather.

Suddenly, by a common impulse, we glanced up at the sword. It was quivering, and the lamplight ran and danced along its polished surface. In a moment, throwing the other weapons to the floor by the movement, it sprang point-first from the rack. It flashed hissing toward Ahmed. He had no time to step aside. The blade struck him full in the breast, and he threw up his arms with a wild cry. I saw his face as he half-turned in falling; it was a frozen mask of fear, horror and amazement.

Leaving him there with the sword in his body, six inches of the blade sticking out at the back to testify to the force with which it had been driven, I went out into the streets. I wandered about half the night, scarcely knowing where I went, and almost in a state of collapse. It was long after midnight when I returned and summoned courage to re-enter and face the thing that had been my friend.

I laid down and went to sleep from sheer mental and physical exhaustion. When I awoke I found myself in the town prison; certain busybodies of the neighbourhood who had entered and found Ahmed dead and myself in a stupour, having taken it upon themselves to have me arrested for murder. I was tried, and told my story. Some believed me and others deemed me a dreamer or a madman. But as my close friendship with Ahmed was well-known, few suspected me of his murder, and I was speedily acquitted.

I immediately sold all my possessions, and bringing only the money and the sword with me, I came to Delhi and took service under the Feringhees. My obstinacy persisted, even in the face of the fate that had befallen my friend, and I would not part with the blade. Or was it that I could not? Perhaps there was some fateful spell about it. Who knows?

There was a certain young Moslem from Lahore in my regiment with whom I became great friends. One day I told him the story of the sword. He was very thoughtful for awhile before he spoke.

"Pir Mohammed," said he, "this blade once belonged to the Rajah of Johore, a large Central Indian state. Two years ago, as the Hindu of whom thy friend bought it, said, it was stolen from him. He made great searches for the thief, but without success. He valued the sword greatly, for it was one that had long been in the hands of the Rajahs of Johore, and there was a tradition among them that it made the owner invulnerable and insured him against defeat. It was welded many centuries ago in Benares by the famous Hindu swordsmith, Amaru Cheynab, to the chanting of mantras, or spells, by the priests of Siva. Thus the superstition. There was also another belief to the effect that the Rajah, could, in time of need, if the sword were not then at hand, call it to him.

"Shortly after the theft the Rajah became engaged in a war with the Feringhees. I was in one of the regiments that were sent against him. It was a lengthy campaign, for the Rajah had a large and well-disciplined army, and he put up a desperate fight. He won several skirmishes, but when our forces met him in a more decisive battle, he was worsted, though not after a severe struggle. Several more battles had to be fought though, before he could be vanquished, and in these the Rajah and his men, Kshatriyas of the purest blood, fought with a valour worthy of Khoumbou and Qudey Singh. But he lost every battle, and slowly but surely, we drove him back toward his capital, the great walled city of Johore.

"Finally his army, or the shattered remnant of it, stood at bay on the plains before the city. It was said that the Rajah would retreat no further, but would stay on the field with his remaining force and fight to the last man, disdaining to take shelter behind the walls.

"We advanced a little before noon, expecting to terminate the battle with one short, decisive struggle, but the Rajputs fought like the lions after which so many of them are named and surpassed all their previous records of bravery. Man to man we really outnumbered them, but victory was only to be purchased at a fearful price. Hour after hour they stood firm against our charges, though their ranks thinned momentarily, and their dead lay piled in heaps. Night drew on, but still a number of them, the Rajah at the head, held the field.

"The fight continued well into the evening, and might have held out longer had not the Rajah fallen by the sword of a Feringhee officer. Then his few remaining followers surrendered, we afterwards learned, by the Rajah's instructions.

He paused a little and went on: "This last battle was fought on the fifteenth of Saphar, the same day on which thy friend was killed by the sword."

Now light broke upon me and I saw the explanation of the sword's actions. Each time when it had leaped from the rack it had been at the Rajah's call, commanding it to return to him in his need. But he had not possessed the requisite will-power to compel it to the full obedience of the command, or perhaps the distance was too great. On the fifteenth of Saphar, in the extremity of his need, his call had been more vehement than previously, and so the blade had sprung with tremendous force, but only to sheath itself in Ahmed's body.

# The Red Turban

Mir Abdul Ali, chief of the Delhi police, was the narrator of the following story:

A wealthy merchant, one Lejut Puri, came to me telling of a theft which had recently occurred. A large and valuable sapphire, which had been in his possession for many years, was missing. It had been kept, he told me, in a small casket, to which he alone possessed a key. This had been broken open, apparently with some heavy object, and the stone taken out. He had no reason to suspect any of his household of the theft.

I went to Lejut Puri's house, accompanied by two officers, and we made a thorough examination of the room in which the sapphire had been kept. The casket, which was of some dark, heavy wood, was shattered into splinters. At first sight I did not perceive anything of importance—any clue that might point to the thief. Finally I perceived a red turban lying on a divan. I asked Lejut Puri if it belonged to him or to any of his family. Lejut, seeing it for the first time, gave a cry of surprise. "Sirdar," said he, "The turban is not mine, nor has it been worn by any of the household. Therefore it must have belonged to the thief, who dropped it in his haste."

Though somewhat perplexed that anyone should be so incautious as to leave his turban behind him, I took the merchant's view of the case.

I picked up the turban and examined it closely. It was a bright red, of the finest silk, and of a texture such as is worn only in Benares.

"This is a valuable clue." I remarked to Lejut Puri. "The thief, whoever he was, had very good taste in turbans, and the money wherewith to gratify it. Such as this are worn only by the wealthy."

I continued my examination of the room, but found nothing further of interest. I then called the merchant's servants together and subjected them to a rigid cross-examination. They were a badly frightened lot, and even had they known anything regarding the theft, I doubt if I could have elicited it from them, so great was their apprehension. They had neither seen nor heard the thief nor knew anything of the matter until their master had told them of it that morning.

Concluding that I could learn nothing more of value, I left taking the turban with me. I afterwards handed it over to one of my officers, with orders to take it to all the clothing shops in Delhi, and learn, if possible, from which it had been sold, and to whom.

I then dismissed the matter from my mind, having several important cases on hand.

My subordinate, Lal Singh, a Sikh, reported the following morning. "Sirdar," he said, "I have obeyed your orders. The turban was sold by one Ibrahim Marrash, a clothing dealer whose place of business is in the Chandui Chowk. He promptly identified it, and told me that it had been sold two weeks ago to one Indra Singh. Indra Singh is a wealthy and well-known Punjaubi, and is of high caste."

Indra Singh was a personal friend of mine, and therefore you may judge of my surprise upon hearing this. To verify it, I paid a visit in person to Ibrahim Marrash's shop, and received substantially the same story, with some added information, even to the price of the article.

"Indra Singh," said the dealer, "is an old customer of mine, and I have never sold him any but the best goods. Yes, I remember that turban well. I am confident that there is not another like it in Delhi. Sirdar, here are Russia-leather slippers such as a Maharajah might wear, and the price is just seven rupees!"

This affair was very perplexing. How came Indra Singh's turban into the merchant's house? I did not like to think that the Punjaubi was the thief. I knew him to be rich, and besides, he was honorable. High castes are not in the habit of appropriating other people's jewelry.

The Sapphire, in spite of the most stringent search, was not found, nor did I come any nearer to discovering the identity of the thief. As to Indra Singh's part in this matter, I gradually became convinced that there had been some mistake in regard to the turban. And besides, the presence of his turban in Lejut Puri's house by itself, was small proof of the Punjaubi's guilt.

Lejut Puri, who appeared to set a great value on his sapphire, came often, and seemed much disheartened that no progress had been made. The jewel, he told me, had belonged to his father, and had had an eventful history. It had originally been the property of a high-caste Punjaubi family from whom it had been taken during the terrible days of the mutiny. This family, it appeared, had remained true to the English during those times, and in consequence their house, after the mutineers had taken possession of the city and murdered the English inhabitants, had been looted by a mob. The sapphire fell into the hands of a low-caste Mohammedan, and was purchased from this man for a small sum by Leja Puri's father. Leja Puri gave the name of the original owner as Phairon Singh. The mentioning of this name gave me the first clue to the sapphire's disappearance. Phairon Singh was Indra Singh's father. Investigation revealed that he had remained faithful during the mutiny, and that his house had been sacked by an angry mob. I also learned that such a sapphire had been possessed by him, and that it had disappeared at this time.

It did not take long to put these facts and the finding of Indra Singh's turban together. Taking all into consideration, I decided that Indra Singh was the thief.

First the sapphire had belonged to his father. Then by a low-caste it had come into Leja Puri's family. Lawfully, it was the Punjaubi's property, and Puri had no more right to it than the low-caste. I became convinced that Indra Singh, learning of this, and wishing for some reason to regain the sapphire, had entered Puri's house and stolen it. How he had come to lose his turban I could not surmise. There were very many other things that I did not understand in the case. However, everything pointed to Indra Singh as the thief.

Several days later I paid a visit to the Punjaubi, with the full determination of getting to the bottom of the case. Nothing could be proved by inaction. The only thing was to get the truth out of Indra himself. I was morally convinced of his guilt, but could not prove it unless I obtained his confession.

Indra Singh was a man perhaps thirty years of age. He was tall, even for a Punjaubi, and wore a heavy, black beard.

He greeted me cordially. I could detect nothing in his manner which might indicate apprehension. If he were indeed guilty, it was clear that he did not connect my visit with the sapphire, or else he was an adept at hiding his feelings.

I stated the object of my visit at once.

"Indra," I said, drawing forth the red turban, "does this belong to you?" He started at seeing the article, but beyond that betrayed no emotion. He hesitated a while before answering.

"Sirdar," he said at last, "It is mine." I proceeded to tell him where it had been found, and my suspicions in regard to himself.

"Yes," he confessed slowly. "I may not lie. It was I who stole the sapphire from Leja Puri." He stopped, drew a small metal case from his bosom, and opened it. Within lay a sapphire of perhaps six carats weight, and which I, who am no expert in such matters, saw plainly to be flawless.

"Six hundred years," he continued, "this stone remained in our family. It is of great value apart from its intrinsic worth—for a legend no one knows how old, deems that it will bring good luck to the possessor. Six hundred years—and then the mutiny, when India was drenched in blood, and a madness more terrible than midsummer heat lay upon all the land. The stone was stolen. Till the day of his death my father, Phairon Singh, sought to regain it but in vain. And after him, I, his son, took up the search, and carried it to the end which you have seen. It was no easy matter to trace the thief—why detail?—but success crowned my efforts, and I learned that the sapphire had been sold to Leja Puri's father, and that it was now in the former's possession.

"The only method of regaining it which suggested itself, was theft. There was much risk, but my courage, nerved by determination to regain the sapphire, was equal to the deed. I learned from Puri's servants where he kept his jewels, and selecting a dark night, entered his house. I found the room, broke open the case containing the sapphire and was about to leave when I heard footsteps in the next room.

"Fearing that I was detected, a panic seized me, and in my haste to escape, a loose fold of my turban became entangled and I left the turban behind. I afterwards regretted this greatly, fearing that it might furnish a clue and have always cursed myself for my carelessness. Doubtless the person whose footsteps I heard was totally unaware of my presence, and had no intentions toward me."

"Of course," said I, "as the jewel was stolen from your father, it is legally your property. The fact that the thief sold it to Leja Puri's father does not entitle the latter to it. But there is another side of the case. You had no right to enter Leja Puri's house secretly, even for the purpose of regaining what was legally yours. Had you been caught in the act, there would have been little difficulty in convicting you for burglary.

"For over thirty years the sapphire was in the possession of the Puri family, having been purchased by Leja's father." I paused, and then went on.

"I have come here to urge you to return the sapphire. You will hand it over to me. I guarantee that the matter will be dropped. Leja will be only too happy to have it back, and will not make close inquiries as to the identity of the thief or the method of recovery."

I went on to inform him that if this demand was not complied with, it would be regretfully necessary to place him under arrest.

"I should be very sorry," I said, "for you have always been a good friend to me. But in the performing of duty, friendship is not to be considered, and my duty would be to arrest you for entering Leja Puri's residence for purposes of burglary."

Indra Singh thought the matter over, and recognized the justice of my remarks. I pointed out the situation to him in detail, and he finally, though reluctantly, assented, and gave me the sapphire. Fear of arrest perhaps had much to do with this but, from my knowledge of his character, I think that he really came around to my views.

Leja Puri received the sapphire. The tale which I told him of how I had discovered the thief, and of the jewel's recovery, I have always regarded as a masterpiece.

# Prince Alcouz and the Magician

Alcouz Khan was the only son of Yakoob Ullah, Sultan of Balkh. Unruly and vicious by nature, he was anything but improved by the luxury and power of his position. He grew up overbearing, cruel, and dissolute, and with mature years his faults and vices only became more pronounced. He was exactly the opposite of his father, who was a wise and just ruler and had endeared himself to the people.

The prince spent his time in reprehensible sports and dissipation and kept evil companions. His father often remonstrated with him, but without effect. He sighed when he thought of the day not far distant, for he was growing old, when Alcouz would come to the throne. The prince's succession, indeed, was universally dreaded, for well the people knew what manner of Sultan the cruel, dissipated youth would make.

There came to Balkh from Hindustan a noted magician, by name Amaroo. He soon became famous for his skill in foretelling the future. His patrons were many and of all stations in life, for the desire to tear aside the veil of the future is universal.

Alcouz, actuated by the common impulse, visited him. The magician, a small man with fiery, gleaming eyes, who wore flowing robes, arose from the couch whereon he had been sitting wrapped in meditation, and salaamed low.

"I have come to thee," said Alcouz, "that thou mayest read for me the hidden and inscrutable decrees of fate."

"In so far as lies my ability, I will serve thee," replied the Hindu. He motioned his visitor to be seated and proceeded with his preparations,

He spoke a few words in a tongue Alcouz could not understand and the room became darkened except for the dim, flickering light from a brazier of burning coals. Into this Amaroo cast various perfumed woods, which he had at hand. A thick black smoke arose, and standing in it, his figure half-hidden and seemingly grown taller and more impressive, he recited incantations in the strange and unknown tongue.

The room lightened and seemed to widen out indefinitely, with it the black vapor. Alcouz could no longer see the walls and the room seemed some vast cavern shut in at a distance by darkness. The smoke formed itself into curling, fantastic shapes which took on rapidly the semblance of human beings. At the same time the walls of the darkness contracted till they limited a space as large as the Sultan's throne room. More smoke arose from the brazier and grew to longs rows of pillars and to a dais and a throne. A shadowy figure sat upon the throne before which the other figures assembled and knelt. They rapidly became clearer, more distinct, and Alcouz recognized them.

The place was the royal throne-room, and the seated figure was himself. The others were officers of the court and his personal friends. A crown was placed on Alcouz's head and his courtiers knelt down in homage. The scene was maintained awhile and then the shapes re-dissolved into black vapor.

Amaroo stood at the prince's side. "What thou hast beheld will in time come to pass," he said. "Now thou shalt look upon another event."

Again he stood in the whirling smoke and chanted incantations, and again the vapor grew to pillars and a throne occupied by the solitary figure of Alcouz. He was sitting with unseeing eyes, absorbed in meditation. Anon a slave entered and seemed to speak to him, then withdrew.

Then came a figure which Alcouz recognized as that of Amaroo, the Hindu magician. He knelt before the throne and seemed to present some petition. The seated shape was apparently about to reply, when the Hindu, springing suddenly to his feet, drew a long knife from his bosom and stabbed him.

Almost at the same instant, Alcouz, who was watching horror-stricken, gave a wild cry and fell dead, stabbed to the heart by the magician, who had crept up behind him unobserved.

# The Malay Krise

"Sahib," said the sword-dealer, "this blade, which came from far Singapore, has not its equal for sharpness in all Delhi."

He handed me the blade for inspection. It was a long krise, or Malay knife, with a curious boat-shaped hilt, and, as he had said, was very keen.

"I bought it of Sidi Hassen, a Singapore dealer into whose possession it came at the sale of Sultan Sujah Ali's weapons and effects after the Sultan's capture by the British. Hast heard the tale, sahib? No? It runs thus:

"Sujah Ali was the younger son of a great Sultan. There being little chance of his ever coming to the throne, he left his father's dominions, and becoming a pirate, set out to carve for himself a name and an empire. Though having at first but a few *prahus* (boats) and less than a hundred men, he made up this lack by his qualities of leadership, which brought him many victories, much plunder and considerable renown. His fame caused many men to join him, and his booty enabled him to build more *prahus*. Adding continually to his fleets, he soon swept the rivers of the Peninsula, and then began to venture upon the sea. In a few years his ships were held in fear and respect by every Dutch merchantman or Chinese junk whose sails loomed above the waters of the China sea. Inland he began to overrun the dominions of the other Sultans, conquering, amongst others, that of his elder brother, who had succeeded to his father's throne. Sujah Ali's fame reached far, and its shadow lay upon many peoples.

"Then the English came to the Peninsula and built Singapore. Sujah Ali despatched ships to prey upon their vessels, many of whom he succeeded in capturing. The English sent big ships after him, bearing many heavy guns and many armed men.

"The Sultan went to meet them in person, with the greater part of his fleet. It was a disastrous day for him. When the red sun sank into the sea, fully fifty of his best *prahus,* and thousands of his men, amongst whom he mourned several of his most noted captains, lay beneath the waters. He fled inland with the shattered remnant of his fleet.

"The British resolved to crush him decisively, sent boats up the rivers, and in numerous hard-fought battles they sunk most of Sujah Ali's remaining *prahus,* and cleared land and water of the infesting pirates. The Sultan himself, however, they sought in vain. He had fled to a well-nigh inaccessible hiding-place—a small village deep in a network of creeks, swamps, and jungle-covered islands. Here he remained with a few fighting-men while the English hunted unsuccessfully for the narrow, winding entrances.

"Amina, his favorite wife, was among those who had accompanied him to this refuge. She was passionately attached to the Sultan, and, although such was his wish, had positively refused to be left behind.

"There was a beautiful girl in the village, with whom Sujah Ali became infatuated. He finally married her, and she exercised so great an influence over him that Amina, who had hitherto considered herself first in her husband's estimation, grew jealous. As time passed, and she perceived more clearly how complete was his infatuation, her jealousy grew more intense and violent, and at last prompted her to leave the village secretly one night, and to go to the captain of a British vessel which had been cruising up and down the river for weeks. To this man, one Rankling Sahib, she revealed the secret of Sujah Ali's hiding place. In thus betraying him, her desire was probably more for revenge upon her rival than upon the Sultan.

"Rankling Sahib, guided by Amina, passed at midnight through the network of creeks and jungles. He landed his crew and entered the village. The Malays, taken completely by surprise, offered little or no resistance. Many awoke only to find themselves confronted by loaded rifles, and surrendered without opposition.

"Sujah Ali, who had lain awake all evening wondering as to the cause of Amina's absence, rushed out of his hut with half a score of his men, and made a futile attempt at escape. A desperate fight ensued, in which he used his krise, the same that thou seest, with deadly effect. Two of the English he stretched dead, and a third he wounded severely.

"Rankling Sahib had given orders that the Sultan be taken alive, if possible. Finally, wounded, weary and surrounded by his foes on all sides, the Sultan was made prisoner. And the next morning was taken down river to Singapore.

"This is the krise you see on the wall."

# The Ghost of Mohammed Din

"I'll wager a hundred rupees that you won't stay there over-night," said Nicholson.

It was late in the afternoon, and we were seated on the veranda of my friend's bungalow in the Begum suburb at Hyderabad. Our conversation had turned to ghosts, on which subject I was, at the time, rather skeptical, and Nicholson, after relating a number of bloodcurdling stories, had finished by remarking that a nearby house, which was said to be haunted, would give me an excellent chance to put the matter to the test.

"Done!" I answered, laughing.

"It's no joking matter," said my friend, seriously. "However, if you really wish to encounter the ghost, I can easily secure you the necessary permission. The house, a six-roomed bungalow, owned by one Yussuf Ali Borah, is tenanted only by the spirit who appears to regard it as his exclusive property.

"Two years ago it was occupied by a Moslem merchant named Mohammed Din, and his family and servants. One morning they found the merchant dead—stabbed through the heart, and no trace of his murderer, whose identity still remains unrevealed.

"Mohammed Din's people left, and the place was let to a Parsee up from Bombay on business. He vacated the premises abruptly about midnight, and told a wild tale the next morning of having encountered a number of disembodied spirits, describing the chief one as Mohammed Din.

"Several other people took the place in turn, but their occupancy was generally of short duration. All told tales similar to the Parsee's. Gradually it acquired a bad reputation, and the finding of tenants became impossible."

"Have you ever seen the ghost yourself?" I asked.

"Yes; I spent a night, or rather part of one, there, for I went out of the window about one o'clock. My nerves were not strong enough to stand it any longer. I wouldn't enter the place again for almost any sum of money."

Nicholson's story only confirmed my intention of occupying the haunted house. Armed with a firm disbelief in the supernatural, and a still firmer intention to prove it all rot, I felt myself equal to all the ghosts, native and otherwise, in India. Of my ability to solve the mystery, if there were any, I was quite assured.

"My friend," said Nicholson to Yussuf Ali Borah an hour later, "wishes to spend a night in your haunted bungalow."

The person addressed, a fat little Moslem gentleman, looked at me curiously.

"The house is at your service, Sahib," he said. "I presume that Nicholson Sahib has told you the experiences of the previous tenants?"

I replied that he had. "If the whole thing is not a trumped-up story, there is doubtless some trickery afoot," said I, "and I warn you that the trickster will not come off unharmed. I have a loaded revolver, and shall not hesitate to use it if I meet any disembodied spirits."

Yussuf's only answer was to shrug his shoulders.

He gave us the keys, and we set out for the bungalow, which was only a few minutes' walk distant. Night had fallen when we reached it. Nicholson unlocked the door and we entered, and lighting a lamp I had brought with me, set out on a tour of inspection. The furniture consisted chiefly of two charpoys, three tabourets, an old divan quite innocent of cushions, a broken punkah, a three-legged chair and a dilapidated rug. Everything was covered with dust; the shutters rattled disconsolately, and all the doors creaked. The other rooms were meagerly furnished. I could hear rats running about in the dark. There was a compound adjoining, filled with rank weeds and a solitary pipal tree. Nicholson said that the ghost generally appeared in one of the rooms opening upon it, and this I selected as the one in which to spend the night. It was a fitting place for ghosts to haunt. The ceiling sagged listlessly, and the one charpoy which it contained had a wobbly look.

"Sleep well," said Nicholson. "You will find the atmosphere of this spirit-ridden place most conducive to slumber."

"Rats!" said I.

"Yes, there are plenty of rats here," he answered as he went out.

Placing the lamp on a tabouret, I lay down, with some misgivings as to its stability, on the charpoy. Happily, these proved unfounded, and laying my revolver close at hand, I took out a newspaper and began to read.

Several hours passed and nothing unusual happened. The ghost failed to materialize, and about eleven, with my skepticism greatly strengthened, and feeling a trifle ashamed concerning the hundred rupees which my friend would have to hand over the next morning, I lay down and tried to go to sleep. I had no doubt that my threat about the revolver to Yussuf Ali Borah had checked any plans for scaring me that might have been entertained.

Scarcely were my eyes closed when all the doors and windows, which had been creaking and rattling all evening, took on renewed activity. A light breeze had sprung up, and one shutter, which hung only by a single hinge, began to drum a tune on the wall. The rats scuttled about with redoubled energy, and a particularly industrious fellow gnawed something in the further corner for about an hour. It was manifestly impossible to sleep. I seemed to hear whisperings in the air, and once thought that I detected faint footsteps going and coming through the empty rooms. A vague feeling of eeriness crept upon me, and it required a very strong mental effort to convince myself that these sounds were entirely due to imagination.

Finally the breeze died down, the loose shutter ceased to bang, the rat stopped gnawing, and comparative quiet being restored, I fell asleep. Two hours later I awoke, and taking out my watch, saw, though the lamp had begun to burn dimly, that the hands pointed to two o'clock. I was about to turn over, when again I heard the mysterious footsteps, this time quite audibly. They seemed to approach my room, but when I judged them to be in the next apartment, ceased abruptly. I waited five minutes in a dead silence, with my nerves on edge and my scalp tingling.

Then I became aware that there was something between me and the opposite wall. At first it was a dim shadow, but as I watched, it darkened into a body. A sort of phosphorescent light emanated from it, surrounding it with pale radiance.

The lamp flared up and went out, but the figure was still visible. It was that of a tall native dressed in flowing white robes and a blue turban. He wore a bushy beard and had eyes like burning coals of fire. His gaze was directed intently upon me, and I felt cold shivers running up and down my spine. I wanted to shriek, but my tongue seemed glued to the roof of my mouth. The figure stepped forward and I noticed that the robe was red at the breast as though with blood.

This, then, was the ghost of Mohammed Din. Nicholson's story was true, and for a moment my conviction that the supernatural was all nonsense went completely to pieces. Only momentarily, however, for I remembered that I had a revolver, and the thought gave me courage. Perhaps it was a trick after all, and anger arose in me, and a resolve not to let the trickster escape unscathed.

I raised the weapon with a quick movement and fired. The figure being not over five paces distant, it was impossible to miss, but when the smoke had cleared it had not changed its position.

It began to advance, making no sound, and in a few moments was beside the charpoy. With one remaining vestige of courage I raised my revolver and pulled the trigger three times in succession, but without visible effect. I hurled the weapon at the figure's head, and heard it crash against the opposite wall an instant later. The apparition, though visible, was without tangibility.

Now it began to disappear. Very slowly at first it faded, then more rapidly until I could make out only the bare outlines. Another instant and all was gone but the outline of one hand, which hung motionless in the air. I got up and made a step toward it, then stopped abruptly, for the outlines again began to fill in, the hand to darken and solidify. Now I noticed something I had not before seen— a heavy gold ring set with some green gem, probably an emerald, appeared to be on the middle finger.

The hand began to move slowly past me toward the door opening into the next apartment. Lighting the lamp, I followed, all fear being thrown aside and desiring to find the explanation of the phenomenon. I could hear faint footfalls beneath the hand, as though the owner, though invisible, were still present. I followed it through the adjoining apartment and into the next, where it again stopped and hung motionless. One finger was pointed toward the further corner, where stood a tabouret, or stand.

Impelled, I think, by some force other than my own volition, I went over and lifting the tabouret, found a small wooden box, covered with dust, beneath.

Turning about I saw that the hand had disappeared.

Taking the box with me, I returned to my room. The thing was made of a very hard wood and in size was perhaps ten inches in length by eight in width and four in length. It was light, and the contents rustled when I shook it. I guessed them to be letters or papers, but having nothing to pry the box open with, I concluded to wait until morning before trying to.

Strange as it may seem I soon fell asleep. You would naturally think that a man would not feel inclined to slumber immediately after encountering a disembodied spirit. I can give no explanation of it.

The sun was streaming through the window when I awoke, and so cheerful and matter-of-fact was the broad daylight that I wondered if the events of the night were not all a dream. The presence of the box, however, convinced me that they were not.

Nicholson came in and appeared much surprised and a trifle discomfited to find me still in possession.

"*Well,*" he inquired, "what happened? What did you see?"

I told him what had occurred and produced the box as proof.

An hour afterwards, Nicholson, with a short native sword and considerable profanity, was trying to pry the thing open. He finally succeeded. Within were a number of closely-written sheets of paper and some letters, most of which were addressed to Mohammed Din.

The papers were mostly in the form of memoranda and business accounts such as would be made by a merchant. They were written in execrable Urdu, hopelessly jumbled together, and though all were dated, it was no small task to sort them out. The letters were mostly regarding business affairs, but several, which were written in a very fair hand, were from a cousin of Mohammed Din's, one Ali Bagh, an Agra horse-trader. These, too, with one exception, were commonplace enough. Nicholson knitted his brows as he read it, and then handed it to me. The greater part, being of little interest, has escaped my memory, but I recollect that the last paragraph ran thus:

"I do not understand how you came by the knowledge, nor why you wish to use it to ruin me. It is all true. If you have any love for me, forbear."

"What does that mean ?" asked Nicholson. "What secret did Mohammed Din possess that he could have used to ruin his cousin?"

We went through the memoranda carefully, and near the bottom found the following, dated April 21, 1881, according to our notation:

"To-day I found the letters which I have long been seeking. They are ample proof of what I have long known, but have hitherto been unable to substantiate, that Ali Bagh is a counterfeiter, the chief of a large band. I have but to turn them over to the police, and he will be dragged away to jail, there to serve a term of many years. It will be a good revenge—part compensation, at least, for the injuries he has done me."

"That explains Ali Bagh's letter," said Nicholson. "Mohammed Din was boastful enough to write to him, telling him that he knew of his guilt and intended to prove it."

Next were several sheets in a different hand and signed "Mallek Khan." Mallek Khan, it seemed, was a friend of Ali Bagh's, and the sheets were in the form of a letter. But being without fold, it was quite evident that they had not been posted.

The communication related to certain counterfeiting schemes, and the names of a number of men implicated appeared. There was another unfolded letter, this time from Ali Bagh, and relating to similar schemes. This, plainly, was the proof alluded to by Mohammed Din, and which he had threatened his cousin to turn over to the police.

There was nothing else of interest save the following in Mohammed Din's hand, dated April 17th, 1881:

"To-morrow I shall give the papers to the authorities. I have delayed too long, and was very foolish to write to Ali Bagh.

"I passed a man in the street to-day who bore a strong resemblance to my cousin.... I could not be sure... But if he is here, then may Allah help me, for he will hesitate at nothing..."

What followed was illegible.

"On the night of April 21st," said Nicholson, "Mohammed Din was killed by a person or person unknown." He paused and then went on: "This Ali Bagh is a man with whom I have had some dealings in horses, and an especially vicious crock it was that he got three hundred rupees out of me for. He has a bad reputation as a horse-dealer, and the Agra police have long been patiently seeking evidence of his implication in several bold counterfeiting schemes. Mallek Khan, one of his accomplices, was arrested, tried and sentenced to fifteen years' imprisonment, but refused to turn State's evidence on Ali Bagh. The police are convinced that Ali Bagh was as much, if not more implicated, than Mallek Khan, but they can do nothing for lack of proof. The turning over of these papers, however, as poor Mohammed Din would have done had he lived, will lead to his arrest and conviction.

"It was Ali Bagh who killed Mohammed Din, I am morally convinced, his motive, of course, being to prevent the disclosure of his guilt. Your extraordinary experience last night and the murdered man's papers point to it. Yet we can prove nothing, and your tale would be laughed at in court."

Some blank sheets remained in the bottom of the box, and my friend tilted them out as he spoke. They fluttered to the veranda and something rolled out from amongst them and lay glittering in the sunshine. It was a heavy gold ring set with an emerald—the very same that I had seen upon the apparition's finger several hours before.

A week or so later, as the result of the papers that Nicholson sent to the Agra police, accompanied by an explanatory note, one Ali Bagh, horse-trader, found himself on trial, charged with counterfeiting. It was a very short trial, his character and reputation going badly against him, and it being proven that he was the leader of the gang of which Mallek Khan was thought to be a member, he was sentenced to a somewhat longer term in jail than his accomplice.

# The Mahout

Arthur Merton, British Resident at Jizapur, and his cousin, John Hawley, an Agra newspaper editor, who had run down into Central India for a few weeks' shooting at Merton's invitation, reined in their horses just outside the gates of Jizapur. The Maharajah's elephants, a score of the largest and finest "tuskers" in Central India, were being ridden out for their daily exercise. The procession was led by Rajah, the great elephant of State, who towered above the rest like a warship amongst merchantmen. He was a magnificent elephant, over twelve feet from his shoulders to the ground, and of a slightly lighter hue than the others, who were of the usual muddy grey. On the ends of his tusks gleamed golden knobs.

"What a kingly animal!" exclaimed Hawley, as Rajah passed.

As he spoke, the mahout, or driver, who had been sitting his charge like a bronze image, turned and met Hawley's eyes. He was a man to attract attention, this mahout, as distinctive a figure among his brother mahouts as was Rajah among the elephants. He was apparently very tall, and of a high-caste type, the eyes proud and fearless, the heavy beard carefully trimmed, and the face cast in a handsome, dignified mold.

Hawley gave a second exclamation as he met the mahout's gaze and stared at the man hard. The Hindu, after an impressive glance, turned his head and the elephant went on.

"I could swear that I have seen that man before," said Hawley, at his cousin's interrogatory expression. "It was near Agra, about six years ago, when I was out riding one afternoon. My horse, a nervous, high-strung

Waler, bolted at the sight of an umbrella which someone had left by the roadside. It was impossible to stop him, indeed, I had all I could do to keep on. Suddenly, the Hindu we have just passed, or his double, stepped out into the road and grabbed the bridle. He was carried quite a distance, but managed to keep his grip, and the Waler finally condescended to stop. After receiving my thanks with a dignified depreciation of the service he had done me, the Hindu disappeared, and I have not seen him since.

"It is scarcely probable, though, that this mahout is the same," Hawley resumed, after a pause. "My rescuer was dressed as a high-caste, and it is not conceivable that such a one would turn elephant-driver."

"I know nothing of the man," said Merton, as they rode on into the city. "He has been Rajah's mahout ever since I came here a year ago. Of course, as you say, he cannot be the man who stopped your horse. It is merely a chance resemblance."

The next afternoon, Hawley was out riding alone. He had left the main road for a smaller one running into the jungle, intending to visit a ruined temple of which Merton had told him. Suddenly he noticed elephant tracks in the dust, exceedingly large ones, which he concluded could have been made only by Rajah. A momentary curiosity as to why the elephant had been ridden off into the jungle, and also concerning the mahout, led Hawley to follow the tracks when the road branched and they took the path opposite to the one that he had intended to follow. In a few minutes he came to a spot of open ground in the thick, luxuriant jungle, and reined in quickly at what he saw there.

Rajah stood in the clearing, holding something in his trunk which Hawley at first glance took to be a man, dressed in a blue and gold native attire, and with a red turban. Another look told him that it was merely a dummy — some old clothes stuffed with straw. As he watched, the mahout gave a low command, reinforced with a jab behind the ear from his ankus, or goad. Rajah gave an upward swing with his trunk, and released his hold on the figure, which flew skyward for at least twenty feet, and then dropped limply to earth. The mahout watched its fall with an expression of what seemed to be malevolence upon his face, though Hawley might have been mistaken as to this at the distance. He gave another command, and a jab at the elephant's cheek—a peculiar, quick thrust, at which Rajah picked the dummy up and placed it on his back behind the mahout in the place usually occupied by the howdah. The Hindu directing, the figure was again seized and hurled into the air.

Much mystified, Hawley watched several repetitions of this strange performance, but was unable to puzzle out what it meant. Finally, the mahout caught sight of him, and rode the elephant hastily away into the jungle on the opposite side of the clearing. Evidently he did not wish to be observed or questioned. Hawley continued his journey to the temple, thinking over the curious incident as he went. He did not see the mahout again that day.

He spoke of what he had seen to Merton that evening, but his cousin paid little attention to the tale, saying that no one could comprehend anything done by natives, and that it wasn't worth while to wonder at their actions anyway. Even if one could find the explanation, it wouldn't be worth knowing.

The scene in the jungle recurred to Hawley many times, probably because of the resemblance of the mahout to the man who had stopped his horse at Agra. But he could think of no plausible explanation of what he had seen. At last he dismissed the matter from his mind altogether.

At the time of Hawley's visit, great preparations were being made for the marriage of the Maharajah of Jizapur, Krishna Singh, to the daughter of the neighboring sovereign. There was to be much feasting, firing of guns, and a gorgeous procession. All the Rajahs, Ranas, and Thakurs, etc., for a radius of at least a hundred miles, were to be present. The spectacle, indeed, was one of the inducements that had drawn Hawley down into Central India.

After two weeks of unprecedented activity and excitement in the city of Jizapur, the great day came, with incessant thunder of guns from the Maharajah's palace during all the forenoon, as the royalty of Central India arrived with its hordes of picturesque, tattered, dirty retainers and soldiery. Each king or dignitary was punctiliously saluted according to his rank, which in India is determined by the number of guns that may be fired in his honor.

At noon a great procession, the Maharajah heading it, issued from the palace to ride out and meet the bride and her father and attendants, who were to reach Jizapur at that hour.

Hawley and Merton watched the pageant from the large and many-colored crowd that lined the roadside without the city gates. As Rajah, the great State elephant emerged, with Krishna Singh in the gold-embroidered howdah, or canopied seat, on his back, a rising cloud of dust in the distance proclaimed the coming of the bride and her relatives.

Behind the Maharajah came a number of elephants, bearing the nobles and dignitaries of Jizapur, and the neighboring princes. Then emerged richly caparisoned horses, with prismatically-attired riders—soldiers and attendants. Over this great glare of color and movement was the almost intolerable light of the midday Eastern sun.

The two Englishmen were some distance from the city gates, so that when the Maharajah's slow, majestic procession passed them, that of the bride was drawing near—a similar one, and less gorgeous only because it was smaller.

Perhaps fifty yards separated the two, when something happened to bring both processions to a halt. Hawley, who happened at the moment to be idly watching the elephant Rajah, and his driver, saw the mahout reach swiftly forward and stab the animal's cheek with his goad, precisely as he had done on that day in the jungle when Hawley had come unexpectedly upon him. Probably no one else noticed the action, or, if they did, attached any importance to it in the excitement that followed.

As he had reached with his trunk for the dummy seated on his back, so Rajah reached into the howdah and grasped Krishna Singh about the waist. In an instant the astonished, terror-stricken Maharajah was dangling in mid-air where the elephant held him poised a moment. Then, in spite of the shouts, commands, and blows of his mahout, Rajah began to swing Krishna Singh to and fro, slowly at first, but with a gradually increasing speed. It was like watching a giant pendulum. The fascinated crowd gazed in a sudden and tense silence for what seemed to them hours, though they were really only seconds, before the elephant, with a last vicious upward impetus of his helpless victim, released his hold.

Krishna Singh soared skyward, a blot of gold and red against the intense, stark, blazing azure of the Indian sky. To the horror-stricken onlookers he seemed to hang there for hours, before he began to fall back from the height to which the giant elephant had tossed him as one would toss a tennis-ball. Hawley turned away, unable to look any longer, and in an instant heard the hollow, lifeless thud as the body struck the ground.

The sound broke the spell of horror and amazement that had held the crowd, and a confused babble arose, interspersed with a few wails and cries. One sharp shriek came from the curtained howdah of the bride. The Maharajah's body guard at once galloped forward and formed a ring about the body. The crowd, to whom the elephant had gone "musth," or mad, began to retreat and disperse.

Hawley, in a few words, told his cousin of what he had seen the mahout do, and his belief that the elephant's action had thus been incited.

The two Englishmen went to the captain of the body-guard, who was standing by the side of the fallen Maharajah. Krishna Singh lay quite dead, his neck broken by the fall. The captain, upon being informed of what Hawley had seen, directed some of his men to go in search of the mahout, who, in the confusion, had slipped from Rajah's neck, disappearing no one knew where. Their search was unsuccessful, nor did a further one, continued for over a week, reveal any trace of the elephant-driver.

But several days afterward Hawley received a letter, bearing the Agra postmark. It was in a hand unfamiliar to him and was written in rather stiff, though perfectly correct English, such as an educated native would write. It was as follows:

> TO HAWLEY SAHIB :
>
> I am the man who stopped the Sahib's horse near Agra one day, six years ago. Because I have seen in the Sahib's eyes that he recognized and remembers me, I am writing this. He will then understand much that has puzzled him.
>
> My father was Krishna Singh's half-brother. Men who bore my father an enmity, invented evidence of a plot on his part to murder Krishna Singh and seize the throne. The Maharajah, bearing him little love and being of an intensely suspicious nature, required little proof to believe this, and caused my father and several others of the family to be seized and thrown into the palace dungeons. A few days later, without trial, they were led out and executed by the "Death of the Elephant." Perchance the Sahib has not heard of this. The manner of it is thus: The condemned man is made to kneel with his head on a block of stone, and an elephant, at a command from the driver, places one of his feet on the prisoner's head, killing him, of course, instantly.
>
> I, who was but a youth at the time, by some inadvertence was allowed to escape, and made my way to Agra, where I remained several years with distant relatives, learning, in that time, to speak and write English. I was intending to enter the service of the British Raj, when an idea of revenge on Krishna Singh, for my father's

death, suddenly sprang into full conception. I had long plotted, forming many impracticable and futile plans for vengeance, but the one that then occurred to me seemed possible, though extremely difficult. As the Sahib has seen, it proved successful.

I at once left Agra, disguising myself as a low-caste, and went to Burma, where I learned elephant-driving—a work not easy for one who has not been trained to it from boyhood. In doing this, I sacrificed my caste. In my thirst for revenge, however, it seemed but a little thing.

After four years in the jungle I came to Jizapur and, being a skilled and fully accredited mahout, was given a position in the Maharajah's stables. Krishna Singh never suspected my identity, for I had changed greatly in the ten years since I had fled from Jizapur, and who would have thought to find Kshatriya in the person of such a low-caste elephant-driver?

Gradually, for my skill and trustworthiness, I was advanced in position, and at last was entrusted with the State elephant, Rajah. This was what I had long been aiming at, for on my attaining the care of Krishna Singh's own elephant depended the success or failure of my plan.

This position obtained, my purpose was but half-achieved. It was necessary that the elephant be trained for his part, and this, indeed, was perhaps the most difficult and dangerous part of my work. It was not easy to avoid observation, and detection was likely to prove fatal to me and to my plan. On that day when the Sahib came upon me in the jungle, I thought my scheme doomed, and prepared to flee. But evidently no idea of the meaning of the performance in the jungle entered the Sahib's mind.

At last came my day of revenge, and after the Maharajah's death I succeeded in miraculously escaping, though I had fully expected to pay for my vengeance with my own life. I am safe now—not all the police and secret emissaries in India can find me.

The death that my father met has been visited upon his murderer, and the shadow of those dreadful days and of that unavenged crime has at last been lifted from my heart. I go forth content, to face life and fate calmly, and with a mind free and untroubled.

# The Rajah and the Tiger

There was more than one reason why Bently did not view his appointment as British Resident at Shaitanabad with enthusiasm. The climate was reported to be particularly hot even for India, the population largely composed of snakes, tigers, and wild boars, and the attitude of the natives from the Rajah down unfriendly. The last Resident had died of sunstroke, so it was said, and the one before him departed suddenly for an unknown destination without taking the trouble to apply for leave of absence. But as somebody had to occupy the position, Bently went to Shaitanabad; from the nearest railway station one hundred miles by camel and bullock cart over parched hills and sandy desert.

His early impressions of the place were hardly reassuring. His first glimpse of it was from the summit of a cactus-covered hill through a red haze of dust-laden heat. The principal feature which caught his eye was the Rajah's fortress-palace perched on a high rock on the northeast side and grimly overlooking the flat-roofed city. It was known as the Nahargarh, or Tiger Fort. For the rest Shaitanabad may be summed up as a place of narrow, irregular alleys, bazaars with shops little larger than dry-goods boxes, bad smells, a perpetual plague of insects, gaily clothed people, and a general Arabian Nights atmosphere. A thousand years ago it was the same, and so it will be a thousand years hence. The local temperature was 120° in the shade, sometimes more. Except the Resident, there were no other Englishmen in the place, not even a missionary. That is sufficient testimony as to Shaitanabad's character.

Bently regarded it as fortunate that the Residency was situated outside the city, and that his predecessor's staff of Bengali and Rajput servants were waiting to receive him. A bath, a fairly well-cooked meal, and a good night's rest, in spite of the heat, removed the exhaustion of the journey and made the outlook appear more satisfactory.

His first duty being to call on the Rajah, he early proceeded to the palace accompanied by his servant, Lal Das. Ascending a flight of steps cut in the towering sandstone rock, which was the only means of access to the fort, Bently passed through a great gate into a courtyard. There he was left to stand in the full rays of the Indian sun while the Rajah's attendants went in to announce the Resident's arrival. Finally they returned and conducted him through a deep veranda into a hall, from which another room opened. This room, carpeted with Persian rugs and hung with rare kinkhab draperies, seemed cool and pleasant after the heat without.

The Rajah, Chumbu Singh, was seated on a cushioned *gadi,* surrounded by several attendants. He was a tall, slender man of about forty, and wore the peculiar Rajput side whiskers. His attire consisted of a pearl-embroidered coat, trousers of white tussah silk, and an elaborately embroidered turban. One hand toyed with the gem-encrusted hilt of a short sword stuck in a broad silk cummerbund.

At this first meeting conversation was short and formal. The Rajah asked after Bently's health, and requested his opinion of such matters as the climate. He spoke fluent English, and seemed well educated and intelligent.

"I hope you will like Shaitanabad," he said, finally. "Sport here is good. If at any time you care to hunt tigers, I shall be glad to place all the facilities in my power at your disposal."

Bently retired on the whole rather favorably impressed with the Rajah, and inclined to treat certain adverse reports of his conduct as exaggerated. Native princes are always more or less prone to irritation at the ways of British Residents. Probably such was the basis of Chumbu Singh's offense in British official quarters.

During the next two or three weeks Bently thought he had reason to be pleased at his judgment of native character. Chumbu Singh fell so readily into certain administrative reforms proposed by Bently that there appeared little doubt of his earnestness to walk in the path of modern progress. So far things looked much better than he had been led to anticipate, even the temperature dropping to 98° at midnight. It was after the settlement of a land ownership case, in which Bently's assistance had been requested, that the Rajah made a proposal.

"I have arranged for a tiger hunt tonight," he said. "Would you like to go?"

Bently eagerly responded in the affirmative.

"This is a terrible animal, Sahib," continued the Rajah. "He has killed many people. His den is in the hills—an old cave temple, haunted, my people say, by ghosts and devils. However that may be, the tiger is many devils in himself. He stalks both cattle and villagers in broad daylight, and kills not only when hungry, but out of the devilishness of his heart. We have planned to get him at the cave."

When the last rays of the sun had faded from the hot red sandstone of the Nahargarh, and the grey veil of dusk had fallen over Shaitanabad, Chumbu Singh and several followers came to the Residency to announce that all was ready. They were armed and mounted on wiry Baluchi ponies. Bently joined them, accompanied by Lal Das, and the party set off across the rapidly darkening plain. Their destination, as indicated by Chumbu Singh, was a mass of low-lying, jungle-clad hills two miles to the north-east. The plain, or rather desert, between was barren with scarce a tree or shrub, and its monotony was broken only by a series of nasty wadis or gullies, which gave much trouble, necessitating careful horsemanship and slow traveling.

Reaching the hills without mishaps, the horses were left near an old tomb in the charge of the servants. The Rajah, Bently, Lal Das, and two Rajputs continued afoot. They first followed a bullock trail, and then a narrow foot-path, one of the Rajputs acting as guide. The path, winding up and down, through cactus jungle, deep ravines, and among great boulders, led well into the hills.

The moon had risen, and as they emerged from a patch of jungle, Bently saw the cave temple of which Chumbu Singh had spoken. It was in a steep hillside, where the formation changed from sandstone to light granite. In front was a level space overgrown with cactus, jungle plants, and a few larger trees. There were three entrances, the central one being about fifteen feet high, and the other two smaller. The larger one was open, but the others were choked with debris.

The hunters toiled up the hillside, scrambling over boulders and through the thick scrub. There was no path, and it was not pleasant traveling. A handful of cactus spines, even on a moonlit night in the presence of ancient and interesting ruins, is more productive of profanity than enthusiasm.

"This is the ancient temple of Jains," said the Rajah when they at last came panting to the entrance.

Bently peered within to behold the moonlight shining on huge indistinct figures, old forgotten gods carved in the solid granite. There were also great footprints in the thick dust, evidently those of the tiger. Undoubtedly he was a monster animal, for Bently had never seen pads to equal them.

The two Rajputs examined the pads carefully, and gave it as their opinion that the tiger had crept forth, bent on stalking about nightfall, and would probably not return until morning. They were sure he was not in the cave. The Rajah seemed annoyed at the prospect of a long wait, and abused the Rajputs for not arranging matters so that they might have arrived at the cave earlier and so intercepted the tiger.

"I owe you many apologies," he said, turning to Bently. "You see what comes of trusting to these fellows. But since it is such an effort to get here, I suggest that we wait for the tiger."

"Certainly," agreed Bently. "I am willing to wait as long as you like for a shot at that beast."

"Very well," the Rajah nodded. "In the meantime suppose we take a look at the cave temple. It is an interesting place, of its kind without equal in India."

To this Bently readily assented. Thereupon the Rajah sent off one of the Rajputs and Lal Das with an order for the rest of the retainers to keep watch in case the tiger returned unexpectedly. The other Rajput then produced a torch, and the party of three entered the cave. First they passed through a sort of peristyle, or antechamber, which, thirty yards from the entrance, opened into a vast grotto. This was the main excavation. Huge stone pillars, elaborately sculptured, supported the roof, and around the sides great gods and goddesses of the Jain mythology, called Arhats, glared downward. The torch illuminated dimly, leaving much in shadow, and in the shadow imagination created strange fantasies. A narrow passage from the grotto ended in a smaller chamber littered with fallen fragments. It was more than once necessary to climb over some god whose face was in the dust. Another short passage led to an arched entrance two-thirds blocked with debris.

"We cannot go any further," said the Rajah, "but if you take the torch and climb up on that pile, you will be able to see into a greater cave beyond. My superstitious retainers believe that it is the abode of ghosts and devils, the guardians of the temple."

Bently's curiosity was stimulated. Torch in hand he surmounted the obstruction, and peered into a gulf of black darkness. He seemed on the verge of a great precipice, the limits and bottom of which the torchlight failed to reach. From far beneath he fancied he caught a splash of water tumbling over a rocky bed, and strange echoes floated upward, but he could see nothing. It was an appalling abyss, which, for all he knew, might sink into the foundations of the earth.

Suddenly he received a violent push from behind, accompanied by a muttered curse hurled from the Rajah's lips. Bently tumbled forward, and, in doing so, threw out an arm wildly to save himself. It caught the barrel of the Rajah's rifle, swept it from his grasp, and hurled it clattering into the chasm beneath. Bently promptly followed the Rajah's rifle down a steep crumbling slope to what would have been certain death, had his own rifle not brought him up with a jerk by becoming lodged to half its length between two rocks. As it were, there he hung in midair with the buttress of his rifle for his only support. A shower of following pebbles swept on down into nothingness.

For some moments he remained almost stunned by the peril of the situation, but presently his mind began to gather in the slender chances of escape. He had apparently been brought up with his back against a side-wall of rock and with one foot resting on a narrow projection. Reaching out a hand, and groping with it, he discovered that the narrow projection was one of a flight of irregular steps cut in the rock and leading upward. If a hazardous foothold, he presumed it had been used at some period, and decided to attempt its course.

He balanced himself carefully, and disengaging his rifle, crept slowly upward step by step. Once his foot slipped, and he almost fell, but throwing himself inward he found he had stumbled into the entrance of a narrow passage. That meant safety from the chasm at any rate, and he gave vent to a huge breath of relief. His next act was to test the springs of his rifle, and so far as he was able to judge in the darkness he was further gratified to find that it was uninjured. Then he went cautiously forward, guiding his progress by a hand on the side-wall. Presently he came to a broad flight of steps partly choked up with fallen debris. Climbing up this, he emerged into the grotto of the temple.

Then he drew back suddenly. A coughing snarl echoed through the cavern. Bently softly moved behind the stone image of a god, and looked out from its shadow. From a clift in the roof of the temple a stream of moonlight fell within, and toned with silver the yellow body and velvet stripes of a monster tiger. It also shone upon the prostrate forms of the Rajah and his Rajput retainer, held beneath the huge paws of the Lord of the Jungle. Again the coughing snarl echoed through the temple. The eyes of the beast flashed with a savage thirst for blood as it lowered its head to plunge its fangs into the throat of one of its victims.

Bently raised his rifle to the shoulder, took steady aim, and fired. A terrific roar shook the stone gods, a gigantic convulsion seized upon the body of the tiger as it rolled over. Bently fired again, and then strode from his place of concealment. Another shot at closer range finished the death struggle of the tiger. Its last breath went forth in a choking growl of defiance.

It took but a cursory examination to convince Bently that both the Rajah and the Rajput were past rendering any account of their treachery on this earth, and a lack of response to his shouts made it plain that the Rajah's retainers had promptly bolted when the tiger unexpectedly returned. The Rajah and the Rajput had thus been left to encounter the powerful beast unarmed.

How Bently regained the Residency was a matter he was unable to explain except by instinct, but daylight had already broken when he reached the compound. Then he acted with swift decision.

He sent orders for the Rajah's retainers to appear at the Residency for an investigation, which eventually led to a thorough exploration of the temple. By another entrance the bottom of the abyss was gained, and sundry relics discovered there proved how the Rajah had relieved himself of the undesirable presence of those who had interfered with his dubious proceedings.

# Something New

"Tell me something new," she moaned, twisting in his arms on the sofa. "Say or do something original—and I'll love you. Anything but the wheezy gags, the doddering compliments, the kisses that were stale before Antony passed them off on Cleopatra!"

"Alas," he said, "there is nothing new in the world except the rose and gold and ivory of your perfect loveliness. And there is nothing original except my love for you."

"Old stuff," she sneered, moving away from him. "They all say that."

"They?" he queried, jealously.

"The ones before you, of course," she replied, in a tone of languid reminiscence. "It only took four lovers to convince me of the quotidian sameness of man. After that, I always knew what to expect. It was maddening: they came to remind me of so many cuckoo clocks, with the eternal monotony of their advances, the punctuality of their compliments. I soon knew the whole repertory. As for kissing—each one began with my hands, and ended with my lips. There was one genius, though, who kissed me on the throat the first time. I might have taken him, if he had lived up to the promise of such a beginning."

"What shall I say?" he queried, in despair. "Shall I tell you that your eyes are the unwaning moons above the cypress-guarded lakes of dreamland? Shall I say that your hair is colored like the sunsets of Cocaigne?"

She kicked off one of her slippers, with a little jerk of disgust.

"You aren't the first poet that I've had for a lover. One of them used to read me that sort of stuff by the hour. All about moons, and stars, and sunsets, and rose-leaves and lotus-petals."

"Ah," he cried hopefully, gazing at the slipperless foot. "Shall I stand on my head and kiss your tootsie-wootsies?"

She smiled briefly. "That wouldn't be so bad. But you're not an acrobat, my dear. You'd fall over and break something—provided you didn't fall on me."

"Well, I give it up," he muttered, in a tone of hopeless resignation. "I've done my darndest to please you for the past four months; and I've been perfectly faithful and devoted, too; I haven't so much as looked corner-wise at another woman—not even that blue-eyed brunette who tried to vamp me at the Artists' Ball the other night."

She sighed impatiently. "What does that matter? I am sure you needn't be faithful unless you want to be. As for pleasing me—well, you did give a thrill once upon a time, during the first week of our acquaintance. Do you remember? We were lying out under the pines on the old rag that we had taken with us; and you suddenly turned to me and asked me if I would like to be a hamadryad.... Ah! there is a hamadryad in every woman; but it takes a faun to call it forth.... My dear, if you had only been a faun!"

"A real faun would have dragged you off by the hair," he growled. "So you wanted some of that caveman stuff, did you? I suppose that's what you mean by 'something new.'"

"Anything, anything, providing it is new," she drawled, with ineffable languor. Looking like a poem to Ennui by Baudelaire, she leaned back and lit another cigarette in her holder of carved ivory.

He looked at her, and wondered if any one female had ever before hidden so much perversity, capriciousness, and incomprehensibility behind a rose-bud skin and harvest-coloured hair. A sense of acute exasperation mounted in him—something that had smouldered for months, half-restrained by his natural instincts of chivalry and gentleness. He remembered an aphorism from Nietzsche: "When thou goest to women, take thy whip."

"By Jove, the old boy had the right dope," he thought. "Too bad I didn't think to take my whip with me; but after all, I have my hands, and a little rough stuff can't make matters any worse."

Aloud, he said: "It's a pity no one ever thought to give you a good paddling. All women are spoiled and perverse, more or less, but you—"

He broke off, and drew her across his knees like a naughty child, with a movement so muscular and sudden that she had neither the time nor the impulse to resist or cry out.

"I'm going to give you the spanking of your life," he growled, as his right hand rose and descended.... The cigarette holder fell from her lips to the Turkish carpet, and began to burn a hole in the flowered pattern.... A dozen smart blows, with a sound like the clapping of shingles, and then he released her, and rose to his feet. His anger had vanished, and his only feeling was an overpowering sense of shame and consternation. He could merely wonder how and why he had done it.

"I suppose you will never forgive me," he began.

"Oh, you are wonderful," she breathed. "I didn't think you had it in you. My faun! My cave-man! Do it again."

Doubly dumbfounded as he was, he had enough presence of mind to adjust himself to the situation. "Women are certainly the limit," he thought, dazedly. "But one must make the best of them, and miss no chances."

Preserving a grim and mysterious silence, he picked her up in his arms.

# The Flirt

Someone introduced him to her as she stepped from the surf at the bathing beach. She was blonde as a daffodil, and her one-piece suit of vivid green clung to her closely as a folded leaf to the flower bud. She smiled upon him with an air of tender and subtle sadness; and her slow, voluptuous eyelids fell before his gaze with the pensive languor of closing petals. There was diffidence and seduction in the curve of her cheek; she was modest and demure, with an undernote of elusive provocation; and her voice was a plaintive soprano.

Twenty minutes later, they sat among the dunes at the end of the beach, where a white wall of sand concealed them from the crowd. Her bathing suit, only half-dry, still clung and glistened; but their flirtation had already ripened and flourished with an ease that surprised him.

"Surely I knew you in ancient Greece," he was saying. "Your hair retains the sunlight of the Golden Age, your eyes the blue of perished heavens that shone on the vale of Tempe. Tell me, what queen or goddess were you? In what fane of chalcedony, or palace of ebony and gold did I, a long-forgotten poet, sing before you the hymns or lyrics of my adoration? … Do you not remember me?"

"Oh, yes, I remember you," she said, in her plaintive soprano. "But I was not a queen or a goddess: I was only a yellow lily, growing in a forest glade on the banks of some forgotten stream; and you were the faun who passed by and trampled me."

"Poor little flower!" he cried, with a compassion he did not need to feign. It was impossible to resist the dovelike mournful cadence of her voice, the submissive sorrow and affection of her gaze. She said nothing, but her head drooped nearer to his shoulder, and her lips took on a more sorrowful and seductive curve. Even if she were not half so lovely and desirable, he felt that it would be unpardonably brutal not to kiss her.... Her lips were cool as flowers after an April rain, and they clung softly to his, as if in gratitude for his tenderness and pity....

The next day, he looked for her in vain among the bathers at the beach. She had promised to be there—had promised with many lingering kisses and murmurs. Disconsolate, remembering with a pang the gentle pressure of her mouth, the light burden of her body so loath to part from his arms, he strolled toward the dune in whose shelter they had sat. He paused, hearing voices from behind it, and listened involuntarily, for one of the voices was hers. The other, low and indistinct, with a note of passion, was a man's voice.... With the dove-like soprano whose tones were so fresh and vibrant in his memory, he heard her say:

"I was only a yellow lily, growing in a forest glade by the banks of some forgotten stream; and you were the faun who passed by and trampled me."

# The Perfect Woman

Once there was an idealist who sought for the Perfect Woman. In the course of his search, which lasted many years, and was thorough and painstaking, he acquired the reputation of a rake, and lost his youth, his hair, his illusions, and most of his money. He made love to actresses, ingénues, milkmaids, nurses, nuns, typists, trollops, and married women. He acquired an expert knowledge of hairpins and lingerie, and much data on feminine cussedness. Also, he sampled every known variety of lipstick. But still he failed to find the Ideal.

One day, to continue the weary tale, he lost whatever reason his experiences had left (or given) him; and, seized with the fury of a fiercer mania, threw a Charlotte Russ at the perfectly nice debutant with whom he was drinking. Two days later he received a membership in a home for the Mentally Exalted. Whether his insanity came from disappointment, excess, prohibition, booze, or a Streptococcic infection, the M.D.'s were never quite able to determine.

On his way to the asylum, guided by two stalwart keepers, he saw a rubber doll in a shop window, and fell in love with it like a college-boy with a soubrette. He had the price of the doll in his purse, so the keepers kindly permitted him to buy it, and bring it with him to enliven his sojourn in the Refuge for the Ecstatic.

"Gee, ain't he the nut?" they grinned.

However, he was happy at last, and did not mind. He believed he had found the Perfect Woman.

He still believes it, for the doll (one of the squeekless and unmechanized kind) has never said or done anything to disillusion him. He loves it with an absolute and ideal devotion, and believes his love is returned. He is perfectly happy.

# A Platonic Entanglement

They were sitting a fairly proper distance apart, on their favorite moss-grown boulder, at the end of the leaf-strewn autumn trail they had taken so often.

"Do you know that people are talking about us?" Her voice was hardly more than a whisper, failing on a mournful cadence almost inaudible, and he moved nearer, to catch the faint silver of its tones. As always, he found something vaguely pleasurable in the nearness of the plump olive neck under its coil of unbobbed hair, and the tender oval cheek that was exquisitely innocent of rouge.

"We have been seen together too often," she continued, with trouble and sadness in the droop of her eyelids, in the fall of her voice. "This town is full of cats, like all villages, and they are all the more willing to tear me in shreds because I am living apart from my husband. I am sorry, Geoffry ... because our friendship has meant so much to me."

"It has meant much to me, too, Anita," he responded. He felt disturbed and even a little conscience-stricken. It had been very pleasant, in his loneliness, to call upon her with increasing frequency throughout the summer, and to take these little walks in the autumn woods, now that the air was cooling and the leaves were aflame with saffron and crimson. It had all been so harmless and platonic, he assured himself—the natural drifting together of two lonely people with certain tastes in common. But assuredly he was not in love with her nor she with him: his attitude toward her had always been rather shy and respectful, and it was she who had somehow increased the familiarity of their friendship by subtle and imperceptible degrees. Indeed, had she not urged him, he would never have had the boldness to call her by her first name. She was a little the older and much the maturer of the two.

"Those horrid tattle-cats!" she went on, raising her voice in a silver burst of indignation. "If they would only be content to do their ripping and rending and clawing behind my back! But some of them must always come and tell me about it—'My dear, I think you ought to know what people are saying!'" She made an exquisite little *moue* of disgust. He reflected, not for the first time, that her mouth was eminently kissable; but, being a somewhat shy and modest young man, and not at all in love with her, he put the thought away as speedily as he could.

"What will your husband do if he hears the gossip?" he queried cautiously.

"Oh, George wouldn't care." Her tone was reckless, with an undertone of contempt. "As long as I leave him alone, he will leave me alone.... He wouldn't have the decency to give me a divorce; but, on the other hand, he is too indifferent to make trouble. George doesn't matter, one way or the other: what I hate and dread is this dirty small-town gossip; I feel as if unclean hands were pawing me all the time."

Shuddering a little, she pressed against him, ever so gently. Her mournful eyelids fluttered, and she gave him a brief and almost furtive glance, in which he could read nothing but sadness. She lowered her eyes hastily, as tears crept out and hung on the thick lashes.

"Oh! it is hateful—hateful!" There was a melodious break in her voice. "I don't know what to do.... But I can't give up seeing you, Geoffry; and you don't want to give me up, do you?"

"Of course not," he hastened to reassure her. "But I can't see what all the excitement is about. We are good friends, of course, but—" He broke off, for she was sobbing openly, seeming not to hear him. Somehow—he never quite knew how it all happened—her head fell on his shoulder, and her white arms, clinging forlornly and tenaciously, were about his neck. Slightly terrified, in a turmoil of sensations that were by no means unpleasant, he returned the embrace and kissed her. It seemed to be the thing to do.

Afterwards, as she rearranged the coil of her disordered hair, she murmured:

"I have always loved you, Geoffry.... It simply had to happen, I suppose.... Do you love me?"

"Of course I love you." He put the correct period to his reply with another kiss. After all, what else could he say or do?

# The Expert Lover

"Tom is terribly in love with you, Dora. He'd stand on his head in a thistle-patch if you told him to. You won't find a better provider in Auburn."

"Yes, I know Tom is fond of me. But, Annabelle, he is such a complete dud when it comes to love-making. All he can say is: 'Gee, but you're pretty, Dora,' or: 'I'm sure crazy about you,' or: 'Dora, you're the only girl for me.'"

"I suppose Tom isn't much on romantic conversation. But what do you expect? Most men aren't."

"Well," sighed Dora, impatiently, "I'd really like a little romance. And I can't see it in Tom. He's about as romantic as potatoes with onions. Everything about him is so obvious and commonplace—even his name. And when he tries to hug me, he makes me think of a grocer grabbing a sack of flour."

"All the same, there are worse fish in the sea, dearie."

Dora Cahill, a dreamy-looking blonde, and her bosom-friend, Annabelle Rivers, a vivacious and alert brunette, were sitting out a dance at Rock Creek hall. Tom Masters, the object of their discussion, who was Dora's escort, had been sent off to dance with one of the wallflowers. Dora was a little tired, and, as usual, more than a little bored. She knew that Tom's eyes, eager and imploring, were often upon her as he whirled past in the throng on the dance-floor; but vouchsafing him only an occasional languid glance, she continued to chat with Annabelle.

"I wish I could meet a real lover," she mused—"someone with snap and verve and technique—someone who was eloquent and poetic and persuasive, and could carry me away, in spite of myself."

"That kind has usually had a lot of practice," warned Annabelle. "And practice means that they have the habit."

"Well, I'd rather have a Don Juan than a dumbbell."

"You can take your choice, dear. Personally, I'd prefer something dependable and solid, even if he didn't scintillate."

"Pardon me, Miss Cahill." The two girls looked up. The speaker was Jack Barnes, a man whom Dora knew slightly; another man, whom she was sure she had never seen before, stood beside him.

"Permit me to introduce my friend, Mr. Colin—Lancelot Colin," said Barnes. Dora's eyes met the eyes of the stranger, and she acknowledged the introduction, a little breathlessly. Her first thought was: "What a heavenly name!" and then: "What a heavenly man!" Mr. Colin, who stood bowing with a perfect suavity and an ease that was Continental rather than American, was really enough to have taken away the breath of more than one girl with romantic susceptibilities. He was dark and immaculate, with the figure of a soldier and the face of an artist. There was an indefinite air of gallantry about him, a sense of mystery, of ardour and poetry. Dora contrasted him with Tom, who was broad and ruddy, and about whom there was nothing to excite one's imagination or tease one's curiosity. She was frankly thrilled.

Annabelle was now included in the introduction, but, beyond a courteous murmur of acknowledgment, the newcomer seemed to show no interest in her. His eyes, large and full-lidded, with a hint of weariness and sophistication in their brown depths, were fixed with a sparkling intensity upon Dora.

"May I have the pleasure of dancing with you, Miss Cahill?" His voice, a musical and vibrant baritone, completed the impression of a consummately romantic personality.

Dora consented, without her usual languid hesitation, and found herself instantly whirled away in the paces of a fox-trot. She decided at once that Mr. Colin was a superb dancer; also that he was what is commonly known as a "quick worker," for no sooner were they on the floor than he murmured in her ear:

"You look as if you had just stepped out of a bower of roses. I've been watching you all evening, and I simply had to know you."

"There really isn't much about me that is worth knowing." Dora gave him her demurest smile.

"Ah! but you are wonderful!" rhapsodized Mr. Colin. "Your eyes are the blue of mountain lakes under a vernal sky, your cheeks are softer than wild rose petals. And you dance like a dryad in the April woods."

He continued in the same strain, so eloquently and to such good effect that Dora was convinced by the end of the dance that she had found the expert lover for whom she had been expressing her desire to Annabelle only a few minutes before. When the music stopped, and Mr. Colin suggested that they go for a few minutes' stroll in the moonlight, she assented readily, and she did not even notice the disconsolate Tom, who followed them with a look of glum and glowering astonishment.

Outside, the large and mellow moon of a California May was just freeing itself from the tree-tops. Automobiles were parked all about the country dance-hall, and in some of them low murmurs and laughter were audible.

"We could sit in my car," observed Mr. Colin, pointing out a stylish roadster. "But you'd rather take a little walk, wouldn't you? It would be more romantic, somehow."

He had accurately gauged her preferences, for Dora had a poetic streak in her nature, and loved moonlight and idyllic surroundings. When they paused, a minute later, in a grassy meadow encircled by oaks and alders, she felt that one of her dearest dreams was coming true. How often she had pictured to herself a moonlight stroll with a handsome and fervent and eloquent lover!

"I adore you! I loved you madly from the very first moment that I saw you tonight!" There was a convincing ardor in his low tones, and Dora thrilled.

"But how can you? You don't know anything about me." Dora made the usual feminine demurs. She was already more than half in love with Mr. Colin, and wholly in love with romance; but she knew, or had been told, that men were prone to despise immediate conquest or concession.

He caught her in his arms, pouring out passionate and half-incoherent words, and would have kissed her; but she turned her lips aside and resisted firmly; and after a little he did not persist. He was learned in the ways and reactions of women, and he knew that it was something more than the moonlight that had softened her lips and brightened her eyes. He could afford to wait. So he contented himself with taking her hand and pressing his lips to it with a fervor and a courtliness of gesture that were new to Dora's experience. From that moment she adored him.

Both were a little silent as they returned to the dance-hall. But the air was full of vibrant potentialities, of things unsaid and undone as yet, but not to be long deferred. Another fox-trot, and still another, in the course of which Mr. Colin managed to say some more charming things.

"Will you go riding with me tomorrow afternoon?" he queried. "More than one nook of Arcady could be explored in an afternoon."

"Yes," breathed Dora, assenting to the observation as well as to the question.

It was now late in the evening, and the gay throng of dancers and onlookers had begun to thin out.

"It is time for me to go home," said Dora, "so I'll have to say goodnight." She had become aware, as one who awakens partially from a blissful dream, that Tom was hovering gloomily somewhere in the near background.

"I wish that tonight were eternal—or that it were already tomorrow," murmured Mr. Colin, with a gallant bow and a glance full of ardor and passion that caused Dora to flush and the waiting Tom to grit his teeth quite audibly.

"Say, who is that fellow anyway?" Tom demanded when he and Dora were seated in his Buick and were on their way back to Auburn.

"A Mr. Lancelot Colin." For ears duller even than Tom's, the unwonted warmth and softness of her tone would have betrayed something of the inward thrill with which she uttered the syllables.

"Never heard of him. Must be a newcomer," Tom snorted, and stepped on the gas. The way in which the car leapt forward was more eloquent of his mood than many words. He said nothing more till they were inside the town limits. Then:

"Do you like him?" he snapped.

"Very much." Dora's tone was sweet and tranquil. She ignored Tom's bruskness. Her thoughts were far away, in a delicious land of glamour and romance and perpetual moonlight.

Tom relapsed into sulky silence, and nothing more was said till they stopped in front of Dora's home.

"Tomorrow is Sunday," Tom observed. "What are you planning to do? I'd like to take you for a drive."

"I'm sorry, Tom, but I've already made an engagement."

"With that Colin bird, I suppose."

"Tom, you are really quite rude tonight."

"Sorry," he grumbled, in a tone that was scarcely apologetic. "Well, I guess I'd better be going. Good night." And he drove away at a speed that was somewhat in excess of the official limit.

Sunday morning came and passed for Dora in a mellow haze of sunlit dreams, of golden glowing anticipations. With the early afternoon arrived Mr. Colin, in his roadster. Dora was in the front yard among her mother's roses when he drove up and got out, immaculately dressed as on the previous evening, and, to Dora's romantic eyes, even more handsome and dashing.

"I suspected that you dwelt among roses," he said, as he came up the garden walk and bowed in his courtier fashion. "Now I know it."

Dora dimpled. "Who taught you to be so gallant, kind sir?"

"You have taught me—you alone."

"I don't see how I could teach anything to anyone."

"You can inspire—and that is the best kind of teaching."

"You must come in and meet my parents," said Dora, a little later. "You can talk to them while I powder my nose."

Dora's mother and father, both stout and staid and placidly middle-aged, gave Mr. Colin a welcome that was tinged with little more than the usual amount of interest that they manifested toward her beaux. For them, he was merely one more possible suitor of a girl who seemed uncommonly "choosy" and difficult to marry off. Perceiving that he was handsome, obviously a gentleman, and apparently well-to-do, they surveyed him with a regard that was hopeful rather than otherwise—but not too hopeful.

"Mr. Colin is going to take me for a ride," announced Dora. She went upstairs to perform the perennial feminine rite of re-powdering her nose, which, to a superficial masculine eye, would have seemed little in need of such ministrations. When she returned, Mr. Colin was chatting agreeably and successfully with her parents, who appeared to look upon him with increased favor. It was evident that he was really a clever young man.

When they were seated in the roadster, he said with a mysterious air: "I know a perfectly wonderful place where I shall take you. But you aren't to know where it is beforehand."

"How heavenly!" breathed Dora. "I'm sure it will be wonderful."

"For me, any place would be fairyland with you. But when one can have the ideal companion and the ideal setting, then true perfection is to be attained. Life can offer no more."

He turned the car northward on the Colfax road. As they drove along, she turned the conversation to himself with feminine deftness. He told her that he had artistic ambitions, possessed independent means, and had come to Auburn with the idea of painting a few landscapes of the local scenery, which he had visited and explored years before and of which he had become much enamored. He was from San Francisco, where his people lived. His father, he explained, was a wealthy realtor and was none too favorably disposed toward his artistic ambitions. His mother, however, was on his side.

Dora was fascinated. She had never known an artist, and all that Mr. Colin told her served to confirm the romantic interest that he had aroused.

"Well, I think that's really enough about myself," he laughed. "Now let's talk about something worth while." He began to ply her with compliments, which, to Dora's ear, were marvellously poetic; but, for the time, he did not speak of the passion he had avowed on the previous evening.

Now they had left the highway and were traveling a narrow side-road that ran toward Bear River. This was soon abandoned for a still narrower road that turned and twisted among brush-oak, chaparral and manzanita. Presently Mr. Colin turned the car aside in a grassy meadow, in front of a grove of tall pines. Except for the road, there was no trace of human life.

They left the car and plunged into the pine grove for several hundred yards. Suddenly, and, for Dora, quite unexpectedly, they came upon a little glade in which there grew a solitary redwood. Here they might have been a hundred miles from civilization, in the midst of the primeval mountain forest, for any evidence to the contrary. Sunlight sifted goldenly through the pine-tops, and a jay scolded them from somewhere in the dark-green branches. Dora exclaimed with delight.

There was a fallen log at hand to provide them with a seat, and of this they availed themselves at Mr. Colin's suggestion.

"Do you like this?" The very tone of his query was a caress.

"I adore it."

"And I adore you. Say that you love me a little, Dora."

"I like you very much."

"Can't you do better than that?" He was very close beside her and his breath was in her hair as she half-averted her face, fearing that he would see the traitorous softness of her eyes, the tender flush of her cheeks.

"We hardly know each other, Lancelot."

"I know you well enough to realize that no one else could ever make me feel what I feel for you." His arm was about her now, and she did not resist. She had intended to make him wait, to prolong the wooing; but now, in a flash, her will to do so had fled, and all her thoughts seemed to dissolve in a delicious langour.

With a gentle hand he turned her face toward him, and kissed her—a long, passionate, full-blooded kiss, that seemed as if it could never end. Finally she withdrew her lips and hid her face against his shoulder.

"Do you love me?" he whispered, almost fiercely.

"Yes, I love you."

Two weeks had passed for Dora in a golden and fire-shot mist of romance. At first she was very happy, with the sensation of treading on air that sometimes accompanies the first stages of a great emotion. There were many long walks, rides and cosy evenings with Mr. Colin, who was manifestly a model of devotion and ardor. For some reason, which he told her he would explain later, he had wished to delay the announcement of their engagement; and he had hinted that it would be at least a year before he would be in a position to marry. This had not troubled her—she had been too happy not to trust her lover implicitly. But of late he had appeared self-absorbed and not quite so unfailingly attentive as at first. She wondered, anxiously, if he were growing a little tired. Even when he told her that he was at work upon a new painting which he hoped would mark a real achievement, she was not entirely reassured. She had seen some of his pictures—amateurish watercolors, not lacking in a certain shallow feeling for tonal harmony—and had thought them quite wonderful. She tried to content herself with his explanation, reflecting that an artist must work, after all, even if he were in love.

One day, in the Auburn post-office, she came upon Mr. Colin chatting gaily with her friend Annabelle, who was smiling at him with all of her wonted animation. Dora was a little surprised, remembering that he had shown no interest in that vivacious brunette on the evening when they had met at Rock Creek. Absorbed entirely in her lover, she had seen little of Annabelle since that occasion.

"Hello, dearie," warbled Annabelle. "I was just asking Mr. Colin what had become of you. You and he seem to have pre-empted each other entirely, and no one else has a look-in."

"I have been busy," said Dora, vaguely.

"I know all about that," laughed Annabelle. "I'll say you have. Well, so long." She walked away with a mirthful glance that included both, but lingered somehow a little longer upon Mr. Colin than upon Dora.

"Since when have you been chumming with Annabelle?" Dora turned to her lover with mock-earnestness.

"I'd hardly call it that." His tone was negligent. "She asked me about you, and I was trying to be civil. She's really quite amusing, though."

Dora thought little of the incident; but one afternoon, a few days later, it occurred to her that she would really like to see Annabelle; also, that Annabelle might well be feeling neglected. She was still vaguely discontented, and troubled by Mr. Colin's fits of preoccupation and by something that was almost absent-minded about his kisses and gallantries. She felt the need of renewing her old friendship with Annabelle, who had always cheered her in hours of depression or boredom.

The Rivers home was on the other side of Auburn from where Dora lived. She sauntered slowly through the winding streets under the shade of elms and maples and eucalypti, and went in at the familiar picket-gate. She was going down the garden-path to the house when she heard Annabelle's voice nearby, in an arbor that was thickly covered with Cherokee rose-vines, now in full flower. She could not see Annabelle or her companion, but the words came clearly:

"I thought you were in love with Dora.... Now behave ... or I'll tell on you." There followed a voluptuous giggle, and then the voice of a man, Mr. Colin's vibrant baritone:

"Your lips are too sweet for anything but kisses. You look as if you had always lived in a rose-arbor."

"If Dora heard you say that...."

"Why be always mentioning Dora, when we have you to talk about? ... And when there are better things to do even than talk?"

"Now you behave... or...." The sentence was cut short by the unmistakable sound of a kiss.

Dora had the sensation of stumbling blindly among ashes and ruins when she left the garden of Annabelle's home. By an automatic rather than conscious impulse she closed the gate behind her as quietly as she could. Her throat was dry, and she could scarcely control the tears that welled beneath her eyelids. Somehow, she reached her home, and flung herself on the sofa in the sitting-room.

She began to weep. Her parents were away, and for this she was vaguely thankful. No one would see her in the first overwhelming shock of her grief and disillusionment.

An hour later the telephone rang, and she sprang automatically to answer it. The voice was that of Tom Masters, whose occasional gruff but recurrent invitations she had refused ever since her meeting with Mr. Colin.

"Say, Dora, how about the dance at Rock Creek next Saturday night?" There was an almost forlorn stubbornness in his tone. "I thought I'd ring up and ask."

"Oh, all right, Tom, I guess I can go with you."

# The Parrot

The pawnshop was so crowded with unredeemed articles, that neither electricity nor sunlight could dissipate fully the murk of its doubtful corners. The windows were always unwashed and the cobwebs were unswept. It was even darker and grimier than usual, on this late afternoon of April; and the sea-fog that had inundated San Francisco was visibly mingled with the dust that hovered always in its air. No one who was unfamiliar with the place would have noticed the parrot, which occupied a perch in the corner farthest from the door. The bird was in one of its taciturn moods, and had apparently forgotten its extensive repertoire of thieves' argot, water-front oaths, and Jewish idioms, for it had not spoken a word since morning.

"Vell, Micky Horgan, vot you vant?" The huge, swarthy, furtive-looking person thus hailed by Jacob Stein, the proprietor, was better known as Black Mike to the local underworld and police circles. He was peering about uncertainly for Stein, who was stooping behind the counter. The Jew was so small and dingy that he blended in with his surroundings as if he had taken on a sort of protective coloration.

"I want one hundred dollars." Horgan's voice was a peremptory growl.

"For vot should I gif you so much money?"

"For this." Horgan took an amber necklace from his coat-pocket and laid it on the counter, where it gleamed like a circle of solidified sun-rays.

Stein peered at the necklace through his heavy-rimmed goggles and shook his head with a vehement grimace.

"I gif you fifteen," he said dubiously.

"The hell you will. That's real amber. I didn't swipe it from any hall-bedroom, either. And I'm offering it mud-cheap because I've got to have a hundred bucks to-night."

Stein came out from behind the counter and began to expostulate.

"For vot you take me? No one buys amber. I'm a poor man, and I haf a family. Fifteen tollars I gif you, but no more."

Horgan sensed finality in the tones of the Jew. Sinister, desperate thoughts arose in his brain. His need of a hundred dollars was indeed urgent, for the sum had been demanded by a sweetheart whom he loved with ferocious ardor. He knew her coldness and contempt if he should go to her without the money—knew the merciless vituperations with which she would greet him. Also, he thought of all the former occasions on which Stein had defrauded him of his rightful due for some stolen article.

"You rotten Sheeny—I'm damned if you'll gouge me this time!" Horgan's desperation was tinged with a stealthy, rat-like anger.

"Fifteen tollars—und I'm robbing myself, Micky." The Jew rubbed his hands together, turned his head away, and looked indifferently through the smeared windows. He did not seem to notice the ugly and precarious mood of his client.

A murderous calculation crept into Horgan's thoughts. He peered about. The street outside was very quiet, and the fog was thickening into a drizzle. It was not likely that anyone would come in at the moment. Furtively, with careful slowness, he reached for the revolver in his hip-pocket. He pulled it out, raised it aloft with a flourish incredibly swift, and brought down the heavy butt on the pawn-broker's head. Stein fell, sprawling at full length between a crowded table and the metal base of a floor-lamp. He did not move; and stooping over him, Horgan saw that blood was beginning to ooze from the crushed crown of his skull. The horn-rimmed goggles had not fallen from the eyes, and they lent a grotesque air of life and peering animation to the corpse. It was hard to believe that Stein was dead, for even as he lay, he seemed to be inspecting some dubious article or customer.

The burglar stood up and looked about hastily. He could not afford to delay. He went over to the counter, stuffed the necklace back into his pocket, and then took a step toward the cash-register.

"Vell, Micky Horgan, vot you vant?" The voice came from a shadowy corner, and was an exact mimicry of Stein's. Horgan gave a violent start, and his heart missed one or two beats, while a surge of ancestral Irish superstition clamored in his brain. Then he remembered that there was a parrot which he had seen on several previous occasions.

"I want one hundred dollars," continued the voice.

"Damn that bird," thought Horgan. "I've got to wring its neck before I go." He seemed to hear the parrot uttering his name in Stein's voice to the San Francisco police, and repeating various bits of the late dispute. He started for the corner where the perch stood, and collided with a chair in his blind haste. He almost fell, but caught himself in time and went on, cursing aloud with the pain of a bruised knee. There was so much furniture and bric-a-brac in the place, that he could not locate the perch for a few moments.

"For vot should I gif you so much money?" The voice was at his very elbow. He saw the bird, which seemed to be inspecting him, with its green head cocked to one side and a sardonic gleam in its eye. His hand shot out to clutch its legs, but he was not quick enough. The parrot fluttered away from the perch and settled with a leisurely flap of its wings on an empty coat-hanger among the pawned garments at one end of the shop.

"Damn you to hell!" Horgan was not aware that he had yelled the words. He lurched toward the coat-hanger, obsessed by one frantically imperative idea, that he must catch the bird and wring its infernal neck. This time, the parrot flew off before he came within reach, and established itself on the cash-register. There it continued to repeat word for word the conversation he had had with Stein.

"I gif you fifteen," it screeched.

Horgan picked up a little bronze bust of Dante from a table covered with art-objects and bric-a-brac, and hurled it at the parrot. The bust struck the cash-register with a reverberant clang, loud as that of an alarm-gong, and the bird rose again and seated itself on the parchment shade of the floor-lamp above the pawn-broker's body. It yelled raucously all the while, and sailors' oaths and Yiddish idioms were intermingled with more scraps of the dialogue that had ended in Stein's death.

The murderer flung himself at the floor-lamp, tripped on the insulated wire, and brought the lamp down, as he fell across the corpse of his victim. The top of the lamp-stand struck a loaded table, and there was a terrific crash of Chinese pottery and cut-glass.

"Hey, what's going on here?" The door had opened and a policeman was entering. He had heard the gong-like clang of the bust against the cash-register, and had decided to investigate. He drew a revolver very quickly and levelled it at Horgan, when he saw the body of Jacob Stein, from whose head a little pool of blood had oozed.

Horgan picked himself up slowly and sullenly. As he rose to his feet before the levelled muzzle, he heard once more the voice of the parrot, which had now returned to its perch.

"I gif you fifteen," it screamed, with a note that was like malicious laughter.

# A Copy of Burns

Andrew McGregor and his nephew, John Malcolm, were precisely alike, except for one particular. Both were unmistakably Scottish, to an extent that was almost caricatural; both were lean-faced and close-lipped, and ropy of figure; both were thrifty to the point of penuriousness; and both loved with a dour love the rugged soil of their neighbouring hillside ranches in El Dorado. The difference lay in this, that McGregor, a native of Ayrshire, was fantastically enamored of the poetry of Burns, whom he quoted on all possible occasions, regardless of whether or not the verse was appropriate. But young Malcolm, who was Californian by birth, had a secret disdain for anything in rhyme or meter, and looked upon his uncle's literary enthusiasm as an odd weakness in a nature otherwise sound and admirable. This opinion, however, he had always been careful to conceal from the old man; though his reasons for concealing it were not altogether those of respect for an elder and affection for a relative.

McGregor was now close upon eighty; and a lifetime of rigorous toil had bowed his back and consumed his vitality. In the space of a few months, his health had broken, and he was now quite feeble. It was generally thought that he would leave his well-kept orchard, as well as a tidy deposit in the Placerville bank, to John Malcolm, the son of his sister Elizabeth, rather than to his own sons, George and Joseph, who had tired of country labor years before and were now prospering after their own fashion in Sacramento. Young Malcolm, certainly, was deserving; and the ranch left him by his parents was of poorer soil than McGregor's, and had never yielded more than a scant living, despite the industry of its owners.

One day, McGregor sent for his nephew. The young man found the elder sitting in an arm-chair before the fire-place, pitiably weak; and his fingers trembled helplessly as they turned the worn pages of the copy of Burns he was holding. His voice was a thin, rasping whisper.

"My time is about come, John," he said, "but I want to gie ye a gift with my own hand before I jany. Take this copy of Burns. I recommend that ye peruse it diligent-like."

Malcolm, a little surprised, accepted the gift with proper thanks and with all due expressions of solicitude regarding his uncle's health. He took the volume home, placed it on a shelf which contained an almanac, a Bible, and two mail-order catalogues; and forgot all about it henceforward.

A week later, Andrew McGregor died. After he had been interred in the Placerville cemetery, a search was made for his will. It was never found; and in due course of time, his sons laid claim to the property. Afterwards, they sold the ranch, not caring to keep it themselves.

John Malcolm swallowed his disappointment in a dour silence, and went on plowing his rocky slope of grape-vines and pear-trees. He saved a little money, purchased a little more property, and eventually found himself in a position of tolerable comfort, which however could be maintained only at the cost of incessant work. He married; and one daughter was born to him. He named her after his aunt Elizabeth, of whom he had been fond. Twenty years later, the long hours of back-breaking toil, plus an addiction to El Dorado moonshine, had finally done their work. Prematurely worn out at fifty, John Malcolm lay dying. Double pneumonia had set in; and the doctor made no pretense of hopefulness.

Malcolm's wife and daughter sat at his bedside. Usually a silent man, delirium had now loosened his tongue, and he babbled for hours at a time. Mostly, he talked of the money and property he had once hoped to inherit from Andrew McGregor; and regret for its loss was mingled with reproaches toward his uncle. The lost will had been forgotten by everyone else long ago; and no one had dreamt that he had cared so much, or borne the matter so much in mind all these years.

His wife and daughter were shocked by his babbling. In an effort to pre-occupy her mind, the girl Elizabeth took from the shelf the copy of Burns which McGregor had once presented to his nephew, and began to turn the sheets. She read a poem here and a stanza there; and with a mechanical feverishness her fingers contrived to flick the pages. Suddenly she came upon a thin sheet of writing-paper, which had been cut to the exact size of the book and had been pasted in so unobtrusively that no one could have detected its presence without opening the volume at the right place. On this sheet, in faded ink, was written the last will and testament of Andrew McGregor, in which he had left all his property to John Malcolm.

Silently the girl showed the will to her mother. As the two bent over the yellowed sheet, the dying man ceased to babble.

"What's that?" he said, peering toward the woman. Evidently, he was now aware of his surroundings, and had become rational again.

Elizabeth went over to the bed and told him how she had found the will. He made no comment whatever, but his face went ashen and lifeless, with a look of bleak despair. He did not speak again. He died within thirty minutes. It is probable that his death was hastened several hours by the shock.

# Checkmate

"I'm afraid he has found your letters to me, Leonard."

"He? Who is he?"

"My husband, of course, stupid!"

"The devil! That's awkward, if true. What makes you think your husband has found them?"

"The letters are missing—and who else could have taken them? You remember where I kept them—under that pile of lingerie in my middle bureau drawer? Well, the whole packet is gone. Also, Jim has changed toward me the last few days. He's so grouchy all the time. And he has a kind of sly look, too, as if he knew something and were watching me."

"What do you think he'll do about it?"

"I don't know, I'm sure. But it makes me very uncomfortable. The present question is, what are we going to do? Have you anything to suggest?"

Ethel Drew and her lover, Leonard Alton, stared at each other in mutual alarm. Also, their consternation was touched with more than a hint of critical appraisal. In the light of the danger that menaced their affair, Ethel wondered if Leonard were quite the ideal gallant she had imagined him to be. And Leonard wondered for the first time if Ethel's blonde deliciousness were not becoming slightly over-mature. However, they had had a lot of pleasant times together; and neither of them relished the idea of an interruption to those good times. Then, there were other considerations. Ethel was indifferent to her husband; but there were reasons why she did not care to lose him. He was a convenient wage-earner and provider of luxuries—even if not of romantic thrills. And Leonard, on his part, was hardly intrigued by the vision of a divorce suit in which he would find himself playing the expensive role of co-respondent. Also, he might have to marry Ethel… and support her.

"Supposing he decides to divorce me?" Ethel, with feminine frankness, was the first to voice the thought.

"We can't have anything of that sort."

"Jim *might* do it. Certainly he could, with your letters for evidence."

Leonard recalled certain passages of the perfervid phraseology which he had used in writing to Ethel. Also, the many direct references to episodes of their passion. What an indiscreet idiot he had been!

"I'll say he could," he rejoined ruefully.

"Well, haven't you anything to suggest?" The tone was perceptibly tart.

"If he has the letters, he must have put them away somewhere. Have you looked for them?"

"Of course I have. I went through Jim's bed-room and clothes-closet as soon as I found they were missing. Then, I searched his den. But the letters aren't in the house. It was useless to look—he wouldn't leave them around like that."

"Have you searched his office? Bet you he's got them pigeon-holed in his desk."

"I haven't looked there yet—no chance to do it so far. But I thought of it. I'll try to get hold of the office-key as soon as I can. Jim may go out of town for a day or two before long, on some business deal."

"You've got to find the letters, Ethel."

"That's evident. *You* wouldn't be much good at finding them. Of course, it's up to me."

"But I'll come with you, if you like."

"Oh, all right. I'll ring you up when I get the key."

"Bet you anything he's got the letters filed away in his desk."

"Maybe—if he hasn't filed them with a lawyer."

Ethel Drew and her husband were at breakfast the next morning. Jim had been gulping his coffee and oatmeal in sulky silence. And Ethel was pretending a blithe unconsciousness of his manner and its implications. Jim did not speak till he arose from the table. Then:

"I'm going out of town to-day. Have to see the Chalmers Co.—also, Reed Bros. I won't be back till late to-morrow night…. And I'd advise you to behave while I'm gone."

It was the first direct verbal insinuation which Jim had made.

"What do you mean?" Ethel's tone was crisp and cool.

"Just what I say. You'd better be good ... if you want me to go on paying for your lingerie and breakfast bacon."

"I don't understand you. And your remarks are rather insulting."

"The hell they are."

"I think you might explain your insults."

"Is it necessary? You certainly have your nerve, Ethel. I know all about you and your little play-mate."

"Are you crazy, Jim? I don't know what you are driving at."

Jim glowered at Ethel as he drew on his overcoat.

"Oh, yes you do. Take it from me, you can't get away with this Leonard Alton business. No lounge-lizard is going to make a monkey of me. He'll have the job of supporting you, if there's any more of that stuff.... And you'll like that, won't you, hey? He'll certainly make a grand provider, with his peanut income."

"Jim, you are ridiculous."

"A great little bluffer, aren't you? Well, I know all about it.... Red-hot letters to a red-hot mama!" He fairly sneered the last words. "Bye-bye. And don't forget what I told you."

He was gone before Ethel could think of another rejoinder.

"Well, that's that," she thought, biting her lip. "I've simply got to get Leonard's letters back and destroy them. They're the only evidence. Jim can be nasty, of course—but he couldn't really prove anything without them."

Five minutes later, she was ransacking Jim's room, hoping desperately that he had not taken his key-ring with him. Where would it be? It was not on the bureau, where he often left it. But sometimes he left it in his pocket. She remembered that he had been wearing a suit of brown and black checks that morning, instead of the blue serge suit he usually wore in the office.

She opened the clothes-closet. The blue serge was hanging next to the door. And thank heaven, the key-ring was in one of the coat-pockets. She knew the office-key by sight. There it was, between the door-key of their bungalow and the key of an old trunk.

She called Leonard on the phone.

"Jim is out of town until late to-morrow. And I have the key. Will you help me to do a little burglarizing?"

"Any time, darling."

"Not till tonight, of course. The stenographer might be there during the day. You can take me to dinner, if you want to, and we'll visit the office afterwards."

"That's a good plan. Nothing like combining pleasure with business. Shall I call for you at the house about six-thirty?"

"That will be fine, Leonard. But you needn't be so flippant. Supposing we don't recover the letters?"

Ethel and Leonard were very gay that evening; and neither spoke of the missing letters, as they sat in an alcove of a fashionable restaurant. There was a tenseness beneath their gaiety, however; and they were repeating to themselves over and over the same unanswered query with which their phone conversation had ended. The tenseness grew. With a tacit agreement, they did not linger over their dessert.

A short drive in Leonard's car, and then they entered a downtown building. They boldly took the elevator to the third story. Before them, in a long, deserted hall, was the lettered glass of an office door, with the words: JAMES DREW, Fire Insurance. Ethel took the key-ring from her vanity bag and unlocked the door.

She turned on the light and began to examine her husband's desk. It was strewn with unsorted papers; and none of the drawers had been locked. She pulled them out one by one and went through them systematically. Nothing of interest in the first two—only business documents. But what were these letters in the third drawer, lying beneath some legal papers?

The letters were not those for which she was looking. But nevertheless, what were they doing in her husband's desk? They were addressed to Jim; and the writing and stationery were feminine. Indeed, they fairly reeked of femininity: the mauve paper had been perfumed with sandalwood. Ethel did not recognize the writing; but her natural curiosity was not lessened by this fact.

She opened one of them and began to read it. The letter began: "Darling Piggy," and was full of endearments and amorous allusions, couched in the diction of a demimonde. It was signed, "Your red-hot tootsie-wootsie, Flora," with a row of crosses before and after the name.

Ethel's cheeks and eyes were burning as she turned to Leonard. She was shocked and amazed—also indignant. She would not have believed Jim capable of this sort of thing. Who was this low woman with whom he had gotten himself involved?

"Have you found something?" asked Leonard.

"I've found plenty." She gave him the letter with no further comment and proceeded to open and read the next.

"Why, the old devil!" exclaimed Leonard, when he had caught the purport of the epistle. "This is rich." He ended with a chuckle.

"Do you think it so funny?" Ethel asked stiffly.

"Well, I'll be—" Leonard wisely checked himself, reflecting that no man could foresee a woman's emotional reactions.

Ethel gave him the second letter and opened the third. There were nearly two dozen in the pile. She and Leonard read them all. Most of them were damnatory proof of a vulgar liaison. Many referred to secret meetings, even to nights that had been spent together in hotels by Jim and the writer, under assumed names. One of them enclosed a snapshot, showing Jim with his arm around a plump and luscious brunette in a one-piece bathing suit of extreme brevity. The snap-shot commemorated one of their outings. The woman's full name, Flora Jennings, was signed to one of her letters—a comparatively formal note which evidently dated from the beginning of the acquaintance.

"I'll divorce him!" cried Ethel when she had finished the last letter.

"But how about my letters? We haven't found them yet."

Ethel did not reply. She was re-reading one of the mauve-tinted epistles. Then, as she stuffed the whole packet into her vanity bag, she said:

"I'm going to take these letters with me—even if I haven't found yours."

"A fair exchange is no robbery," chuckled Leonard.

Jim had returned from his business trip. He and Ethel were at the breakfast table again.

"Did you do what I told you?" he asked gruffly, after a period of sullen pre-occupation with his food.

"What was that, Jim?" Ethel's tone was very sweet and guileless.

"What I told you about that d—n lounge-lizard," he snapped.

"And who is the lounge-lizard, pray?"

"Don't try any more bluff with me.... I told you to watch your step with Leonard Alton."

"Oh, I remember now. You said some silly things about Leonard.... Which reminds me that the dear boy took me out to dinner, night before last."

"What?" Jim was almost apoplectic with rage. "Say, do you think you can go on getting away with murder? I found a bunch of billets-doux from this Leonard person in your bureau the other day. They certainly told me all I needed to know—they ought to have been written on asbestos instead of paper. Do you think I'm going to stand for any more of this? I've got those letters in a safety deposit box at the bank. But I'll deposit 'em with a lawyer, if there's any more funny business."

"Why, what an odd coincidence," laughed Ethel. "I put some letters in a box at the bank, myself, only yesterday."

"You did? What letters?" Jim was plainly puzzled.

"Oh, some letters on mauve paper, scented with sandalwood. They were written to you, Jim, by someone named Flora Jennings.... So I think you'd better not say anything more about Leonard."

# The Infernal Star

Accursed forevermore is Yamil Zacra, star of perdition, who sitteth apart and weaveth the web of his rays like a spider spinning in a garden. Even as far as the light of Yamil Zacra falleth among the worlds, so goeth forth the bane and the bale thereof. And the seed of Yamil Zacra, like a fiery tare, is sown in planets that know him only as the least of the stars...

—*Fragment of a Hyperborean tablet.*

## Foreword

From a somewhat prolonged acquaintance with Oliver Woadley, I can avow my belief that the story he told me, in explanation of the dire embarrassment from which I had rescued him, was absolutely beyond his powers of invention.

Returning on the train at 2 A.M., after a month in Chicago, to the large Mid-western city of which we were both denizens of long standing, I had gone to bed immediately with the hope that no one would interrupt my slumber for many hours to come. However, I was awakened at earliest dawn by a telephone call from Woadley, who, in a voice rendered virtually unrecognizable by agitation and distress, implored me to come at once and identify him at the local police station. He also begged me to loan him whatever clothing I could spare.

Hastening to comply with the twofold request, I found a pitifully dazed and bewildered Woadley, garbed only in the blanket with which the police had decorously provided him. Piecing together his own vague and half-coherent account with the story of the officer who had arrested him, I learned that he had been trying to reach his suburban home a little before daybreak, via one of the main avenues, in a state of what may be termed Adamic starkness. At the time, he seemed unable to provide any clear explanation of his plight. Concealing my astonishment, I bore witness to the sanity and respectability of my friend, and succeeded in persuading the forces of the law that his singular promenade *in puris naturabilis* was merely a case of noctambulism. Though I had never known him to be thus afflicted, I believed sincerely that this was the only conceivable explanation; though, it was quite staggering that he should have appeared in public or anywhere else without pajamas or night-gown. His evident confusion of mind, I thought, was such as would be shown by a rudely awakened sleepwalker.

After he had dressed himself in the somewhat roomily fitting suit which I had brought along for that purpose, I took Woadley to my apartments and fortified him with cognac, hot coffee and a generous breakfast, all of which he manifestly needed. Afterwards he became vociferously grateful and explanatory. I learned that he had summoned me to his assistance because he deemed me the only one of his friends sufficiently broad-minded and unconventional to make allowance for the plight into which he had fallen. Especially, he had feared to call upon his own valet and housekeeper; and he had hoped to reach his home and enter it unobserved. Also, for the first time, he began to hint at a strange series of happenings which had preceded his arrest; and finally, with some reluctance, he told me the entire tale.

This story I have re-shaped hereunder in my own words. Unfortunately, I made no notes at the time; and I fear that some of the details are more impressionistic than precise in my memory. It is now impossible for Woadley to clarify them, since he forgot the whole experience shortly after unburdening himself, and denied positively that he had ever told me anything of the sort. This forgetfulness, however, must now be regarded as a tacit confirmation of his tale, since it merely fulfills the doom declared against him by Tisaina.

# Chapter I:
# The Finding of the Amulet

Woadley, it would seem, was the last person likely to undergo a translation in which the familiar laws of time and place were abrogated. For one thing, his faith in these laws was so implicit. Least of all, in the beginning, was he aware of any nascent impulse or aspiration toward things beyond the natural scope of mundane effort. The strange and the far-away had always bored him. His interest in astronomy and other orthodox but abstract sciences was very mild indeed; and sorcery was a theme that he had never even considered, except with the random superciliousness of the well-entrenched materialist. Evil, for him, was not the profound reverse ascension of the mind and soul, but was wholly synonymous with crime and social wrong-doing; and his own life had been blameless. A middle-aged bibliophile, with the means and leisure to indulge his proclivities, he asked nothing of life, other than a plenitude of Elzevirs and fine editions.

The strange process, which was to melt the solid world about him into less than shadow, began with the irritating error made by a book-dealer on whom he had always relied for infallible service. He had ordered from this dealer the well-known Hampshire edition of the novels of Jane Austen; and, opening the box, found immediately that Volume X of the set was missing. In its place was a book that resembled the other volumes only through the general form and black leather binding. The cover of this book was conspicuously worn and dull, and without lettering of any sort. Even before he had examined its contents, the substitution impressed Woadley as being an unpardonable piece of carelessness.

"I should never have believed it of Calvin," he thought. "The man must be in his dotage."

He lifted the lid of the unattractive volume, and discovered to his further surprise that it was a bound manuscript, written in a clear but spidery hand, with ink that showed a variety of discolorations, on paper brown and slightly charred at the edges. Apparently it had been saved from a conflagration; or perhaps someone had started to burn it and changed his mind. After reading a few sentences here and there, Woadley was inclined to the latter supposition, but could not imagine why the burning had been prevented.

The manuscript was untitled, unsigned, and appeared to be a collection of miscellaneous notes and jottings, made by some eccentrically minded person who had lived in New England toward the latter end of the era of witchcraft. References were made in the present tense to certain notorious witches of the time. Most of the entries, however, bore on matters that were fantastically varied and remote, and which had no patent relationship to each other aside from their common queerness and extravagance. The erudition of the unknown writer was remarkable even if misguided: as he turned the leaves impatiently, the attention of Woadley was caught by unheard-of names and terms wholly obscure to him. He frowned over casual mentionings of Lomar, Eibon, Zemargad, the Ghooric Zone, Zothique, the Table of Mordiggian, Thilil, Psollantha, Vermazbor, and the Black Flame of Yuzh. A little further on, he came to the following passage, which was equally holocryptic:

"The star Yamil Zacra, which shines but faintly on Earth, was clearly distinguished by the Hyperboreans, who knew it as the fountain-head of all evill. They knew, moreover, that in every peopled world to which the beams of Yamil Zacra have penetrated, there are beings who bear in their flesh the fierie particles diffused by this star throughout time and space. Such beings may pass their days without knowledge of the perilous kinship and the awefull powers acquired by virtue of these particles; but in others the evill declares itself variously. All who are witches or wizards or necromancers, or seekers of any forbidden lore or domination, have in them more or less of the seed of Yamil Zacra. Most mightily do the fires awaken, it is said, in him that wears on his person one of the black amulets which were brought to Earth in elder time from the great planetary world that circles eternally about Yamil Zacra and its dark companion, Yuzh. These amulets are made of a strange mineral, and upon each of them, as upon a seal, is graved the head of an unknown creature. They were once five in number, but now there are only two of them left on Earth, since the other three have been translated with their wearers back to the parent world. The manner of such translation is hard to comprehend; and the thing can occur only to one who has in himself the highest and most potent of the severall kinds of atomies emitted by Yamil Zacra. These, if he wear the amulet, may master within him in their fierie flowering the seeds of all other suns; and, being brought by virtue of this change beneath the full magneticall sway of the parent star, he will see the walls of time and place dissolve about him, and will walk in the flesh on the planet that is near to Yamil Zacra. Howbeit, there are other mysteries concerned, of which nothing is known latterly: for this lore was mainly lost with the elder continents; and lost likewise are the very names of the three men who were transported formerly from Earth. But Carnamagos, in his *Testaments*, prophesied that a fourth transportation would occur during the present cycle of terrene time; and the fifth would not occur till the final cycle, and the lifting of the last continent, Zothique."

Appended to this passage, in the form of a footnote, was another entry: "The star Yamil Zacra is unnamed by astronomers, and is seldom noted, being insignificant to the eye because of the brighter orbs that surround it. He who would find it must look midway between Algol and Polaris."

Woadley was unable to account for the patience he had shown in perusing this ineffable farrago.

"What stuff!" he exclaimed aloud, as he closed the volume and dropped it on the library table with a vehemence that bespoke his indignation. "I had no idea that Calvin went in for astrology and such rot. I must give him a piece of my mind about this damnable mistake."

His eye returned to the volume, noting with fresh displeasure that the somewhat shabby binding, which was plainly the work of an amateur, had cracked a little at the back from the violence with which he had let it fall. Gingerly he picked it up again, to examine the damage. Behind the rent in the shoddy leather, which ran diagonally down from the book's top, he discerned the rim of a small flat article, dark but scintillant, that was lodged in the interstices of the binding. Moved by a half-unwilling curiosity, he pried the thing very carefully from its hiding-place with a thin paper-cutter, without lengthening the rift.

"Well, I'll be damned," he said to himself, aloud. The profanity was almost without precedent for Woadley, but, in justification, the object that lay in the palm of his hand was nothing less than unique. It was a kind of miniature plaque or seal-like carving, little larger or thicker than an Attic mina, made of a carbon-black material which seemed to emit phosphorescent sparklings and was impossibly heavy, being at least double the weight of lead. Its outlines were unearthly, but, in the absence of any data to enlighten him, he assumed that the thing represented a sort of profile. This profile possessed a sickle-like beak and a semi-batrachian mouth whose underlip curved down obscurely and divided into swollen wattles. Far back in the corrugated face, there was a round, protuberant eye that gave the uncomfortable illusion of revolving in its socket beneath the least change of light. Above this eye, the head arose in a series of bosses, each of which was armed with a formidable upward-jutting spike. The monster was neither bird, beast nor insect, and it seemed to express a diabolism beyond anything in nature or human art. A medieval gargoyle, or an Aztec god, would have been mild and benignant in comparison. Shimmering as if with black hell-fire, it appeared to twist and writhe in malign fury as it lay in Woadley's hand. He turned it over rather hastily, but found that the obverse side repeated the figure in every hideous detail, like the other half of a face. He noticed also, for the first time, that certain worm-like characters or symbols were repeated in the clear space between the profile and the rim.

Owning himself utterly at a loss, he put this thing in his coat-pocket, with the intention of showing it to the curator of a local museum. This curator, with whom he was on friendly terms, would no doubt be able to identify it. Later, he would return it to the book-seller, together with the offensively substituted volume.

He looked at the clock, and saw that the closing time of the museum was nearly at hand. The curator seldom lingered after hours, and he lived in a remote suburb; so Woadley decided to defer his visit till the following day. It still lacked an hour of his customary dinner-time; and a curious languor, a disinclination toward any effort, either mental or physical, had come upon him all at once. The annoyance of the book-dealer's error, the bothersome riddle of the carving, began to slip from his mind. He sat down to peruse the evening paper, which his manservant had brought in a little while before.

Amid the heavier headlines of crime and politics, his eye was drawn almost immediately to an unobtrusive item relating to a new scientific discovery. It was headed: INFRA-MICROSCOPIC SUNS IN LIVING BODY-TISSUE. Woadley seldom read anything of the sort; but for some reason his interest was inveigled. He found that the gist of the article was in the following paragraph:

"It has now been proved that the human body contains atoms which burn like infinitesimal suns at a temperature of 1500° Centigrade. They stimulate vital activity, and many of their functions and properties are not yet wholly comprehended. In the most literal sense, they are identical with sun-fire and star-fire. Their arrangement in the tissue is like the spacing of constellations."

"How queer!" thought Woadley. "Bless me, but that's like the stuff in the astrological manuscript—the 'fierie particles,' etc. What are we coming to anyway?"

After dining with the moderation that marked all of his habits, Oliver Woadley was overcome by an unwonted and excessive drowsiness, which he could hardly attribute to his single glass of port. Being a respectable bachelor, he commonly spent his evenings in his own home, or else at one of the ultra-conservative clubs to which he belonged. In either case, with an unfailing punctuality, he was in bed by 10:30 P.M. This time, however, to the mild scandalization of his valet and housekeeper, he fell asleep in an easy chair among his books, after vainly trying to keep himself awake with Volume I of *Sense and Sensibility* from the new and strangely incomplete set of Jane Austen. There was a feeling of insidious narcotic luxury, a dim and indolent drifting as if upon Lethean clouds or vapors or exotic perfumes. At moments he was vaguely troubled by this infinite relaxation, which seemed to have in it something of decadent sensuality and sybaritism. However, he quickly resigned himself, and slumber bore him away on a tide softer than drifted poppy petals.

His sleep was soon troubled by a feeling of vast subliminal unrest and activity. In a state midway between oblivion and coherent dream, he seemed to apprehend the muttering of myriad voices, the opening of many doors, the lighting of myriad lamps and furnaces in the secret subterranes of his mind, that had lain dark and stirless heretofore. The muffled tumult rose and grew louder, the flames brightened, as if a resurrection of dead things were taking place. Then, like an ever-streaming pageant called up by necromancy, the dreams began.

His dreams, as a rule, were no less ordinary, no less innocuous, than the doings and reveries of the daytime. But now, with no violation of congruity, and no sense of strangeness or revulsion, he found himself playing the chief role in dramas from which the waking Woadley would have recoiled with horror.

In one of the dreams he was a medieval sorcerer taking part in the gross abominations of the Sabbat, amid the hysterical laughter of witches, the moaning of succubi, and the leaping of flames that flung their bloody gules on the black, enormous Creature presiding over all. In a second dream, he was an alchemist who sought the elixir of immortal life. He breathed the vapors of poisonous chemicals, he delved in volumes of unholy lore and madness, he tampered with the secrets of death and mortality, in the effort to reach his goal. Then he became an Atlantean scientist who had mastered the creation of living protoplasm and the disintegration of the atom, and who, by virtue of this knowledge, had attained tyrannic empire over the peoples of the crumbling continent. He made war on rebel cities with armies of artificial monsters; till, threatened in his citadel by the deadly fungi sent against him by a rival savant, he loosed the cataclysmic forces that would shatter the last foundations of Atlantis and bring upon it the engulfing sea. Subsequently, by turns, he was a Shaman of some Tartar tribe, performing rude sacrifice to barbarous gods; a Yezidee devil-worshipper, serving the baleful Peacock; and a witch of Salem who called upon demons and hurled venomous maledictions at the bystanders as she was led to the stake.

Centuries, cycles of wild and various visions followed, with no other thread of unity than the lust for unlawful knowledge and power, or pleasure beyond the natural limits of the senses, which was common to all the selves of the dreamer. Then, with casual suddenness, the phantasmagoria took an even stranger turn.

The scene of these latter dreams was not the earth, but an immense planet revolving around the sun Yamil Zacra and its dark companion, Yuzh. The name of the world was Pnidleethon. It was a place of exuberant evil life, and its very poles were tropically fertile; and the lowliest of its people was more learned in wizardry, and mightier in necromancy, than the greatest of terrene sorcerers. How he had arrived there, the dreamer did not know, for he was faint and blinded with the glory of Yamil Zacra, burning in mid-heaven with insupportable whiteness beside the blackly flaming orb of Yuzh. He knew, however, that in Pnidleethon he was no longer the master of evil he had been on Earth, but was an humble neophyte who sought admission to a dark hierarchy. As a proof of his fitness, he was to undergo tremendous ordeals, and tests of unimaginable fire and night.

There was, he thought, a terrible terraced mountain, lifting in the air for a hundred miles between the suns; and he must climb from terrace to terrace on stairs guarded by a million larvae of alien horror, a million chimeras of the further cosmos. Death, in a form hideous beyond the dooms of Earth, would be the price of the least failure of courage or any momentary relaxation of vigilance. On each of the lower terraces, when he had attained it after incalculable jeopardy, there were veiled sphinxes and hooded colossi of ill to whose interrogations he must give infallible answer. And having answered them correctly, thus evading the special doom assigned for the ignorant or forgetful, he must commit himself to the care of those Gardeners whose task was the temporary grafting of human life on the life of certain monstrous plants. And after the floral transmigration, in which he must abide for a stated term of time, there were other transmigrations for the acolyte to undergo on his way to the mountain-summit, so that no order of life and sentience should be foreign to his understanding...

In another dream, he had nearly gained the summit, and the rays of Yamil Zacra were upon him like ever-falling sheets of levin-flame in the cloudless air. He had passed all of the mountain's guardians, except Vermazbor, who warded the apex, and was the most terrible of all. Vermazbor, who had no visible form, other than that derived from the acolyte's profoundest and most secret fear, was taking shape before him; and all the pain and peril and travail he had endured in his ascent would be as nothing, unless he could vanquish Vermazbor...

## Chapter II: The Wearing of the Amulet

When Woadley awakened, all of these monstrous and outré dreams were like memories of actual happenings in his mind. With bewilderment that deepened into consternation, he found that he could not dissociate himself from the strange avatars through which he had lived. Like the victim of some absurd obsession, who, knowing well the absurdity, is nevertheless without power to free himself, he tried vainly for some time to disinvolve the thoughts and actions of his diurnal life from those of the seekers after illicit things with whom he had been identified.

Physically, his sensations were those of preternatural vigor, of indomitable strength and boundless resilience. This, however, contributed to his alarm and mental dislocation. Almost immediately, when he awakened, he became aware of the heavy carving, pressing against him like a live and radiant thing in his pocket. It thrilled him, terrified him inexpressibly. An excitement such as he had never known, and bordering on hysteria, mounted within him. In a sort of visual hallucination, it seemed that the early morning room was filled with the lambence of some larger and more ardent orb than the sun.

He wondered if he were going mad: for suddenly, with a sense of mystic illumination, he remembered the passage in the old manuscript regarding Yamil Zacra and the dark amulets; and it came to him that the thing in his pocket was one of these amulets, and that he himself was the fleshly tenement of certain of the fiery particles from Yamil Zacra. His reason, of course, tried to dismiss the idea as being more than preposterous. The information on which he had stumbled was, he told himself, a fragment of obscure folklore; and like all such lore, was crass superstition. In spite of this argument, which could have seemed incontrovertible to any sane modernist, Woadley drew the carving from his pocket with a fumbling haste that was perilously near to frenzy, and laid it on the library table beside the dilapidated volume that had been its repository.

To his infinite relief, his sensations quickly began to approximate their normal calmness and sanity. It was like the fading of some inveterately possessive nightmare; and Woadley decided that the whole phenomenon had been merely a shadowy prolongation of his dreams into a state between sleeping and waking. The removal of the plaque from his person had served to dissipate the lingering films of slumber. Reiterating to himself this comfortable assurance, he sat down at once and wrote a letter of protest to the dealer who had mistakenly supplied him with the volume of ungodly and outrageous ana. Still further relieved by this vindication of his natural, everyday self, he repaired to the bathroom. The homely acts of shaving and bathing contributed even more to the recovery of his equanimity; and after eating an extra egg and drinking two cups of strong coffee at breakfast, he felt that the recovery was complete.

He was now able to re-approach the engravure with the courage and complacency of one who has laid a phantom or destroyed a formidable bogy. The malignant profile, jetty and phosphorescent, seemed to turn upon him like a furious gargoyle. But he conquered his revulsion, and, wrapping it carefully in several thicknesses of manila paper, he sallied forth toward the local museum, whose curator, he thought, would be able to resolve the mystery of the carving's nature and origin.

The museum was only a few blocks away, and he decided that a leisurely saunter through the spring air would serve as a beneficial supplement to the hygiene of the morning. However, as he walked along the sun-bright avenue into the city, there occurred a gradual resumption of the dream-like alienage, the nervous unease and derangement, that had pursued him on awakening from that night of prodigious cacodemons. Again there was the weird quickening of his vital energies, the feeling that the flat image was a radiant burden against his flesh through raiment and wrapping-paper. The phantoms of foundered and unholy selves appeared to rise within him like a sea that obeyed the summoning of some occult black moon.

Abhorrent thoughts, having the clearness of recollections, occurred to him again and again. At moments he forgot his destination…He was going forth on darker business, was faring to some sorcerers' rendezvous. In an effort to dispel such ridiculous fantasies, he began to tell over the treasures of his library…but the list was somehow confused with dreadful and outlandish volumes, of which the normal Woadley was altogether ignorant or had heard but vaguely. Yet it seemed that he was familiar with their contents, had summarized their evil formulas, their invocations, their histories and hierarchies of demons.

Suddenly, as he walked along with half-hallucinated eyes and brain, a man jostled him clumsily, and Woadley turned upon the offender in a blaze of arrogant fury, the words of an awful ancient curse, in a rarely studied language, pouring sonorously from his lips. The man, who was about to apologize, fell back from him with ashen face and quaking limbs, and then started to run as if a devil had reached out and clawed him. He limped strangely as he ran, and somehow Woadley understood the specific application of the curse he had just fulminated in an unknown tongue. His unnatural anger fell away from him, he became aware that several bystanders were eyeing him with embarrassing curiosity, and he hurried on, little less shaken and terrified than the victim of the malediction.

How he reached the museum, he was never quite able to remember afterwards. His inward distraction prevented him from noticing, except as a vague, unfeatured shadow, the man who descended the museum steps as he himself began to climb them. Then, as if in some dream of darkness, he realized that the man had spoken to him in passing, and had said to him in a clear voice, with an elusively foreign accent: "O bearer of the fourth amulet, O favored kinsman of Yamil Zacra, I salute thee."

Needless to say, Woadley was more than astonished by this incredible greeting. And yet, in some furtive, unacknowledged way, his astonishment was not altogether surprise. Recalled by the voice to a more distinct awareness of outward things, he turned to stare at the person who had accosted him, and saw only the back of a tall, gaunt figure, wearing a formal morning coat and a high-piled purplish turban. Apparently the man was some kind of Oriental, who had compromised between his native garb and that of the Occident. Without turning his head, so that Woadley could have seen his face or even the salient portions of his profile, he went on with an agile gait that appeared to betoken immense muscular vigor. Woadley stood peering after him, as the man strode quickly along the avenue toward the low-hanging matutinal sun; and, dazzled by the brilliant light, he closed his eyes for a moment. When he opened them again, the stranger had disappeared in a most unaccountable fashion, as if he had dissolved like a vapor. It was impossible that he could have rounded the corner of the long block in that brief instant; and the nearby buildings were all private residences, a little withdrawn from the pavement, and with open lawns that could hardly have offered concealment for a figure so conspicuous.

Two hypotheses occurred to Woadley. Either he was still dreaming in his arm-chair, or else the man who had spoken to him on the steps was an hallucinatory figment of the aberration that had begun to submerge his normal consciousness. As he climbed the remaining stairs and entered the hall, it seemed that circles of fire were woven about him, and his brain whirled with the vertigo of one who walks on a knife-edge wall over cataracts of terror and splendor pouring from gulf to gulf of an unknown cosmos. He fought to maintain corporeal equilibrium as well as to regain sanity.

Somehow, he found himself in the curator's office. Through films of dizzying, radiant unreality, he was conscious of himself as a separate entity who received and returned the greeting of his friend Arthur Collins, the plump and business-like curator. It was the same separate entity who removed the carving from his pocket, unfolded it from the quadruple wrapping of brown paper, laid it on the desk before Collins, and asked

Collins to identify the object.

Almost immediately, there was a reunion of his weirdly sundered selves. The floor became solid beneath him, the webs of alien glory receded from the air. He realized that Collins was peering from the carving to himself, and back again to the carving, with a look of ludicrous puzzlement on his rosy features.

"Where on earth did you find this curio?" said Collins, a note of faint exasperation mingling with the almost infantile perplexity in his voice. The fresh color of his face deepened to an apoplectic ruby when he held up the carving in his hand and perceived its unnatural weight.

Woadley explained the circumstances of his finding of the object.

"Well, I'll be everlastingly hornswoggled if I can place the thing," opined Collins. "It's not Aztec, Minoan, Toltec, Pompeiian, Hindu, Babylonian, Chinese, Graeco-Bactrian, Cro-Magnon, Mound-Builder, Carthaginian, or anything else in the whole range of archaeology. It must be the work of some crazy modern artist—though how in perdition he obtained the material is beyond me. No mineral of such weight and specific gravity has been discovered—if you don't mind leaving it here for a few hours, I'll call in some expert mineralogists and archaeologists. Maybe someone can throw a little light on it."

"Surely, keep the thing as long as you like," assented Woadley. There was a blessed feeling of relief in the thought that he would not have to carry the carving on his person when he returned home. It was as if he had rid himself of some noxious incubus.

"You don't even need to return it to me," he told Collins. "Send it directly to Peter Calvin, the book-dealer. It belongs to him if to anyone. You know his address, I dare say."

Collins nodded rather absently. He was staring with open, semi-mesmeric horror at the baleful gravure. "I wouldn't care to meet the original of this creature," he observed. "The mind of its creator was hardly imbued with Matthew Arnold's 'sweetness and light.'"

Toward evening of that day, Woadley had convinced himself that his morning experiences, as well as the dreams of the previous night, were due to some obscure digestive complaint. It was, he told himself again and again, preposterous to imagine that they were connected in any way with the star Yamil Zacra or a dark amulet from Yamil Zacra or any other place.

By some kind of sophistry, the vague, elastic explanation had somehow included the disturbing incident of the curse; and he was willing to admit the possibility of an element of auto-suggestion in the strange greeting he had heard, or seemed to hear, from the man on the museum stairs. The foundations of his being, the fortified ramparts of his small but comfortable world, which had been sorely shaken in that hour of tremendous malaise, were now safely re-established.

He was perturbed and irritated, however, when a messenger came from the museum about sunset, with a note from Collins and a package containing the little plaque. He had thought himself permanently rid of the thing; but evidently Collins had forgotten or misunderstood his instructions. The note merely stated, in a fashion almost curt, that no one had been able to place either the material or the art-period of the carving.

Leaving the package unopened on his library table, he dined early and went out to spend the evening at one of his clubs. Returning home at the usual hour of 10:30, he retired very properly to his bedroom with the hope that his unholy nightmares would not be repeated.

Sleep, however, betrayed him again to forgotten worlds of blasphemy, of diabolism and necromancy. Through eternal dreams, through peril, wonder, foulness, ghastliness and glory, he sought once more the empire barred by a wise God to finite man. Again he was alchemist and magician, witch and wizard. Reviling and scorn, and the casting of sharp stones, and the dooms of thumbscrew and rack and *auto-da-fé*, he endured in that quest of the absolute. He dabbled in the blood of children, in filth and feculence unspeakable, and the ultimate putrefaction of the grave. He held parley with the Dwellers in pits beyond geometric space, he gave homage to hideous demons seen by the aid of Avernian drugs that blasted the user. From sea-corroded Atlantean columns, he gleaned a lore that seared his very soul in the gleaning; on lost papyri of prehistoric Egypt, and tablets of green brass from Eighur tombs, he found the wisdom that was henceforth as a mordant charnel-worm in his brain. And great, by virtue of all this, was the reward that he won and the masterdom he achieved.

His stupendous dreams of Pnidleethon were not resumed on that night; but with certain other dreams the pristine tradition of Yamil Zacra and the five amulets was interwoven. He sought to acquire one of the fabled amulets, seeking it throughout his avatar as a Hyperborean wizard, in archetypal cities and amid subhuman tribes. A lord of earthly science and evil, he had aspired madly to that supreme evolution possible only through the amulet, by which he would return through the riven veils of time and place to Yamil Zacra. It seemed that he pursued the quest in vain through life after life, till the great ice-sheet rolled upon Hyperborea; and the night of nescience came upon him, and he was swept away from his antique wisdom by other lives and deaths. Then there came darker visions, and more aimless seekings unlit by the legend of Yamil Zacra, in ages when all wizards had forgotten the true source of their wizardry; and after these, he dreamed that he was Oliver Woadley, and that somehow he had come into possession of the longed-for talisman, and was about to recover all that he had lost amid the dust and ruining of cycles.

From his final dream, he awakened suddenly and sat bolt upright in bed, clutching at the pocket of his old-fashioned nightgown. There was a glowing weight against his heart, and the grey morning twilight about him was filled with an illumination of infernal splendor. In an exaltation of rapturous triumph, no longer mingled with any fear or doubting or confusion, he knew that he wore the amulet and would continue to wear it thereafter.

Early in his sleep, he must have risen like a noctambulist to untie the thing from the parcel on the library table, where, later, he found the small cardboard box and crumpled paper in which Collins had returned it to him.

## Chapter III:
## "I am Avalzant, the Warden of the Fiery Change."

In telling me his story, Woadley was somewhat vague and reticent about his psychological condition on the day following the second night of necromantic dreams. I infer, though, that there were partial relapses into normality, fluctuations of alarm and horror, moments in which he again mistrusted his own sanity. The complete reversal of his wonted habits of thought, the flight of his strait horizons upon vertiginous gulfs and far worlds, was not to be accomplished without intervals of chaos or conflict. And, yet, from that time on, he seems to have accepted his incredible destiny. He wore the amulet continually, and his initial sensations of vertigo and semi-delirium were not repeated. But under its influence, he became literally another person than the mild bibliophile, Oliver Woadley...

His outward life, however, went on pretty much as usual. In answer to the vehement epistle of complaint he had written to Peter Calvin, he received an explanatory and profusely apologetic letter. The untitled manuscript had belonged to the library of a deceased and eccentric collector, which Calvin had purchased *in toto*. A new and near-sighted clerk had been responsible for the misplacing of the dark volume amid the set of Jane Austen, and the same clerk had packed the set for shipment to Woadley without detecting his error. Calvin was very sorry indeed and he was sending Volume X by express prepaid. Woadley could do whatever he pleased with the old manuscript, which was more curious than valuable.

Woadley smiled over this letter, not without irony; for the manuscript of obscure ana, which had outraged him on his first cursory perusal of its contents, was now of far more interest to him than Jane Austen. Living umbrageously, and avoiding his friends and acquaintances, he had already begun the study of certain excessively rare tomes, such as *The Necronomicon* and the writings of Hali. These he collated carefully with *The Testaments of Carnamagos*, that Cimmerian seer whose records of ultimate blasphemies, both past and future, were found in Graeco-Bactrian tombs. Also, he perused several works of more recent date, such as Vertnain's *Pandemonium*. How Woadley acquired these virtually unheard-of volumes, I never understood; but apparently they came to his hand with the same coincidental ease as the black amulet: an ease in which it is possible to suspect an almost infinitely remote provenance.

To these books, the darkest cabbala of human and demoniac knowledge, he applied himself like an old student who wishes to refresh his memory, rather than as a beginner. Their appalling lore, it seemed, was a thing that he remembered from pre-existent lives, together with the lost words, the primal arcanic symbols that had baffled their translators. The memory had been revived within him by the talisman. It was the flowering of the monads of Yamil Zacra, the eternal, unforgetting atoms which, before entering his body at birth, had been incarnate in a thousand sorcerers and masters of unpermitted wisdom. This esoteric truth, so difficult to believe or understand, he knew with a simple certainty.

His servants, it would appear, were not cognizant of any change in Woadley, and thought nothing of his studies, doubtless taking the tomes he perused so assiduously for quaint incunabula. A general impression that he was out of town seems to have been created in the small social circle to which he belonged; and, by a coincidence that suited well enough with his own inclination, no one came to call upon him for a whole fortnight.

At the end of that fortnight, in the late evening, he received an unexpected visitor. His servants had gone to bed, and he was memorizing a certain ghastly incantation from *The Testaments of Carnamagos*: an incantation which, if uttered aloud, would cause the complete annihilation and vanishment of a dead human body, either before or after the onset of rigor mortis and the beginning of corruption.

Why he was so intent on learning this formula, he hardly knew; but he found himself conning it over and repeating it silently with a feeling of actual haste and urgency, as if it were a lesson important for him to master. Even as he came to the end, and made sure that the last abhorrent rune was fixed firmly in his mind, he heard the loud and vicious buzzing of the doorbell. No doubt the bell was like any other in its tonal vibrations; it had never impressed his ear unusually before; but he was startled as if by the clashing of sinister sistra, or the rattling of a crotalus. The electric warning of a deadly danger tingled through all his nerves as he went to open the door.

As if he had already begun to exercise the clairvoyant powers proper to his new state of entity, he was not at all surprised by the extraordinary figure that stood before him. The figure was that of a Tibetan lama, garbed in monastic robe and cap. He was both tall and portly, seeming to fill the entire doorway with his presence. His level, heavy brows, his large eyes that flamed with the cruel brilliance of black diamonds, and the high aquiline cast of his features, bore witness to some obscure strain of non-Mongolian blood. He spoke in a voice that somehow suggested the purring of a tiger; and Woadley was never sure afterwards as to the language employed: for it seemed then that all languages were an implicit part of his weirdly resurrected knowledge.

"Bearer of the fourth amulet," said the lama, "I crave an audience. Permit me to enter thy lordly abode." The tone was respectful, even obsequious; but behind it, Woadley was aware of a black blaze of animosity toward himself, and a swollen venom as of coiled cobras.

"Enter," he assented curtly, and without turning his back, allowed the lama to pass by him into the hall and precede him to the library. As if to impress Woadley with his subservient attitude, this lama remained standing, till Woadley pointed to a chair beneath the full illumination of a floor-lamp. Woadley then seated himself in a more shadowy position from which he could watch the visitor continually without appearing to do so. He was close to the oaken library table, on which *The Testaments of Carnamagos* lay open at the lich-destroying formula, with the leaves weighted by a small Florentine dagger which he often used as a paper-knife. Before going to answer the bell, he had switched off the light that shone directly on the table; and the floor-lamp was now the only light burning in the room.

"Well, who are you, and what do you want?" he demanded, in an arrogant, peremptory tone of which he would scarcely have been capable a fortnight previous.

"O master," replied the lama. "I am Nong Thun, a most humble neophyte of the elder sciences. My degree of illumination is as darkness compared to thine. Yet has it enabled me to recognize the wearer of the all-powerful amulet from Pnidleethon. I have seen thee in passing; and I come now to request a great boon. Permit thy servile slave to behold the amulet with his unworthy eyes."

"I know nothing of any amulet," said Woadley. "What nonsense is this that you prate?"

"It pleases thee to jest. But again I beg the boon." The lama had lowered his eyes like a devotee in the presence of deity, and his hands were clasped together as if in supplication on his knees.

"I have nothing to show you." The finality of Woadley's voice was like a barrier of flint.

As if resigning himself to this denial, the lama bowed his head in silence. Apart from this, there was no visible movement or quiver in all his body; but at that moment the floor-lamp above him was extinguished, as though he had risen to his feet and had turned it off. The room was choked with sudden sooty darkness; there was no glimmer through the bay-window from the street-light opposite; nor was there even the least glow or flicker from the table-lamp when Woadley reached out to switch it on. The night that enveloped him, it seemed, was a positive thing, an element older and stronger than light; and it closed upon him like strangling hands. But, groping quickly, he found the Florentine dagger, and held it in readiness as he rose silently to his feet and stood between the table and the arm-chair he had just vacated. As if from deep vaults of his brain, a low minatory voice appeared to speak, and supplied him with an ancient word of protective power; and he uttered the word aloud and kept repeating it in a sonorous, unbroken muttering as he waited.

Apart from that sorcerous incantation, there was silence in the room; and no lightest rustle or creaking to indicate the presence of the lama. The unnatural night drew closer, it smothered Woadley like the gloom of a mausoleum; and upon it there hung a faint fetor as of bygone corruption. There came to Woadley the weird thought that no one lived in the room, other than himself; that the lama was gone; that there had never been any such person. But he knew this thought for a wile of the shrouded enemy, seeking to delude him into carelessness; and he did not relax his vigil or cease the reiteration of the protective word. A monstrous and mortal peril was watching him in the nighted chamber, biding its time to spring; but he felt no fear, only a great and preternormal alertness.

Then, a little beyond arm's-length before him, a leprous glimmering slowly dawned in the darkness, like a phosphor of decay. Bone by fleshless bone, beginning with the stalwart ribs, and creeping upward and downward simultaneously, it illumed the tall skeleton to which it clung; and finally it brought out the skull, in whose eye-pits burned like malignant gems the living eyes of the lama. Then, from between the rows of yellowish vampire teeth, which had parted in a gaping as of Death himself, a dry and rustling voice appeared to issue: the voice of some articulate serpent coiled amid the ruins of mortality.

"Pusillanimous weakling, unworthy fool, give me the black amulet of Yamil Zacra ere it slay thee," hissed the voice.

Like a feinting swordsman who lowers his guard, Woadley ceased for a second his muttering of the word of power which held the horror at bay as if a wizard circle had been drawn about him. In that instant, a long curved knife appeared from empty air in the fleshless hand, seen dimly by the phosphorescent glowing of the finger-bones, and the thing leapt forward, avoiding the chair, and struck at Woadley with a sidelong motion in which its arm-bones and the blade were like the parts of a sweeping scythe.

Woadley, however, had prepared himself for this, and he stooped to the very floor beneath the knife, and slashed upward slantingly with his own weapon at the seeming voidness of thoracic space below the ribs of the phosphor-litten Death. Even as he had expected, his dagger plunged into something that yielded with the soft resistance of living flesh, and the rotten glimmering of the bones was erased in a momentaneous darkness. Then the flames returned in the electric bulbs; and beneath their steady burning he saw at his feet the fallen body of the lama, with a long tear in the robe across the abdomen, from which blood was welling like a spring. With a twisting movement like that of some heavy snake, the body writhed a little, and then became quiescent.

Briefly, while he stood staring at the man he had slain, Woadley felt the nausea, horror and weakness that his former self would have known under such circumstances.

The whole sinister episode through which he had just lived, together with his new self and its preoccupations, became temporarily remote and fantastic. He could realize only that he had killed a man with his own hand, and that the loathsomely inconvenient proof of his crime was lying at his feet with its blood beginning to darken the roses and arabesques of the Oriental carpet.

From this passing consternation, he was startled by a preternatural brightening of the light, as if an untimely dawn had filled the chamber. Looking up, he saw that the lamps themselves were oddly wan and dim. The light came from something that he could define only as a congeries of glowing motes, that had appeared in mid-air at the opposite side of the room, before his longest and highest book-case.

It was as if the thickly teeming suns of a great galaxy had dwarfed themselves to molecules and had entered the chamber. The congeries appeared to have the vague outlines of a colossal semi-human form, wavering slightly, spinning, contracting and expanding through the ceaseless gyrations of the separate particles. These atomies were unsufferably brilliant, and Woadley's eyes soon became dazzled as he regarded them. They seemed to multiply in myriads, till he beheld only a blazing, fulgurating blur. Miraculously, his vision cleared, and the blur resolved itself into a figure that was still luminous but which had now assumed the character of what is known as solid matter. With reverential awe and wonder, wholly forgetful of the corpse at his feet, he saw before him a creature that might have been some ultra-cosmic angel of ill. The giant stature of this being, in the last phase of his epiphany, had lessened till he was little taller than an extremely tall man; but it seemed that the lessening was a mere accommodation to the scale of his terrene environment.

The quasi-human torso of the being was clad in laminated armor like plates of ruby. His four arms, supple and sinuous as great cobras, were bare; and the two legs, powerful and tapering like the rear volumes of pythons standing erect, were also bare except for short greaves of a golden material about the calves. The four-clawed feet, like those of some mythic salamander, were shod with sapphire sandals. In one of his seven-fingered hands, he carried a short-handled spear with a sword-long blade of blue metal from whose point there streamed an incessant torrent of electric sparks.

The head of this being was cuneiform, and its massively flaring lines were prolonged by a miter-shaped helmet with outward-curving horns. His chin sharpened unbelievably, terminating in a dart-like prong, semi-translucent. The ears, conforming to the head, were pierced and fluted shells of shining flesh. The strangely carven nostrils palpitated with a ceaseless motion as of valves that shut and opened. The eyes, far apart beneath the smooth, enormous brow, were beryl-colored orbs that fouldered and darkened as if with the changing of internal fires in the semi-eclipse of their drooping lids. The mouth, turning abruptly down at the corners, was like a symbol of unearthly mysteries and cruelties.

It was impossible to assign a definite complexion to the face and body of this entity, for the whole epidermis, wherever bare to sight, turned momently from a marmoreal pallor to an ebon blackness or a red as of mingled blood and flame.

Rapt and marvelling, Woadley heard a voice that seemed to emanate from the visitant: though the seal-like quietude of the lips remained unbroken. The voice thundered softly in his brain, like the fire and sweetness of a great wine transmuted into sound.

"Again I salute thee, O bearer of the fourth amulet, O favored kinsman of Yamil Zacra. I am Avalzant, the Warden of the Fiery Change, and envoy from Pnidleethon to the sorcerers of outer worlds. The hour of the Change is now at hand, if thy heart be firm to endure it. But first I beg thee to dispose of this carrion." He pointed with his coruscating weapon at the lama's body.

# Chapter IV: The Passage to Pnidleethon

Woadley's brain was filled with a strange dazzlement. Recalling at that moment the half-seen Oriental who had addressed him on the steps of the museum, he stared uncomprehending from his visitor to the corpse.

"Why this hesitation?" said the being, in the tone of a patient monitor. "Were you not conning the necessary spell for the annihilation of such offal when the lama came? You have only to read it aloud from the book if you have already forgotten."

The runes of the lich-destroying formula returned to Woadley, and his doubt and bemusement passed in a flood of illumination. In a voice that was firm and orotund as that of some elder sorcerer, he recited the incantation of Carnamagos, prolonging and accentuating certain words with the required semi-tones and quavers of vowel-pitch. As the last words vibrated in the lamplit air, the clothing and features of the lama became mantled with a still, hueless flame that burned without sound or palpable heat, rising aloft in a smokeless column, and including even the puddled blood on the Persian carpet. At the same instant, flame clothed the blade of the bloody dagger in Woadley's hand. The body melted away like so much tallow, and was quickly consumed, leaving neither ash or charred bone nor any odor of burning to indicate that the eerie cremation had ever occurred. The flame sank, flattened, and died out on the empty floor, and Woadley saw that there was no trace of fire, no stain of blood, to mar the intricate design of the carpet. The stain had also vanished from the dagger, leaving the metal clean and bright. With the pride and complacency of a past-master of such gramaries, he found himself reflecting that this was quite as it should be.

Again he heard the voice of his visitor. "Nong Thun was not the least of the terrestrial children of Yamil Zacra; and if he had slain thee and had won the amulet, it would have been my task to attend him later, even as I must now attend thee. For he lacked only the talisman to assure the ultimate burgeoning of his powers and the supreme flowering of his wisdom.

But in this contest thou hast proven thyself the stronger, by virtue of those illuminated monads within thee, each of which has retained the cycle-old knowledge of many sorcerers. Now, by the aid that I bring, that which was effluent from Yamil Zacra in the beginning may return toward Yamil Zacra. This, if thou art firm to endure the passage, will be the reward of thy perilous seekings and thy painful dooms in a thousand earthly pre-existences. Before thee, from this world, three wizards only have been transported to Pnidleethon; and seldom therefore is my advent here, who serve as the angel of transition to those wizards of ulterior systems, whom the wandering amulets have sought out and have chosen. For know that the amulet thou wearest is a thing endued with its own life and its own intelligence; and not idly has it come to thee in the temporary nescience to which thou wert sunken....

"Now let us hasten with the deeds that must be done: since I like not the frore, unfriendly air of this Earth, where the seed of Yamil Zacra has indeed fallen upon sterile soil, and where evil blossoms as a poor and stunted thing. Not soon shall I come again; for the fifth and last amulet slumbers beneath the southern sea in long-unknown Moaria, and waits the final resurgence of that continent under a new name when all the others have sunken leaving but ocean-scattered isles."

"What is your will, O Avalzant?" asked Woadley. His voice was clear and resolute; but inwardly he quaked a little before the presence of the Envoy, who seemed to bear with him as a vestment more than the vertigo-breeding glory and direness of Death. Behind Avalzant, the shelves of stodgy volumes, the wall itself, appeared to recede interminably, and were interspaced with sceneries lit by an evil, ardent luster. Pits yawned in livid crimson like the mouths of cosmic monsters. Black mountains beetled heaven-high from the brink of depths profounder than the seventh hell. Demonic Thrones and Principalities gathered in conclave beneath black Avernian vaults; and Luciferian Powers loomed and muttered in a sky of alternate darkness and levin.

"First," declared Avalzant, in reply to Woadley's question, "it will be needed for thee to doff this sorry raiment which thou wearest, and to stand before me carrying naught but the talisman; since the talisman alone among material objects may pass with thee to Pnidleethon. The passage is another thing for me, who fare at will through ultimate dimensions, who tread the intricate paths and hidden, folded crossways of gulfs unpermitted to lesser beings; who assume any form desired in the mere taking of thought, and appear simultaneously in more than one world if such be requisite.... It was I who spoke to thee on the stairs before the museum; and since then, I have journeyed to Polaris, and have walked on the colossean worlds of Achernar, and have fared to outermost stars of the galaxy whose light will wander still for a thousand ages in the deep ere it dawn on the eyes of thy astronomers.... But such ways are not for thee; nor without my aid is it possible for thee or for any inhabitant of Earth to enter Pnidleethon."

Submissively, while the Envoy was speaking, Woadley had begun to remove his garments. Hastily and with utter negligence, he flung the dark, conservative coat and trousers of tweed across an arm-chair, tossed his shirt, tie, socks and under-garments on the pile, and left his shoes lying where he had removed them. Trifling as it may have seemed, this negligence was a potent proof of the change he had undergone; for such disorder would have been unthinkable to the neat and somewhat fussy bibliophile.

Presently he stood naked from heel to head before Avalzant, the amulet glowing darkly in the palm of his right hand. Only with the utmost dimness was he able to prevision the ordeal before him; but he trembled with its imminence, as a man might tremble on the shore of uncrossed Acheron.

"Now," said Avalzant, "it is needful that I should wound thee deeply on the bosom with my spear. Art fearful of this wounding? If so, it were well to re-clothe thyself and remain amid these volumes of thine, and to let the talisman pass into hardier hands."

"Proceed." There was no quaver in Woadley's voice, though sudden-reaching talons of terror clawed at his brain and raked his spinal column like an icy harrow.

Avalzant uplifted the strange, blue-gleaming weapon he bore, till the stream of sparks that poured ceaselessly from its point was directed upon Woadley's bare bosom. The neophyte was aware of an electric prickling that wandered over his chest as Avalzant drew the weapon in a slow arc from side to side. Then the spear was retracted and was poised aloft with a sinuous, coiling movement of the arm-like member that held it. Death seemed to dart like a levin-bolt upon Woadley; but the apparent lethal driving-power behind the thrust was in all likelihood merely one more test of his courage and resolution. He did not flinch nor even close his eyes. The terrible, blazing point entered his flesh above the right lung, piercing and slashing deeply, but not deeply enough to inflict a dangerous wound. Then, while Woadley tottered and turned faint with the agony as of throbbing fires that filled his whole being, the weapon was swiftly withdrawn.

Dimly, through the millionfold racking of his torment, he heard the solemn voice of Avalzant. "Even now, it is not too late, if thy heart misgive thee; for the wound will heal in time and leave thee none the worse. But the next thing needful is irrevocable and not to be undone. Holding the amulet firmly with thy fingers, thou must press the graven mouth of the monster into thy wound while it bleeds; and having begun this part of the process, thou hast said farewell to Earth and hast forsworn the sun thereof and the light of the sister planets, and hast pledged thyself wholly to Pnidleethon, to Yamil Zacra—and Yuzh. Bethink thee well, whether or not thy resolution holds."

Woadley's agony began to diminish a little. A great wonder filled him, and beneath the wonder there was something of half-surmised horror at the strange injunction of the Envoy. But he obeyed the injunction, forcing the sickle beak and loathsome wattled mouth of the double-sided profile into the slash inflicted by Avalzant, from which blood was welling profusely on his bosom.

Now began the strangest part of his ordeal; for, having inserted the thin edge of the carving in the cut, he was immediately conscious of a gentle suction, as if the profile-mouth were somehow alive and had started to suck his blood. Then, looking down at the amulet, he saw to his amazement that it seemed to have thickened slightly, that the coin-flat surface was swelling and rounding into an unmistakable convexity. At the same time, his pain had altogether ceased, and the blood no longer flowed from his wound; but was evidently being absorbed through what he now knew to be the vampirism of the mineral monstrosity.

Now the black and shimmering horror had swollen like a glutted bat, filling his whole hand as he still held it firmly. But he felt no alarm, no weakness or revulsion whatever, only a vast surge of infernal life and power, as if the amulet, in some exchange that turned to demoniacal possession, were returning a thousandfold the draught it had made upon him. Even as the thing grew and greatened on his breast, so he in turn seemed to wax gigantic, and his blood roared like the flamy torrents of Phlegethon plunging from deep to deep. The walls of the library had fallen unheeded about him, and he and Avalzant were two colossi who stood alone in the night; and upon his bosom the vampire stone was still suckled, enormous as behemoth.

It seemed that he beheld the shrunken world beneath him, the rondure of its horizons curving far down in darkness against the abyss of stars, with a livid fringe of light where the sun hovered behind the eastern hemisphere. Higher and vaster still he towered, and his whole being seemed to melt with unsufferable heat, and he heard in himself a roar and tumult as of some peopled inferno, pouring upward with all its damned to overflow the fixed heavens. Then he was riven apart in a thousand selves, whose pale and ghastly faces streamed about him in the momentary flashing of strange suns. The sorcerers of Ur and Egypt, of Antillia and Moaria; necromancers of Mhu Thulan and shamans of Tartary; witch and enchantress of Averoigne, Hecatean hag, and sybil from doomed Poseidonis; alchemist and seer; the priests of evil fetiches from Niger; the adepts of Ahriman, of Eblis, of Taranis, of Set, of Lucifer—all these, resurgent from a thousand tombs in demonomaniacal triumph, were riding the night to some cosmic Sabbat. Among them, like a lost soul, was the being who had called himself Oliver Woadley. And upon the bosom of each separate self, as well as upon that of Woadley, a talismanic monster was suckled throughout the black, appalling flight on deeps forbidden save to the stars in their lawful orbits.

# Dawn of Discord

Time was a dimension of space: time was a closed curve, without beginning or end, and space was curved, endless, yet finite. Or so John King had told himself, during those years of study. But now, with war threatening to overwhelm the world, King was through with theory. He was going back into time—or space—or both, if his equations did not lie. And he was going to stop war at its origin.

He took off his acid-stained smock and put on a khaki shirt, breeches, laced boots. King was incongruous among the switchboards and oscillation tubes, the retorts and electric furnaces of the laboratory in the old house on top of Russian Hill; he looked like a man ready to invade the jungle, and he was tall and lean and fit enough for such a task.

One look at the broad bay, at the housetops far below him, at the bridges that spanned the water; one pang of regret as he paused at the door of adventure. His fanatic devotion to science had kept him a stranger to women, and though he resolutely kept them from his thoughts, he wished that he could be sure of returning. There was a shapely blonde girl who must work in an office nearby; he had tried not to notice her on his way to the restaurant where he ate during the afternoon breathing spell.

Then he turned toward the time-traveling machine which was to take back an age when there was no such thing as war. Arrived there, King would cut war off at its root.

The machine had thick metal walls, and was shaped like a bathysphere; its glass ports were built to resist enormous pressure, and it was powered by atomic energy. This would be nothing like the flight of an airplane or rocket ship; there would be no travel in the ordinary sense of the word, for King was putting himself into a magnetic field which would reverse time. This would not be like any three-dimensional journey that any man had ever made.

The self-locking door closed behind him. King wanted to look back once more at the present, but he feared that he would falter; so he stepped to the control levers and the dials that filled all the bulkheads. Two people could have found room beside him, provided they were slender.

He closed the switch; a surge of power shook the machine, and the daylight that came in through the ports became green, then a grey blur. Every atom of his body threatened to leap into space on its own account. King felt knifing pains, a horrible giddiness, and a fear beyond reckoning. Suppose he could not find his way back? Suppose he became an exile from time and space?

When his consciousness ceased whirling, he glanced at the dials that recorded the coordinate of the time-space equation. He had gone back, as nearly as he could calculate from old traditions, to the Golden Age, the fabled era before man learned of hate and iron.

War, King had reasoned, was an insane habit that some bird-brained primitive had devised as a substitute for judgment or intelligence; and thus, a man of the twentieth century, without any illusions as to the glory of strife, might direct the first warrior chief into a happier channel. If these people of the Golden Age, drunk by the novelty of Iron and Power, could see what evolution had finally made of war, they might sober up. War had once been an adventure, but it had long since lost whatever redeeming quality it had possessed.

Through the ports of the time machine, King looked at the green-gold jungles of an infant world. Tall tree ferns trembled in the breeze. The jade waters of a lake lapped a shore fringed with gigantic reeds and grasses; bright insects flashed gold and crimson.

King opened the hatch and stepped to the springy turf. Ages were not as sharply divided as political boundaries, and he would have to reconnoiter to see if he had actually reached the Golden Age.

Then he saw the girl. At the first stirring of the foliage, he had reached for his Colt, not knowing what prehistoric terrors might come out of the jungle; but now his hand dropped. She had the rounded hips and tapered lines of a wood nymph; she moved effortlessly, and the breeze pulled at the translucent tunic that modeled her bosom and the slim curve of her waist. King wondered for a moment if this exquisite creature were just another one of those taunting fancies that had at times crowded equations and integrals from his weary brain.

The girl's blue skirt reached a little below her knees; a costume that reminded him somewhat of the classical drapes worn by women pictured on fragments of Greek pottery. The warm light shaped a golden halo about her head; her unbound hair trailed in copper-colored luxury to her hips.

She started, wide-eyed, when she saw King. Impulsively, he came toward her, and said,

"Don't be afraid, I'm a stranger and maybe you could tell me where I am."

Her grey-green eyes showed her perplexity, but she smiled, recognizing the friendliness of his voice. King could not understand a word of her answer, but that made little difference; her voice warmed him, and made him forget the wonder of having traveled all those centuries into time and space. Whatever she had said, she meant that he was welcome. Then, coming within arm's length, he noted that the skirt was torn, and that scratches crisscrossed her calves and thighs. Her tunic was tattered, and her sides were bruised and scarred. He caught her arm and gestured toward the time machine, saying, "You'd better meet the first aid kit."

He could not understand her answer, but there was meaning in the way she fell in step with him, her hip brushing against him, her arm closing against her side and imprisoning the hand he had laid on her elbow. King's blood sang as if it had been blended with the sap of the young earth.

A rosy flush spread over the girl's cheeks when she looked up and saw King's ardent glance. She held up her free hand, and showed him the small band of yellow metal about her wrist. On this curious bracelet were two golden cases, neither of them much larger than a man's watch; a small reel of fine cable connected them. With her other hand she took off one of the cases and clipped it to King's wrist.

She spoke again, and King could now understand her speech; rather, read her thoughts, in spite of the foreign words.

"I am Ania, a slave, and I ran away from my master, Jurth. He beats me. As you can see—" She half turned, and King saw that her back was seamed with red welts. "He used to be so kind and friendly, like the rest of us. But who are you? I've never seen such strange clothes though they're really becoming."

"I'll give you something to put on those scratches, and while you're doctoring yourself, I'll tell you, though I'm afraid I can't make it very clear. I've come back from what is the future to you; back thirty-two thousand, seven hundred thirteen years—" He lost count of his dial reading, and had to start all over again, for Ania had snuggled up close to him in the cramped cabin of the time cruiser. He finished, "Six months and twenty-two days."

He showed her how to use an iodine swab.

"Oh—that stings! But I can't understand, coming back from the future. It sounds impossible. And why did you do it?"

"We have a disease in our time. A disease called war. Fighting that would be bad enough even if it settled anything, which it never does." He bitterly went on, "Two of my brothers were killed, and a third one is a horrible cripple. I was too young to go. I was sorry then, but when I saw the one who returned, I wished he too had died. So I have come back through time to find the man who started war."

"War?" Ania frowned. "I can say it, but I don't understand."

He was in the Golden Age; her answer assured him of that. His theory was justified. More than that, her master, Jurth, was strangely and unaccountably becoming vicious.

Jurth, the father of strife? Then this was the dawn of discord!

King caught Ania in his arms. "Tell me about Jurth. I won't let him hurt you."

Ania anxiously asked, "You won't go back into the future without taking me with you?"

"Tell me about Jurth," he evaded, and turned toward the shade of the swaying tree ferns.

There he seated himself on the springy turf, and drew in an exhilarating breath. The air of this young world gave him vitality that no human being had had for centuries. He drew Ania closer and kissed her upturned lips; she clung to him, sighed rapturously, and the warmth of her mouth and the pressure of her encircling arms troubled King until there was no room left in his whirling brain for anything but this dawn woman and her possessive beauty.

When King finally got the conversation back to Jurth, Ania explained, "He has studied the forces of nature and bent them to his own use. This thing that makes me understand you—or any other foreigner I might meet—a sort of thought-reading thing, I guess you'd call it, is one of the things Jurth made. But some of his inventions are evil. He makes weapons to kill, to paralyze. Every wise man has servants, lots of them, but Jurth sends out fighting men to take prisoners. That's why he invented this thought-disc, so the strangers could understand his orders."

Pride; greed; restless ambition—this Jurth was moved by the very things that made war. Find Jurth, and give peace to all the centuries to come. For all his horror of killing and wounding, King knew that he had to finish Jurth.

In the meanwhile, the sun was setting, and the time machine, cramped though it was, would be the safest shelter. King rose, gave Ania his hand. "Tomorrow—"

Ania's cry of dismay cut him short. There was a crashing in the brush, and a confusion of deep voices. "That's Jurth!" she cried. "Hurry—before...."

Three men bounded from the edge of the small clearing, and cut off King's retreat to the time machine. The foremost was as tall as King, but heavier of limb and deeper of chest; a black beard jutted aggressively from his craggy face. In one big hand he had a nine-thonged whip. The muscles of his legs and arms were like hawsers. He halted, cracked his scourge, and gestured to Ania. In his other hand he had a rod of bluish metal, tipped with a glass-like bulb; King, taking in the newcomers at a glance, assumed that this was a scepter or other emblem of rank.

Like their chief, Jurth's two retainers wore kilts and short-sleeved jackets, but their weapons were three-pronged spears. King jerked clear of Ania's embrace. "Let go! You run to the machine while I stop these fellows!"

He snapped the telepathic coil and cord from his wrist, and thrust the girl from him. He drew the heavy pistol. The two spearmen were easy targets. But something stayed his hand, and he was glad, for an envoy of peace should certainly not shoot men armed with tridents; so he yelled a warning, and gestured, hoping that they would know enough to stop.

Ania, instead of dashing on, had stopped, unwilling to leave King. One of the spearmen swerved and bounded toward her. King fired, purposely throwing the shot against a rock that jutted up out of the turf, right in front of the big fellow's path. Chips of rock peppered his legs. "Halt, or I'll hit you!" King warned.

The man stopped. Then Jurth raised the rod, and King learned that it was more than a scepter. A tongue of light the length of a man's hand flamed from the glass bulb. King's right arm went numb, and his pistol dropped from his grasp. Amazement froze him; he did not know which way to go, or what to do.

Jurth was now upon him, the scourge hissing in a backward arc. King ducked. While his right arm was still useless, his left was unharmed. He came up, bringing one from the turf, and the blow snapped Jurth's head back. But he had an iron jaw, and instead of dropping in his tracks, Jurth bellowed and slashed home again with the short-lashed scourge.

Apparently he forgot his peculiar ray projector, or else the whip suited his mood. He drove King back with cutting lashes; one peeled his ribs, a second crippled his arm to the shoulder.

King took a third blow. He recoiled, raised his arm as if to shield his face, yelled as if in terror. Jurth laughed and wound up for the cut to lay him out. This was what King had expected. He lunged, letting his legs propel him, and with shoulder and one sound arm he caught Jurth below the knees, just as the whip hissed through empty space.

Jurth thumped to the turf. King followed through, booting his oppressor in the pit of the stomach. He had pretty well forgotten his pacific mission. He cut loose and booted his limp opponent another one, and wondered when he had ever had such a pleasant afternoon.

King was about to get up so he could trample Jurth into the ground when a trident prodded his back. The cold metal brought him to his senses. In his fury he had forgotten the spearmen and Ania. Now, startled and menaced, he realized what he had been trying to do, and he was ashamed. Not but that Jurth deserved a mauling for whipping a girl like Ania; rather, King felt cheap for that ecstasy of rage. Something was undermining his character; he had given up ten years of his life to confer the boon of peace on mankind, and now, a slugging match made him drunk with fighting spirit.

The other spearman had caught Ania. Seeing the trident that prodded King's back, she screamed and broke away. Her captor dropped his weapon and bounded after her, before she could snatch the other spearman's trident. He caught her shoulder, tore her tunic to the waist, and then made another lunge. This time he got her about the waist. Kicking and screaming, clawing and wriggling, Ania ended up with little more than a scrap of skirt and her ruddy hair to cover her. She went limp; her captor grinned, wiped the sweat from his forehead—and then Ania broke loose, and dashed for the time machine.

She had not the faintest idea of how to work it, but a struggle in the instrument compartment could disturb almost any combination of levers and start it off, marooning King in the dawn of discord, and carrying Ania and one of her assailants into the twentieth or any other century, past or future. Terror made King move without thought. He yelled and bounded forward, and the spearman at his back was so startled that for an instant, he did not thrust.

King had no time to retrieve his pistol. He outran the spearman, and overtook Ania's pursuer. He tackled the fellow from the side, and sent him smashing against the trunk of a tree fern. That settled him. "Ania, get in!" King panted, and clawed at a rock, "while I finish this other fellow."

He tore the rock from its bed of moss, and again the fine fury of the young world intoxicated him. He crouched near the hatch of the time machine, ready to heave the heavy missile. His lips were drawn back, his teeth showed.

The spearman backed away. He was afraid of a twentieth-century pacifist. And then Jurth rolled over on his face and got to his knees. He roared, levelled his scepter. King sidestepped, but he was too slow. There was a momentary spurt of flame, and King's legs froze, his whole side and arm went dead, and he toppled over with his missile.

His brain had been touched by this last blast, and while he was not wholly unconscious, he was in a dreamlike haze. He knew only that they were carrying him past a lake, through a jungle, up a mountain. His wits receded, letting him into blackness, and when they returned, he saw a little of his approach to a grey granite fortress whose turrets reached into the clouds.

When King's scrambled senses at last got in step with each other, he was lying on a low couch, and looking through a window which pierced a thick stone wall. A lock clicked, and he sat up. Jurth was coming through a narrow doorway; after him came a dark woman whose beauty was marred by her sullen mouth and stormy eyes.

Her hair had the sheen of a black panther's coat, and her lips were full and luscious as the tawny curves that rounded out the bodice of her silken gown. King was fascinated by the sway of her hips, by the sudden brightening of her black eyes. On one wrist she had the telepathic device, one of whose units she unclasped as she came closer. Her perfume stirred King's blood, and he forgot both Ania and his purpose in traveling back into the remote past.

Jurth remained in the doorway for a moment, then he retreated, closing the door. The dark woman knelt beside King, so close that her shapely body pressed against him; her fingertips were caressing as she fastened the golden clip on his wrist, soft and smooth as her speech. Her voice was like deep-piled velvet, persuasive as her perfume.

"I am Foma, one of Jurth's discarded wives," she purred, "and on the pretext of helping him, I came to help you, Man-From-Times-To-Come. You are in Jurth's palace, high above the great city, Jhaggar, the city older than time. Now Jurth could see that you are stubborn and hard-willed and that he could not win the truth from you with any torture short of killing you, so he depends on me to persuade you to speak. But I can help you, and I will. For all his wisdom, there are things that Jurth does not understand."

Even a scientist would not be ignorant of the wiles of a jealous woman; but King was not certain that Foma actually would help him outwit Jurth, so he said, guardedly, "I am an explorer, seeking the beginning and the end of time. I seek nothing but wisdom."

"Nothing but wisdom?" Her arms slipped about him, and her question ended in the ardent pressure of her lips. "The slave girl told us of your coming out of the future. You could go back into the future, you and I. Take me with you and I'll help you get to your time machine."

Apparently Ania had not spoken of his mission to end war. Perhaps she had feigned ignorance, and Jurth had guessed the nature of the machine.

"Nothing but wisdom," King repeated, though his heart was pounding so that he could hardly speak, and the dark woman's insistent lips were dizzying his judgment and resolution. "And when I return—"

Foma's eager embrace made the contact clip slip from King's wrist, and he could not understand her words; but there was no need of speech.

Later, Foma left the cell; the door opened when she tapped, and King saw the guards posted in the hall. Presently she returned with a tray heaped with roasted meat and ripe fruit that was not quite like any King had ever seen; a golden flagon and golden goblets gleamed from the tray.

She poured an amber-colored wine whose fragrance was as rich as her own perfume, and as he ate, she pillowed her lustrous head against his shoulder. "You don't trust me," Foma reproached. "You are afraid of Jurth, because he and his men handled you roughly, thinking you were a foreigner who had tempted one of his slaves to run away. But he is not really such a violent person. He's keeping you prisoner simply to learn more of the future from which you come."

Straight thinking was difficult, with Foma's curves pressed so close to him, but King resisted the urge to kiss her upturned lips. "For a discarded favorite, you're making a good case for him!"

"You could pretend to tell him the truth, pretend to demonstrate and explain. Otherwise, I don't know how you'll ever get out of here. How can you get to your time machine?"

"You can find a way," King said, evading her tightening embrace. "Tell Jurth I'm still suspicious of you and everyone."

Her eyes gleamed wrathfully when he thrust her away. He was glad, for that one betraying flash of anger told him how narrowly he had missed taking her into his confidence. Then she shrugged, and went to the door; the guards let her out, and bolts slid into place.

King had little time to plan any escape from a cell whose window was so far above the courtyard that only a bird could have left. The clang of iron startled him, and that angry ring shocked him more than the face of the man who entered: Jurth had returned.

*Iron:* a rarity, used only by Jurth's guard; everything else was of gold, but the Golden Age was fading, and the Iron Age was starting. The ancient myths had been more than lovely legends; they were history dimmed by years.

A squad of guards was at Jurth's back. At his gesture, they swooped around on both sides, seizing King before he could begin to resist. By sheer weight and strength, they subdued his struggles, and stretched him flat on the hard stones. Jurth knelt and clipped the telepathic speech transmitter to King's wrist. That done, he drew from his belt a small cylinder with a long, fine needle at one end. With the plunger at the other, it seemed very much like a surgeon's hypodermic. But Jurth's smile made it a fearsome weapon.

"Man of the Future, you are subtle and hard-willed! Foma has kissed the truth out of many men, and seeing you and Ania, I was sure Foma would not fail. But since you are tough as iron, the sacred metal, I will give you something that melts iron unless you tell me why you came back from the future. How do you operate the machine? Tell me, or—"

"Try and make me tell!" To be marooned in the fading years of the Golden Age would be pleasant, but King shuddered at the thought of a savage like Jurth going into the future to make it worse than it actually was. "Kill me if you want, but I won't tell you. Not until I am ready!"

The descending needle stopped an inch from King's chest. Jurth said, "Not until you are ready… well… this may hasten you."

King flinched when the needle sank deep into his flesh; but when Jurth pressed the plunger, sharp agony spread from the puncture and raced through his nerves. His groans made the vault echo; the guards could hardly hold him flat. Jurth snarled, "Steady, you fools! If he drives this in too deep, it'll kill him and you'll wish it had killed you!"

The agony radiated; it was as if King's body were filled with a searing network of electric wires, torturing every nerve. Fire and acid poured through his veins; he could taste the metallic venom in his mouth, he could smell it in his nostrils. His eyes stared through a haze of changing colors. Guards came running from the hall to help those who could hardly restrain the writhing madman.

Finally, King would have spoken. He knew that he was beaten, but he could not speak. His outraged nerves collapsed, and his body with them. The telepathic disc had been displaced during his last struggle, and thus Jurth did not suspect how close he had been to victory. He rose, gestured to his retainers, and stalked toward the door.

King, partially regaining consciousness, understood the derisive gesture. It meant, "There is more. I can give more than you can take."

The sun was setting when the door opened again, and Foma returned. In the ruddy light he saw the dark bruises on her shoulders, the welts that criss-crossed her legs, and showed dimly through the frail cloth of her gown. She ran toward him, without any studied gait or gesture; she was in his arms before he could sit up or inquire, and as she pressed her lips to his, she snapped the clip on his wrist.

"Look—he beat me for failing. I was going to trick you—you were right—but he has beaten me once too often—we'll kill him—and we'll escape into the future—"

She poured it out in a gasp. This could be part of a trick, but the passionate intensity of her voice, the tremor of her body, the insistence of her grasp, these all convinced King. Where before he had sensed a studied cunning, now he felt that a primitive creature revealed herself without reservation.

Her fury for a moment terrified him. Unalloyed, primal rage, a slaying lust: the same ferocity that Ania had described, a new mood and one foreign to that idyllic world until Jurth had delved too deeply into wisdom, and his pride had made him greedy and grasping.

This woman, tainted by Jurth's contagious wrath, would doom the man who was the root of discord. King was more and more pleased by the need of killing Jurth. He knew that he also was succumbing to the murderous vibration with which Jurth made raiders and slayers of his once kindly followers, but this no longer shocked him.

Foma read his thought, and curled up in his arms.

"We'll be happy in the future," she sighed, languidly....

In the days that followed, King saw Jurth's army drilling in the court: fifty men, practicing parries and thrusts with a newly invented weapon that looked like a cross between a scythe and a pike. On other days they marched out, and King saw red against the sky, the flare of burning villages. Then, captives; the capital was growing from these new additions, and Jhaggar's outskirts reached further beyond the original walls.

At first the natives were bewildered. Some tried to share the burdens that the newcomers carried; others hospitably offered the newly captured prisoners cups of wine, but soon they learned to avoid such unpatriotic gestures. Before King had been a captive for many weeks, the natives of Jhaggar were hurling rocks, shaking fists, jeering at the prisoners.

Down in the streets, King saw a modification of the telepathic disc. There was no longer any interlinking cord, and only the slaves wore them. This was a great improvement, for with hordes of foreigners dragged into town by Jurth's ever increasing army, the taskmasters could not possibly have used the old system of communication.

King, kept from torture because Jurth was too busy with war, was biding his time. Foma's visits convinced him that she did have a bitter grudge against Jurth, who had discarded her in favor of a lovely captive. From her, he learned the language, and he questioned the guards about Ania, but with no result. Once, however, he caught a glimpse of her in the corridor, and he was certain that she had seen him.

Late one night the hall door opened, and Foma hurried in, with a faint tinkling of anklets and rustling of silk. Her hand trembled as she caught his shoulder. "John-king, I have found out—it is in the main laboratory—under lock—Jurth has the key—"

King drew her closer, felt her violent heart beat, and the warmth of her mouth as she returned his kiss; but she broke away, saying, "It is different, this time. I told him how stubborn you are. So you will be tortured to the extreme. You must escape. Tonight—when he returns from operating the vibration-thing that makes people eager to fight."

"Get that key—I'll take you with me!" He meant it, for though he was hungry for the sight of Ania, he could not abandon Foma to Jurth's fury. "But the guards?"

"We have another new custom," she explained. "Giving-gifts-to-turn-away-from-duty."

"We have a shorter word for that," King said.

During his captivity, King had felt the operation of the war-vibration machine. The faint, hateful humming was bad enough, after an hour; but there was apparently some ultra-sonic pulsation that aroused fighting fury. His only hope was in the fact that Jurth seemed to need this vibrational irritant to get his people aroused to the right degree of patriotism. So there was hope: destroy the machine whose damnable impulses had poisoned the whole race; had started a cycle of slaying, of destroying the peaceful, until the breed of the twentieth century could by a few newspaper headlines be whipped to insane fury.

Even as he pondered on it, the baleful humming began. He got up and paced the floor, his jaw set, his eyes narrowed; and for lack of anything more definite, he cursed Foma for taking so long about her arrangements. He pounded the door, and shouted at the guards. They answered him with like contempt. One said, "I'm sick of watching that fellow, I've notion to spear him and settle this business."

The other said, "I've been thinking of that—but we better wait—"

"Wait, my eye!"

King taunted them so they would come in to try to kill him. He seized the metal-framed couch, and carried it across the cell, ready to heave against their shins when they came in. The hate-machine was whipping up a vortex of rage. Down below, the city began to mutter; riots were breaking out, and zealous watchmen were clubbing or spearing citizens into order.

Some master raid must be in the making. King began to think of Jurth, but just for the general purpose of killing him. In his fine fury, he had no purpose or aim. And he hated Ania. Damn her spineless soul, all honey and kisses, and had she ever tried to help him?

Then, behind him, King heard the mellow ring of gold. The goblet he had set on the sill was now rolling across the floor. Tiny feet and shapely calves were silhouetted against the moonlight; a woman was sliding down a rope that apparently came from a window still higher in the turret. Curiosity, and the woman's breathtaking peril made King forget his fury.

The skirt hitched up, up, up as she descended, swung in and missed, swung in again, and then got her bare feet on the deeply recessed sill. But before she arched her supple body enough to back from the sill into the cell, King knew that Ania had finally found her way to him.

Breathless, she clung to him, and it was more her gesture than her words that made him understand when she took a key from her bosom. "All these weeks—the time machine—now we can escape—before that awful woman comes back—"

"So you know—?"

"I don't care, she forced herself on you!"

Ania turned to the sill. "I can't climb up, it was bad enough sliding down. But you're strong, John-king, and I'll wait for you to get around to the door and let me out. There are new guards, the old ones go out to war."

King was so glad that not even the hammering waves of hatred could make him warlike.

Then the climb. In the interests of science, he had kept fit, with road work and gymnasium, in that dim future which none of those about him could even picture. Now he needed his training, every bit of it, as he went up, hand over hand. The hard twisted cord cut his palms. He should have removed his boots, but in his excitement, he had overlooked that handicap.

Ania had slipped through the upper window easily enough; for all her shapeliness, she was slender. It had never occurred to her that King's worst struggle would be at the narrow slot that pierced the masonry. His arms were wooden, his palms were drenched with sweat, his legs had no resiliency left. The terror of that deep gulf had tightened him, exhausted him, made it as if he had climbed twice as far. For minutes he lay there, wedged in that narrow slot, not in any danger of sliding back, but certain that if he had to retreat, his strength would not permit him to slip down the cord and back to his prison.

He was close to the hate-vibration. The masonry shivered in resonance with its pulse. Again King felt the whip of wrath. He lurched, bruised and cut himself, wedged tight; but now reckless, he snarled with an insane anger against even himself, and somehow, he tore loose, and dropped in a heap on the floor of the uppermost hall.

Then King heard Jurth's bull-roar, and a woman's scream. A whip cracked. As King dashed down the hall, Jurth snarled and cursed Foma, threatened her with all known tortures if she did not return the key she had stolen.

The laboratory was in the cross passage at King's right. He rounded the corner and saw Jurth and Foma in front of the locked door. Her tawny body gleamed in the light of the torches whose cold flame lined the hall. Jurth's whip had peeled most of the gown from her back. When she flung herself at him, screaming and clawing, he slapped her with the flat of his hand. She stumbled and fell in a heap against the wall.

"Where's that key?" Jurth roared, flicking the whip.

King darted in. This blow had to be good—and it was good. Jurth, question frozen on his lips, toppled to the floor. He was so stiff that he did not make any instinctive move to break his fall.

King jerked Foma to her feet, and hustled her to the laboratory door. He ignored her question as to his escape and his possession of the key. It fitted the lock. He booted the panel open, and spent a moment looking and thinking.

There were coils and alembics, the strange devices which in some ways were primitive, in others ways, far advanced of twentieth-century instruments; at a glance, he sensed that many of the arts he knew had never been known to the ancients, and that on the other hand, a wealth of science had been lost, hopelessly perhaps, in thirty-thousand-odd years.

Looking, and thinking. There was his time machine. There was the war-vibrator whose infra-sonic humming made the room shiver. It had dials and levers and controls, it had focused projectors, traversing wheels; its concentration could be turned in every direction. King saw this, saw all these other things, and wondered whether he should escape, or whether he should patch up a truce with Jurth, and finally go back into the twentieth century with a full knowledge of all the lost arts.

But how to get Ania? Only Foma could enter the cell, or pass the guards.

"Jurth is going to stay unconscious for some time. Run down and get—" He fumbled at his belt. "My pistol."

That was a bad guess. Foma's eyes hardened and her lips curled. "You're trying to trick me! You know you never had those belt-weapons in your cell, there they are—see them—"

He followed her gesture. His pistol was on a bench, apparently ready for an examination Jurth had not yet had time to make. If that demon learned the power of gunpowder! Horror drove King across the laboratory for his weapon.

"How did you get that key?" Foma screamed, dashing after him. "Sending me on a crazy chase—when you had it—trying to get rid of me—after I've been beaten on your account—oh, I know, it's that Ania, that slave girl, that—no wonder she's been playing up to Jurth, you fool, he'll kill her when he finds out!"

He caught her by the shoulders. "Shut up! Shut up!" She thought he was merely trying to sidetrack her; Foma did not realize that Ania was in King's cell, waiting for release. "Wait a second—no, come with me, there are things I have to get, we'll need them in the future."

The war-machine's devilish vibration was whipping King to wrath, and it stirred Foma's sultry temper. If either had been calm, the impending rage would have been drowned in reason, but as it was, she believed nothing that he said. She shrieked, "You'll not go down, you'll not desert me, you'll not get her!"

"Shut up!" King slapped her; she tumbled end for end, cracked her head against the wall, and lay there, moaning.

He had to kill the guards, or he could not get Ania, and he needed a weapon. He dashed about the spacious laboratory, and found one of the axes that Jurth was perfecting. He snatched it from the bench, whirled it. His legs had limbered up again, and he could settle any two soldiers who ever lived! He'd chop Jurth lengthwise and crosswise on the way down to get the guards! He spun, eyed the war-vibrator: ought to chop that to pieces, that was Jurth's work, he hated everything that made him think of Jurth.

Then his frenzy of plans was scrambled by surprise. He had fate in his hands; he had the power to change every day of the following thirty-odd thousand years; but only a god could have done the right thing at the right time.

He paused to buckle on his gun. Something compelled that. Oh, of course, mustn't leave any specimen of gunpowder for Jurth to analyze. Then he heard Ania's voice from the doorway: "John-king! I bribed the guard—I'm free!"

King lowered the axe. "There it is!" He pointed at the time machine. "Get in! I've got to see a man out in the hall!"

Kill Jurth; to wreck the war-vibrator would only make him invent another one. King was confused by the number of things he had to do. He felt that he must hurry, lest enraged fate destroy a man who upset thirty thousand years of history.

Kill Jurth. Then he saw Foma was on her feet. She tugged at a lever, and a great gong rolled and boomed. On the floor just below, men shouted, armor clanged. The guard was turning out. Kill Foma! An insane thing to do, but King was dizzy with hate. Stupefied by his own fury, he stood there, and neither struck Foma nor ran into the hall to finish Jurth.

Foma bounded to the time machine, screaming. Ania, gentle Ania bounded out to meet her; eyes green with rage, nails raking, teeth exposed, she closed in with Foma. The war-vibrator had been too much for her, and she knew all about the dark woman's love for King.

White limbs and tawny, flailing and threshing; brunette with fresh nail marks, blonde with darkening bruises, a tangle of hair and shredded garments. King shouted, "Stop it, you fools, I'll take you both!"

He went to shake sense into them, and dropped the axe. Already, the guards were clanging up the stairway into the hall. And Jurth was bellowing. Shaken by his ever quickening sense of nightmare failure, King picked up the axe. Jurth dropped his whip, and reached for the ray-scepter. King hurled the ponderous axe.

A good throw, but not quite good enough. It made Jurth shake his head. The glancing axe-head bit into the masonry, sparks flew, and the weapon clanged against the opposite wall. Jurth levelled the paralyzer. King ducked. The struggling girls rolled against his calves; he tumbled over them, backwards in a heap.

Jurth shouted to the soldiers, "There he is, paralyzed! Grab him!"

The column of fours came pounding in, tridents levelled. King whirled to seize Ania. But she was locked in Foma's grip; the brunette, catching the full blast of the power that would have paralyzed King had he not tripped, could not let go of her rival. King could not pry them apart, nor lift the two; not through that narrow hatch.

The ray projector blazed again over the heads of the guards, who ran at a crouch. Panic drove King into the time machine. He pulled the hatchway. The blast was wasted on massive metal, and tridents vainly chipped at the port covers and the walls. He thrust the reverse lever home, pushed the starter.

The howling soldiers blurred in a grey haze. When King's senses became normal again, he was in his own laboratory again, and not showing any sign of battering or struggle. But he was not quite the same. He stared at the emptiness between the two hands he held just far enough apart to have pressed the curve of a slender girl's waist. He shook his head, and hated himself.

Outside, newsboys called war extras. He had failed because he had been incited by the same fury he had gone out to destroy. But since the Golden Age people had succumbed to the hate wave, how could he, with the heritage of a thousand warring generations, have resisted it? He let his empty hands meet, and closed his eyes.

No man can alter that which has been, he now realized; inevitably he could not have brought either Ania or Foma back into this century. But he had brought back a memory, and Ania's loveliness blossomed in his fancy. And he thought of Foma as a sense-stirring fragrance, an ardor whose very reflection made him restless.

He went out to eat. He could not believe his watch. Allowing for his period of bewilderment, it seemed that no time had been consumed. His shirt, all torn, could have been damaged by his involuntary struggle against fading consciousness.

An illusion? Then it had in some way given him peace, and the knowledge that no man can undo what has been done. That scent in his nostrils… go out, it told him, look around… that fragrance had come from no laboratory.…

Then he saw the girl, blonde and slender and shapely; the breeze whipped a print skirt against her lovely legs, and tugged at her shimmering hair. Something about her walk made him think of Ania, and so did her profile. Her side glance and her almost-smile. He knew that he would soon meet her, and find what he had almost brought from the dawn of discord.

As King watched the setting sun play tricks with the girl's skirt, he knew that scientific experiments do have practical results. If she had not reminded him of Ania, he'd never have looked long enough to want to follow her.…

# House of the Monoceros

When the 5:37 stopped at Pengyl, I wasn't surprised to see I was the only passenger who got off at that clutter of old masonry houses with thatched roofs; this was the loneliest corner of Cornwall. No one ever arrived there, and no one ever left, except those who disappeared, which was the business that brought me from London. A monster was eating the peasants. Anyway, that was what Lord Treganneth said in his letter.

A fifteen-year-old Rolls-Royce pulled up, and a big man got out. His face was as rugged as the Cornish coast: heavy chin, broad mouth, jutting nose; and his shaggy tweeds made him look even rougher. He said, brusquely, "I'm Treganneth. You're Mr. Dale, I fancy?"

His voice had a rumble like the surf that was shaking the ground under my feet, and filling the air with fine spray. What a place! Even the sea hated it, and tried to pound it to pieces.

If he wanted to be superior, okay; his check for twenty guineas, a hundred bucks in American money, made him a nice guy.

I heaved my bag into the car. He said, "Get in the back seat." Then he took the wheel. That was funny. It made no sense, an earl or something of the sort, not having a chauffeur. I wondered for a second or two whether the monoceros had eaten all the servants.

Judging from the coat of arms on Treganneth's stationery, a monoceros is a kind of a sea monster with a horn like a unicorn; a sea-going dragon with a long spike coming out between his eyes. The motto on the engraving was funny, too: WE SERVE THE MONOCEROS.

In the couple minutes I'd waited in Pengyl, I figured that it was a ghost town. Now I began to see the people, and I wondered where they'd been up till the time Treganneth drove up.

A man in an oilskin coat and hat shook his fist from a doorway. Before we reached the edge of the village, another man popped out. He heaved a cobble stone and yelled, "Where's Harry Penfield, you bloody bastard?"

The rock smashed against the door. A bit higher and, and it'd have knocked Treganneth from the wheel. This struck me as an odd way to treat the earl who owns the country for miles around. Maybe that was why he had sent for me, an American.

I had a sort of reputation wished on me.

I'd come to London to nail an embezzler; bonding company business, you know. The gent couldn't run further, so he hung himself with the cord of his bath robe. The papers made a play of me hounding the man to his death. That must have pleased Treganneth, so here I was.

A rock crashed against the rear quarter. Another knocked out the rear glass, though no pieces hit me. The people did not like Treganneth.

Cornish miners are the best in the world, I've heard, and the most superstitious; too many generations under ground, and the earth whispered to them. And the fishermen are as bad. Whether Treganneth did or did not have a monster around his castle, the peasants all thought he had.

We climbed a brisk grade, and got up through the mist. I was almost shocked to see how much light there was, for I'd gotten the feeling that the sun never shone here. A grey masonry fortress loomed up from a hill; it had a castellated turret, with little windows out through thick walls. For all the light, the place made me think of a second-hand coffin.

"Hold it!" I said to Treganneth. "I want to look from here. If there is funny work, whoever does it is leaving trails. The monoceros comes out of the castle and goes over the hills, or the natives go over the hills to the castle. Like in France, aviators used to spot batteries because some dumb artilleryman cut across a meadow."

Treganneth pulled up, but did not answer; he just sat there. I dug into my bag and got out a pair of highpower glasses. Anyone used to ordinarily fine glasses would never imagine how these binoculars gathered light. This time they surprised me; that was when I saw the girl in the turret.

She was gripping the bars, and her face was pressed against the metal. A blanket was over her shoulders. That was all she wore, and it covered her back. She was high-breasted, and her waist was slim, and her hips had a luscious flare. The sill reached up high enough to block observations on her legs and so forth, but I was ready to okay her, from the sample displayed. Judging from the way she pressed against the bars she gripped, she was a prisoner.

Lucky she moved away before his lordship got wise that I wasn't studying hillsides. I said, "No, no signs of trespassers here. But who's Harry Penfield?"

Treganneth started. "The last man who vanished."

The road curved, dipped, swooped first inland, then along the sea; for a few miles, we were further from the castle than we'd been when I got that not-quite-enough of a look at the blonde with the nice curves pressed against the bars. The road became tougher, the crags wilder; the full roar of the sea burst upon us, and spray drenched the car. And then we were heading for the arched gateway of the castle.

Grass sprouted between the flagstones of the courtyard. The big iron hinges of the door that opened into the donjon were rusty. The whole place was run down. Ivy grew wild, blocking window after window.

Treganneth pulled up in front of the door. The place looked deserted; it was dusky in the court, and dark inside the donjon, and I didn't like it a bit. People that write about sea monsters eating peasants are not what you want to spend the evening with. If it hadn't been for seeing a chance to see a bit more of the blonde girl, I'd have said, "Here's your twenty guineas, my lord, and nuts for you."

I wanted to see more of that dame. She might be locked up, but I understand locks.

The door opened. A woman in a pink gingham house dress stood there with a kerosene lamp. The castle seemed not to be wired for lights, just for death and disappearance.

"Emily, take Mr. Dale's luggage," Treganneth said.

The dark woman set the lamp in a bracket. I said, "Steady, I can juggle it myself."

She had smooth white skin, and black hair, and blue eyes that were almost black. Her thick lashes were a sooty smudge along the lids; the people of Cornwall were Kelts, ancient and unmixed. I knew why I grabbed that bag. Not because she was a woman, but because she made me feel like she owned the place; in the sense that any first inhabitant looks and acts that way.

The wind howled into the court, and pulled her dress tight. She had nice legs, a perfect thirty, speaking of age, not measure; ripe for the picking, and not picked over enough to be spoiled.

I followed her into the castle, and saw that some of the heap had been remodeled maybe a century ago. The panelling of the big living room was oak, all black with smoke. As I followed Emily to my room on the second floor, I shot a look up the staircase that went up into the turret, where the wind was howling, laughing, snarling at the blonde girl. I decided against asking questions about that angle.

Emily pussyfooted around the room, patting things into shape.

I asked, "What is your idea on this monoceros business? I guess you know why I'm here."

She looked up, and from the corners of her eyes. "I can show you a few things he can't. Late tonight, when no one else is awake."

Anyway you took that, the girl was right. "Dinner will be served in an hour. You needn't dress," she added.

The way it turned out, Treganneth didn't come to dinner. I ate alone in that acre of dark dining room; dark, except for the coals on the hearth, and the two candles which whipped and flickered in the drafts. The wind laughed and cried and booooed. Emily served the roast beef, which was perfect; everything else was cooked to death. But the wine was something to write a book about.

She poured some Burgundy, and said, "His lordship's brother laid this down in 1914, years before he disappeared."

"Huh? Disappeared?"

"Yes. Along with my late husband, Mr. Polgate. The steward."

"The monoceros got 'em?"

"If you stay awake late enough, I'll show you something that will amaze you."

As it was, every time she bent over to fill that big glass she showed plenty. She was good enough for an earl, anywhere you looked.

It was after midnight when Emily tapped on my door. Her hair hung in two thick braids. She wore a nightgown with a low neck yoke, and lace panels on each side; it was trimmed with two rosettes placed just right, though what was beneath didn't need markers. Even though she did wear a heavy robe over that gown, it was a treat. "Treganneth is dead drunk," she said.

When I stepped into the hall, the wind sounded as if a woman were crying. Emily carried an old-fashioned lantern, which lighted our way down a murky corridor; then came a stairway that led down into the unmodernized part of the castle, the masonry that was a thousand years old, perhaps a lot more.

It was damp and creepy and there was a funny smell; the iodine odor of the waterfront, the rank salt-marsh smell of tidal flats. There was dust on the floor, except for a blurred trail, as if something had been dragged. I began to think of Harry Penfield, the last man to disappear. Then Emily led on into an alcove, and at the end she pointed to a ring in the floor.

It was like other rings I'd seen, heavy iron, rusty; anchored by an eyebolt which was sunk in lead poured into a hole in the masonry. She said, "Pull hard, and lift it."

I pulled. There was a screech, and a slab of masonry swung on pivots. Stairs led down, dark and narrow. And that sea smell, way too much of it. I hung back.

A gust of stale air came up, and played tricks with Emily's robe. Holding the lantern up made the neck yoke pull tight, and the rose-colored silk shaped itself about her hips.

"Don't you want to see more?"

I didn't; not of the underground works, that is, but I felt foolish about backing down. "Go ahead," I told her, and she led on, as if she owned the place. By now, I had a hunch that she did own it, and that Treganneth was just a stooge; the earl who could make her a lady if he wanted to.

We came out in a vault hewn from bedrock. In the center was a roughly circular pit perhaps twenty feet across. The coping along its edge was not more than halfway to Emily's knees, and the runway between it and the wall was not over a yard wide. It gave me the creeps, getting so close to that hole in the rock.

Emily sat down on the damp rock, and caught her knees with her clasped hands. She'd given me the lantern; she said, "Sit down, and blow it out." So I joined her, on the steps; they were so narrow I had to wedge close against her. This was once that getting a dame alone in the dark was no treat.

This place was so old I could taste the age. Emily's people, the old people, the Druids that used to offer up human sacrifices at Easter, and burn prisoners in wicker cages, had built this. Emily was at home here.

I lifted the shade and blew the light out.

"We may have to wait," she whispered, and leaned close; I could feel her breath in my ear, and her hair against my cheek. "That shaft reaches down to where the monoceros lived, and died, a thousand years ago. When the Treganneths were Cornish lords, pirates, raiders."

"So it's dead."

"It died, but it is coming to life."

The smell of iodine, of concentrated sea became stronger; the pit was breathing. A white mist was rising out of the blackness, it was twisting and writhing.

It took a shape the thickness of a hogshead, and Lord knows how long. The head was a dragon's, a dragon with a yard-long spike growing out of its forehead. This was the monoceros engraved on Treganneth's stationery, and on his carnelian ring of old, soft gold.

Up—up—up—reaching out of the pit. Two men were kicking and clawing in its coils. One looked like Treganneth. Emily yeeped and caught me with both arms. She poured herself over me. I sprawled back against the stairs. I tangled up with her bare legs, and then I made a dive for the treads. She went limp, and I caught her.

In the scramble, I got a look back. The thing was pulling back into the pit, and thinning out to a haze, ribbon-thin. Then it was gone. I was sweating, shaking till my teeth clicked. I grabbed Emily and headed up those stairs, and I didn't stop for the lantern. I reached the head of the stairs long before I had any hope of getting there, and I took a header. Lucky for Emily I twisted as I flopped, or I'd have smashed her flat. As it was, the crash nearly laid me out. And she came to. She moaned, "It's getting worse, it's reaching further each time, it's calling for its prey—get me out of here—"

I fairly dragged her. It's funny, but I headed for my room, as if that were any safer than anywhere else. When I slammed the bolt, I turned around and saw Emily sag at the knees. She keeled over and flopped in the old lounge.

I stumbled after her. "If Treganneth thinks I am hunting that thing, he is nuts! It sounded like some kind of murder racket when he wrote me, someone giving him the run-around to get him out of his castle. But *that*—what's he think I am?"

"He still thinks something human is tricking villagers into the caves under the castle, and killing them. He doesn't know of this place. Promise me you won't tell him, he's so worried now, a shock would drive him mad."

A fellow can't believe everything he sees. Look at that Hindu rope trick.

And the little green men a friend of mine used to see in his room. He threw things at them, only they just weren't there. Neither was that monster.

"Okay, I won't tell him. But how did you find that awful place?"

"My late husband, Mr. Polgate, was steward. He used to tell me things. About sub-cellars of this castle. Then he and the present earl's brother vanished, and no one ever found their bodies. Seven years passed, they were declared legally dead, and I became a legal widow. Jasper—the present earl—came from Australia to take his heritage. And then things happened. Villagers disappeared. People whispered about the monoceros, and brought up that old legend of how the Treganneths traced their descent from it."

What she meant was, it was a sort of totem, like the Indians have wolves, bears, and the like for clan ancestors. She went on, "The ancient Treganneths sacrificed captives to the monster, to keep their luck in war. It lived in that pit, it came in from the sea for its offerings. Then an earthquake blocked the passage, and the thing starved when the Treganneths could not find enough victims."

"And now the ghost of the monoceros is eating?"

Now that I'd quieted down a bit, I began to think. "That was malarkey. I didn't see it, it was hypnotism. Decaying sea stuff, phosphorescent vapors, and me thinking about the monoceros ever since I got the earl's cockeyed letter."

I turned to Emily. "Why don't you check out?"

"I belong to the place."

"I don't. I'm a detective. I brought embezzlers from Algiers. From Honduras. But a monoceros is something else, you can keep it."

As a matter of fact, I was getting sore at myself for having gone hog wild down there, but I was giving Emily a line to see what she'd do. There was a trick somewhere.

Emily jumped up, and before I could get a lamplight view of this and that, she had me with both arms. She squeezed close, and not just with her arms, either. "You must stay—you've got to—for *my* sake!"

I was getting high blood from that armful of woman, but I could still add things up. Emily's gown had store folds in it. I noticed that when the robe fell from one shoulder. A brand new gown like that cost a couple guineas; a damn funny expenditure when the earl drove his own fifteen-year-old bus. And she'd lied when she said she and the earl were alone here. How about the blonde gal in the tower?

I played the sap on purpose. I nudged her toward the door. "You're too scared to know what you're talking about. Come back when the monoceros business is settled, and see if I head you for the door."

The smile over her shoulder was one of those promises only a chump expects a dame to keep.

The more I thought about the monoceros, as I sat there by the grate, the more I said, "Hell, you do it with mirrors."

An hour passed. Then another. I dug up my flashlight and I put on some felt slippers. It was dark as a squaw's pocket, out in that hall. The wind made dirty sounds and ghastly sounds, and then it laughed whenever I jerked back, figuring something was prowling around in the dark. But I got to the stairs that reached up into the hell-blackness of that turret.

By the time I had convinced myself that the monoceros was something I had eaten, I was up as far as the second narrow slot in the two-foot-thick masonry. The moon was full. The crags were shining from spray, and spray jumped up from the roaring sea. If anything was creeping over those hills, it was belly flat.

Then I looked toward the sea again. Something was moving, something white against the dark crags. I knew it was a woman before I could see the curves that made everything certain except her face.

If she wore anything, it wasn't enough to register at night. She was white and shining, and her golden hair rippled in the wind. A man was stumbling over the rocks, waving his arms.

He was gaining. Then she danced ahead, and won a length. Then they both were blotted out by a black tongue.

To think that I could dash down stairs, and over wet rocks in time to keep the guy from overtaking the girl was crazy, but I was on the way. There is something about a scenario like that that makes a fellow want to keep the other fellow from getting familiar with the girl in question, even if she is a stranger.

When I got there, I saw neither girl nor man. Just wet rocks. Cornwall was where King Arthur got his start, where Merlin did his stuff, where the Lady of the Lake used to hang out. The whole Cornish coast is wacky. The only way to keep from going nuts is not to believe anything you see. But even so, I went back to the turret to find out if there really was a blonde there.

I got my kit of lock picks to work. I'd become handy that way because it simplifies the business of snooping on embezzlers. The door opened easy.

The girl wasn't asleep. She was so scared when the door opened that she couldn't yeep. Moonlight reached into the turret and picked out her beautiful legs, the fine curve of throat and cheek.

I said, "It's all right. If you're a prisoner, maybe I can help you."

"Why didn't you knock, warn me—who are you—?"

I could see her knees shaking, where they peeped out from the grey woolen blanket she clutched to her breast. "I'm Jim Dale, monoceros hunter, and I saw you through the window this afternoon, looking out."

She gasped.

"With glasses. What is the idea, no clothes?"

The flashlight made it clear she didn't have a stitch in the whole turret; just the cot, and the blankets.

"I'm Jasper Treganneth's secretary—I mean, I was, when he was in Perth. I followed him when he came to the title. Just imagine, came to this ruin. I was stranded. When my funds were gone, I came to the castle."

"After you'd sold your shoes and clothing, for subsistence while job hunting," I cracked, "you came to hide in Treganneth Castle. What was the name, please?"

She flared. "I'm Diane Rolley!"

Then she doubled up and began crying. I sat down on the cot beside her and slipped an arm about her. "Buck up, Diane. I'm a detective, trying to settle this monoceros business. How did you get up here?"

"Jasper locked me up."

"What for?"

She'd let the blanket slip a bit, and for all her trying to cover up with a jerk, I saw enough to prove Treganneth was crazy. Diane said, "This gossip, these disappearances, it was driving me mad. When I decided to go, he wouldn't let me."

"Huh?"

"He was afraid I'd never come back, that I'd spread wild stories about the place, perhaps have him declared insane. He said that if I stayed until things were cleared up, he'd marry me, even though he did have a title and I was a former employee."

That made sense, but not this business of taking her clothes. When I asked about that, she said, "Just suppose someone did break in and find me, he and that woman could say that I got violent, tore my clothes to shreds.

That they kept me here because he didn't want to send me to a madhouse."

Having an audience, even a stranger, made Diane crack. She hung herself around my neck and sobbed, "Get me out of here, get a closed car. Take me out by night. The villagers would stone me, throw me into the sea, tear me to pieces. They blame me for these deaths, they'll storm the castle if this keeps up."

After what I'd seen of a blonde girl being chased along the cliffs, I could understand why people might pick on Diane.

Well, Diane did persuade me to stick around and plan for her escape, though I insisted on finishing the monoceros business first. But I didn't wait until sunrise. Having cried out her worries, she curled up and went to sleep. The way it was, if I made an immediate get-away, I'd never learn about that ghost monster; the more I saw of this, the more I was sure they did it with mirrors, and I was sore, being played for a chump.

But before I tiptoed out, I did things to the lock. They passed Diane's grub through a wicket, so it was a ten-to-one shot no one would notice the lock was gummed up.

Early in the morning, Emily brought me a pitcher of hot water; the castle didn't have running water, believe it or not. "Did you sleep well?"

"Lonesome, but otherwise okay. How's the earl, sobered up?"

Treganneth was red-eyed. "Didn't want to talk at night. Man's too credulous at night."

We tied into a kidney pie and some bloaters and some porridge. I listened to his yarn about the monoceros. It checked with Emily's account. He made no mention of vaults under the castle except to say, "Blasted nonsense, reptile cult of my ancestors. But the villagers are getting nasty. I want you to explain the disappearances."

"Suppose I inquired around the village?"

"My good man, I disclaim any liability if you get your skull cracked. After what happened yesterday, I have no intention of returning to Pengyl."

"Let me drive your car. How about the keys?"

Treganneth said, "Emily will drive to market. Go with her."

He rose, and headed for the study. I was thoroughly dismissed.

Going to market in Pengyl wasn't fun. Someone heaved a cobble stone at the car and an old hag screeched, "Where's that golden-haired witch, bring her out!"

Emily leaned out. The men who had rocks dropped them. The old woman stopped cursing and muttering. The men said, "We chucked 'em before we saw it was you. But you better not go back."

Emily pulled up. A crowd gathered. An ugly crowd of gnarled old people. There weren't more than half a dozen young men, and girls were even scarcer. A beak-nosed fellow said, "Ye better not go back. Lon Wellman hasn't come home, and we know he ain't coming back, they never come back. Before God, we're going to tear that place stone from stone, Mis' Polgate, and you're one of us. We don't want you hurt, but there's no saying what people do when they go mad."

That wasn't all. There was that man chasing that blonde girl. Out of the chatter, I got it: a golden-haired witch luring young men to the monoceros. Some of these folks had a funny way of saying witch, I guess it was the Cornwall accent or something. It would be bad if they got hold of Diane.

We went to the market. On the way back, I asked Emily, "What's this golden-haired…uh, witch business? The earl held out on me, and so did you."

"That would have distracted you from the monoceros. These young men are mortally afraid, but each one brags about a blonde girl from London or somewhere, spending a weekend at the sea, and being impressed by him, and coming back to meet him. Women—young and attractive women—are scarce—" She sighed. "As scarce as young and attractive men—oh, what a God forsaken edge of nowhere this is!"

"So they sneak out to meet the blonde baby, making a careful sneak so none of the other boys cut in, and—one more lad fades?"

Emily nodded. "The fourth. Or fifth. A witch tempting them into the den of the monoceros. You know how such a story spreads."

When we got back to the castle, Treganneth called me into his study. It was an old, dark room, all lined with old, leather-bound books in oak cases. He had some of them spread out on the big table; and there was a square of parchment written in jet-black ink.

His hand shook when he pointed, and so did his voice: "Dale, I've been finding old records. The way to get to the foundations of this place. There is a crypt. There was a monster, centuries ago, and it did live on human sacrifices the heathen Treganneths offered, long before King Arthur's time. It's utter rubbish, but there is something strange—there was a golden-haired witch who lured victims to the monoceros, once the Treganneths turned against the Druids and became Christians."

"You believe that?"

"I don't know what I believe."

"Another man vanished, last night."

Treganneth groaned, passed one hand before his eyes. "Again!"

I prodded him. He straightened up.

"You're holding out. I want the straight of it, or you can chase yourself."

He got haughty and tough. "What do you mean?"

"Emily Polgate has a hold on you."

He wouldn't say yes, and he wouldn't say no; he just glared. I took another crack at him: "When we stopped on the ridge, and I took out my binoculars, I got a good look at the girl in the turret. Who is the girl, and why?"

Treganneth jumped up, sweating. "Why—you insolent puppy!"

"Take it easy. The first thing you know, the yokels are going to take this place to pieces by hand and then take Blondie to pieces and Emily, and you too. What kind of a game is this, you having a dame trapping yokels? Monster, my eye, the chumps fall over the cliff, the waves pound them to pulp."

Treganneth was white now, and his heavy jaw twitched. "The girl in the tower—she's there for her own good. She's quite mad."

"How about you and Emily Polgate?"

"I prefer not to discuss that."

"Emily has loyally held down the fort, then hell pops, all the servants check out, men disappear. All of them young men."

"For God's sake, shut up! Let's look into this crypt. Show it is empty. Throw the place open to the villagers."

Treganneth took the chart and a flashlight. In a few minutes, we were in that dark tangle of vaults and passages. He hunted a few minutes in the blind alley, and then he saw the trap with the ring.

The smell of iodine, of sea-decay came swooping up. We went down the narrow stairs. Treganneth was a lord, all right. He led the way. That made me feel better. I didn't want him in back of me.

At the bottom of the stairs, he saw the lantern, and pulled up sharp. "By Jove! Someone's been here before us." He turned around, flashed his light into my face. "You?"

"How would I know about this when you just found out?"

He swung the flash back toward the pit. I struck a match to light a smoke. He jumped like he'd been stung. His flashlight went about. Then he made a choking sound and pointed.

I looked. A pink rosette was lying at the foot of the steps. It was one of the frills from Emily's flossy nightgown. It had torn off while we were pawing each other in panic. I cracked off, "All right, your girlfriend is running this show."

"You—damn it—how do you know—?"

The man went wild. He swung at me with the flash, and howled, "Damn you, you're part of a conspiracy to keep me from Diane! You and that—"

He had missed braining me, but the flash smashed on my shoulder. Then he piled in with fists, there in the stinking dark. The smell was awful now; not sea stench, but corpse odor. The dead were crying in the only way they could.

He slugged me a honey. Lucky he couldn't see what he was doing. I popped him one, heard him grunt.

"You damn fool, I'm not in cahoots with Emily, she's tricking them down into this den!"

But he wouldn't listen. He was off his chump. He growled, and came back at me. I smashed against the wall. I'm not sure I could have swapped punches with him by daylight, but here it was impossible.

He was yelling like crazy now, and the echoes made it worse. Every lunge, he promised to kill me. I was sure now that Emily had tried to make him get rid of Diane; he figured that if I knew so much about the dame's nightgown, we had teamed up against him.

Every so often he connected and slugged me dizzy. Then I ducked him, and began bicycling, but there was nowhere to go. I saw a small flash of daylight, overhead. There was an opening I'd naturally not seen when Emily took me down to the pit by night. I began to get the picture now. Some girl was leading the yokels along the cliff, and they'd stumble through and down into this stinking cave.

I yelled at him, and pointed, but he wouldn't listen. He bored in toward the sound. There was a spattering of glass. He tripped on the lantern. Just then I got in a good wallop.

That, and the damp paving did it. There was a thump, and he stopped yelling. Then I heard the soggy splash.

I struck a match. I was shaking all over, I was ready to park my fritters. Then a woman screeched, "So you did tell him, so you did drive him mad, ohhh—"

By the light of the match I saw it was Emily. She had a pistol in one hand, and my flashlight in the other.

"Go down after him! Go down and tell him the villagers are going to finish the blonde witch—he was mine, he would have been—I belonged here, she didn't—go—go or I'll shoot you—"

Emily must have heard me yelling at Treganneth. She knew I had spilled the beans; that if I got loose, she was on the spot.

The light blazed full in my eyes. I backed up a step. She laughed. The back of my legs was against the coping. I couldn't see the gun, I couldn't see a thing. I went wild like everyone else, and made a dive to catch her around the knees.

She cut loose with the pistol, and she missed. Another shot, just as I stumbled and did get her about the knees. Before I could grab the gun, we toppled in a heap.

Behind me, a woman screamed; a woman with a lamp. The lamp shattered on the stones, and the flashlight rolled clear. There was a tangle of legs and feet, and I couldn't get up. Two dames were mixing it.

One had bare legs. I tangled with a blanket shed in the show. The bare legs and the silk legs stumbled clear of me, and the flashlight, though I could see a white shape in the indirect glow. Diane and Emily toppled to the coping.

"Hold it!" I yelled, and kicked clear of the blanket.

I lunged, but I didn't grab Diane in time. Emily went over the side. There wasn't a thump this time; just a scream, the most horrible thing I'd ever heard. I pulled Diane away from the coping.

She was hysterical, and couldn't say anything. I threw the blanket around her, and reached for the flashlight lying on the floor. The switch lock disengaged, and I was shaking too much to make it stick again. Diane was saying, "Something happened to the lock, the door opened by itself. I slipped out to steal some of her clothes, and I saw her sneaking down, with a gun. So I followed her."

Then she hung on tight, and asked me what had happened. We were too shaky to crawl up the stairs. No sound came up from the pit.

I said we were too weak to move.

That's what I thought until a gleaming grey haze came up out of the dark: that dragon head with the long spike in the forehead, those terrific coils. Treganneth was kicking and threshing in one loop of the monster; there were other men, in other coils. But that was pretty compared to what was on the unicorn spike.

Emily was speared clean through. The gleaming horn came out just below her breast. She was clawing, but there was no sound; just that apparition rising, with her draped over its forehead. Only the spike kept her from slipping off. But where the point touched the ceiling of the vault, the living smoke began to fade.

I said we were too sick to move. But when that thing began to thin out, I let out a yell and headed up the stairs, Diane and blanket included. Lucky she was hanging on. I wasn't going back for anything.

I stumbled into daylight. Diane slid from my arms, and steadied herself against my shoulder. We both shook our heads. "Baby, that didn't happen. Don't ever tell anyone it did. Come on—"

I picked the lock of Emily's room, and said, "Get some clothes, I'll hunt the car keys."

Diane grabbed my hand. "You stay right here. Even if you turned your back, I'd not be alone in this awful place."

I turned my back all right. The joke was on Diane. She was too shaken to notice the mirror angle. But that's not the payoff; that came after I'd bundled Diane into the old car and told the cops all about everything except the phantom monster.

The whole village was turned inside out. From that, and from searching the castle, especially Emily's room, we got the story. Treganneth's brother and Emily's husband had quarreled about her, and the two had finished each other. There were letters from yokels, promising they'd kill her if she quit them to team up with the new lord. As I said, women were scarce, and she'd been a widow for seven years, and the village boys liked her.

So she started getting rid of her lovers, powdering her hair gilt, to make Diane, the witch in the tower, take the rap, when the lid blew off. With enough disappearances, something was bound to happen.

We had this all doped out when we went down into that vault. Then we looked over the edge. And that, I say, was the payoff.

There was a skeleton, a monstrous thing, in the pit. Some of the bones were joined, though most were scattered on a ledge, or sunk in the slime. When the tide was low, the dead reeked in the mud; at high tide, the water blanketed them. Now it was low tide, and awful.

Treganneth was there, and so were the yokels. There were old skeletons,

Treganneth's brother and Polgate, the steward who had kicked about a lord playing with Emily.

And Emily was there, speared on the horn that reached from the skull of the monoceros. There had been such a creature. That skull was what kept me from saying I must have been hypnotized.

I had seen the ghost of a monster god that men had worshipped before King Arthur came to town; worshipped by Druids, worshipped by the ancestors of a woman who played for a lord, and lost. Now she belonged to a dead god. If it hadn't been for that skull, I'd never have *known* that I had seen the ghost of a god, of his victims.

Maybe that's why Diane and I stuck together, when it was all over. It's kind of fun telling each other we did see it, that we weren't wacky.

# The Dead Will Cuckold You

## A Drama in Six Scenes

PERSONAE
*Smaragad,* King of Yoros
*Queen Somelis*
*Galeor,* a wandering poet and lute-player, guest of Smaragad
*Natanasna,* a necromancer
*Baltea,* tiring-woman to Somelis
*Kalguth,* Natanasna's negro assistant
*Sargo,* the King's treasurer
*Boranga,* captain of the King's guards
Waiting-women, court-ladies, courtiers, guards and chamberlains.

THE SCENE:
*Faraad, capital of Yoros, in Zothique*

### SCENE I

A large chamber in the Queen's suite, in the palace of Smaragad. Somelis sits on a high throne-like chair. Galeor stands before her, holding a lute. Baltea and several other women are seated on divans, at a distance. Two black chamberlains stand in attendance at the open door.

*Galeor* (*playing on his lute and singing*):
Make haste, and tarry not, O ardent youth,

To find upon the night,
Outlined in fuming fire,
The footsteps of the goddess Ililot.
Her mouth and eyes make fair the bourns of sleep,
Between her brows a moon
Is seen. A magic lute
Foretells her with wild music everywhere.
Her opened arms, which are the ivory gates
Of some lost land of lote
Wherefrom charmed attars flow,
Will close upon you 'neath the crimson star.

*Somelis:* I like the song. Tell me, why do you sing
So much of Ililot?

*Galeor:*
She is the goddess
Whom all men worship in the myrrh-sweet land
Where I was born. Do men in Yoros not
Adore her also? She is soft and kind,
Caring alone for love and lovers' joy.

*Somelis:*
She is a darker goddess here, where blood
Mingles too often with delight's warm foam....
But tell me more of that far land wherein
A gentler worship lingers.

*Galeor:*
By a sea
Of changing damaskeen it lies, and has
Bowers of cedar hollowed for love's bed
And plighted with a vine vermilion-flowered.
There are moss-grown paths where roam white-fleecèd goats;
And sard-thick beaches lead to caves in which
The ebbing surge has left encrimsoned shells
Like lips by passion parted. From small havens

The fishers slant their tall, dulse-brown lateens
To island-eyries of the shrill sea-hawk;
And when with beaks low-dipping they return
Out of the sunset, fires are lit from beams
And spars of broken galleys on the sand,
Around whose nacreous flames the women dance
A morris old as ocean.

*Somelis:*
Would I had
Been born in such a land, and not in Yoros.

*Galeor:*
I wish that I might walk with you at evening
Beside the waters veined with languid foam,
And see Canopus kindle on cypressed crags
Like a far pharos.

*Somelis:*
Be you more tacit: there are ears
That listen, and mouths that babble amid these halls.
Smaragad is a jealous king—(*She breaks off, for at this moment King Smaragad enters the room.*)

*Smaragad:*
This is a pretty scene. Galeor, you seem at home
In ladies' chambers. I am told you entertain
Somelis more than could a dull sad king
Grown old too soon with onerous royalty.

*Galeor:*
I would please, with my poor songs and sorry lute,
Both of your Majesties.

*Smaragad:*
Indeed, you sing
Right sweetly, as does the simorgh when it mates.

You have a voice to melt a woman's vitals
And make them run to passion's turgid sluice.
How long have you been here?

*Galeor:*
A month.

*Smaragad:*
It has been
A summer moon full-digited. How many
Of my hot court-ladies have you already bedded?
Or should I ask how many have bedded you?

*Galeor:*
None, and I swear it by the crescent horns
Of Ililot herself, who fosters love
And swells the pulse of lovers.

*Smaragad:*
By my troth,
I would confirm you in such continence,
It is rare in Yoros. Even I when young
Delved deep in whoring and adultery. (*Turning to the queen*)
Somelis, have you wine? I would we drank
To a chastity so rathe and admirable
In one whose years can hardly have chastened him.

(*The queen indicates a silver ewer standing on a taboret together with goblets of the same metal. Smaragad turns his back to the others and pours wine into three goblets, opening, as if casually, the palm of his free hand over one of them. This he gives to Galeor. He serves another to the queen, and raises the third to his lips.*)

See, I have served you with my royal hand,
Doing you honor, and we all must drink
To Galeor that he persevere in virtue,
And he must drink with us. (*He drinks deeply. The queen raises her goblet to her lips but barely tastes it. Galeor lifts the wine, then pauses, looking into it.*)

*Galeor:*
How strangely it foams.

*Smaragad:* Indeed, such bubbles seem
To rise as if from lips of a drowning man
In some dark purple sea.

*Somelis:*
Your humor is strange,
Nor are there bubbles in the cup you gave me.

*Smaragad:*
Perhaps it was poured more slowly. (*To Galeor*)
Drink the wine,
It is old and cordial, made by men long dead.
(*The poet still hesitates, then empties his goblet at one draught.*)
How does it taste to you?

*Galeor:*
It tastes as I have thought that love might taste,
Sweet on the lips, and bitter in the throat. (*He reels, then sinks to his knees, still clutching the empty goblet.*)
You have poisoned me, who never wronged you. Why
Have you done it?

*Smaragad:*
That you may never wrong me. You have drunk
A vintage that will quench all mortal thirst.
You will not look on queens nor they on you
When the thick maggots gather in your eyes,
And issue in lieu of love-songs from your lips,
And geld you by slow inches.

*Somelis* (*descending from her seat and coming forward*):
Smaragad,
This deed will reek through Yoros and be blazed

Beyond the murky marches of the damned. (*She sinks to her knees beside Galeor, now prostrate on the floor and dying slowly. Tears fall from her eyes as she lays her hand on Galeor's brow.*)

*Smaragad:*
Was he so much to you? Almost I have a mind
That the bowstring should straiten your soft throat,
But no, you are too beautiful. Go quickly,
And keep to your bed-chamber till I come.

*Somelis:* I shall abhor you, and my burning heart
Consume with hate till only meatless cinders
Remain to guest the mausolean maggots. (*Exit Somelis, followed by Baltea and the other women. The two chamberlains remain.*)

*Smaragad* (*beckoning to one of the chamberlains*):
Go call the sextons. I would have them drag
This carcass out and bury it privily. (*Exit the chamberlain. The king turns to Galeor, who still lives.*)
Think on your continence eternalized:
You had not fleshed as yet your rash desire,
And now you never will.

*Galeor* (*in a faint but audible voice*):
I would pity you,
But there is no time for pity. In your heart
You bear the hells that I have never known,
To which the few brief pangs I suffer
Are less than the wasp-stings of an afternoon
Sweet with the season's final fruit.
*(Curtain)*

SCENE II

The king's audience hall. Smaragad sits on a double-daised throne, a guard bearing a trident standing at each hand. Guards are posted at each of the four entrances. A few women and chamberlains pass through the hall on errands. Sargo, the royal treasurer, stands in one corner. Baltea, passing by, pauses to chat with him.

*Baltea:*
Why sits the king in audience today?
Is it some matter touching on the state?
Still thunder loads his brow, and pard-like wrath
Waits leashed in his demeanor.

*Sargo:*
'Tis a wizard,
One Natanasna, whom he summons up
For practice of nefandous necromancy.

*Baltea:*
I've heard of him. Do you know him? What's he like?

*Sargo:*
I cannot wholly tell you. It's no theme
For a morning's tattle.

*Baltea:*
You make me curious.

*Sargo:*
Well,
I'll tell you this much. Some believe he is
A cambion, devil-sired though woman-whelped.
He is bold in every turpitude, as those
Hell-born are prone to be. His lineage
Leads him to paths forbanned and pits abhorred,
And traffic in stark nadir infamies
Not plumbed by common mages.

*Baltea:*
Is that all?

*Sargo:*
Such beings have a smell by which to know them,
As olden tomes attest. This Natanasna
Stinks like a witch's after-birth, and evil
Exhales from him, lethal as that contagion
Which mounts from corpses mottled by the plague.

*Baltea:*
Well, that's enough to tell me, for I never
Have liked ill-smelling men.
*(Enter Natanasna through the front portals. He strides forward, bearing a staff on which he does not lean, and stands before Smaragad.)*

*Sargo:*
I must go now.

*Baltea:*
And I'll not linger, for the wind comes up
From an ill quarter. (*Exeunt Sargo and Baltea, in different directions.*)

*Natanasna* (*without kneeling or even bowing*):
You have summoned me?

*Smaragad:*
Yes. I am told you practice arts forbid
And hold an interdicted commerce, calling
Ill demons and the dead to do you service.
Are these things true?

*Natanasna:*
It is true that I can call
Both lich and ka, though not the soul, which roams
In regions past my scope, and can constrain
The genii of the several elements
To toil my mandate.

*Smaragad:*
What! you dare avow it—
The thing both men and gods abominate?
Do you not know the ancient penalties
Decreed in Yoros for these crimes abhorred?—
The cauldron of asphaltum boiling-hot
To bathe men's feet, and the nail-studded rack
On which to stretch their scalded stumps?

*Natanasna:*
Indeed
I know your laws, and also know that you
Have a law forbidding murder.

*Smaragad:*
What do you mean?

*Natanasna:*
I mean but this, that you the king have filled
More tombs than I the outlawed necromancer
Have ever emptied, and detest not idly
The raising of dead men. Would you have me summon
For witness here against you the grey shade
Of Famostan your father, in his bath
Slain by the toothed envenomed fish from Taur
Brought privily and installed by you? Or rather
Would you behold your brother Aladad,
Whose huntsmen left him with a splintered spear
At your instruction, to confront the fen-cat
That he had merely pricked? Yet these would be
Only the heralds of that long dark file
Which you have hurried into death.

*Smaragad* (*half-rising from his seat*):
By all
The sooted hells, you dare such insolence?
Though you be man or devil, or be both,

I'll flay you, and leave your hide to hang in strips
Like a kilt about you, and will have your guts
Drawn out and wound on a windlass.

*Natanasna:*
These be words
Like froth upon a shallow pool. No finger
Of man may touch me. I can wave this staff
And ring myself with circles of tall fires
Spawned by the ambient space arcane. You fear me,
And you have reason. I know all the secrets
Of noisome deed and thought that make your soul
A cavern where close-knotted serpents nest.
Tell me, was there not yestereve a youth
Named Galeor, who played the lute and sang,
Making sweet music for an evil court?
Why have you slain him? Was it not through your fear
Of cuckoldom, thinking he pleased too much
The young Somelis? But this thing is known
To me, and I know moreover the dim grave
Where Galeor waits the worm.

*Smaragad* (*standing erect, his features madly contorted*):
Begone! begone!
Out of my presence! Out of Faraad!
And here's a word to speed you: when you entered
This hall, my sheriffs went to find your house
And seize Kalguth, your negro neophyte
For whom 'tis said you have the curious fondness
That I might keep for a comely ebon wench.
Ponder this well: Kalguth must lie by now
Embowelled in our dankest dungeon-crypt.
He will rejoin you if tomorrow's sun
Meet you outside the city. If you linger,
I'll give him to my sinewy torturers.

*Natanasna:*
King Smaragad, if young Kalguth be harmed,
Hell will arise and sweep your palace clean
With fiery besoms and with flails of flame. (*Exit Natanasna.*)
(*Curtain*)

## SCENE III

The necropolis of Faraad. Dying and half-decayed cypresses droop over creviced headstones and ruinous mausoleums. A gibbous moon shines through wispy clouds. Enter Natanasna, humming:

A toothless vampire tugs and mumbles
Some ancient trot's whitleather hide,
But he'll fly soon to the abattoir
And the pooling blood where the stuck pig died.
(*Kalguth emerges from behind the half-unhinged door of a tomb close at hand. He carries a dark bag, which he lays on the ground at Natanasna's feet.*)

*Kalguth:* Greetings, O Master.

*Natanasna:*
It was well I sent you
To wait me here among the tacit dead—
Lugging you from your slumber at morning dusk
While none but blind-drunk bowsers were abroad.
As I prevised, the king took advantage
Of my commanded presence in his halls,
And sent his hounds to sniff for you. He'll not
Venture to harry me, who have climbed too high
In magedom's hierarchy, but would fang
His baffled spleen on one not fully armed
And bucklered with arts magical. We must
Depart from Yoros promptly, leaving it
To all its many devils, amid which
This king is not the least. (*He pauses, looking about him at the tombs*

*and graves.*) It is a land
Where murder has made much work for necromancy,
And there's a task to do before we go
That we be not forgotten.... I perceive,
My good Kalguth, that you have found the spot
Which my strix-eyed familiar did describe:
Those yonder are the yellowing cypresses
That death has pollarded, and this the tomb
Of the lord Thamamar, which sheltered you
Daylong from eyes still mortal.... See, where it bears
The lichen-canceled legend of his titles
And the name itself, half-blotted out. (*He paces about, peering closely at the ground, and holding his staff extended horizontally. Over a certain spot the staff seems to twist violently in his hand, like a dowser's wand, until it points downward with the tip almost touching the earth.*)
This is
The grave that covers Galeor. The turf
Was lately broken here, and spaded back
With the grass turned upward. (*He faces in the direction of Faraad, whose towers loom indistinctly beyond the necropolis. Raising both arms, he intertwines his fingers with the thumbs pointing skyward in the Sign of the Horns.*)
By this potent Sign,
O jealous king who dreaded cuckoldom,
Murder shall not avert from your proud head
The horns of that opprobrium: for I know
A spell whereby the dead will cuckold you. (*Turning to Kalguth*)
Now to our ceremonies. While you set
The mantic censers forth, I'll make the circles. (*Taking a short sword, the magic arthame, from under his cloak, he traces a large circle in the turf, and a smaller one within it, trenching them both deeply and broadly. Kalguth opens the dark bag and brings out four small perforated censers whose handles are wrought in the form of the double triangle, Sign of the Macrocosm. He places them between the circles, each censer facing one of the four quarters, and lights them. The necromancers then take their positions within the inner circle. Natanasna gives the arthame to Kalguth, and retains his magic staff, which he holds aloft. Both face toward the grave of Galeor.*)

*Natanasna* (*chanting*):
*Mumbavut, maspratha butu,*
*Varvas runu, vha rancutu.**
Incubus, my cousin, come,
Drawn from out the night you haunt,
From the hollow mist and murk
Where discarnate larvae lurk,
By the word of masterdom.
Hell will keep its covenant,
You shall have the long-lost thing
That you howl and hunger for.
Borne on sable, sightless wing,
Leave the void that you abhor,
Enter in this new-made grave,
You that would a body have:
Clothed with the dead man's flesh,
Rising through the riven earth
In a jubilant rebirth,
Wend your ancient ways afresh,
By the mantra laid on you
Do the deed I bid you do.
*Vora votha Thasaidona*
*Sorgha nagrakronithona.***
(*After a pause*)
*Vachat pantari vora nagraban****

*Kalguth:*
*Za, mozadrim: vachama vongh razan.*****
(*The turf heaves and divides, and the incubus-driven Lich of Galeor rises from the grave. The grime of interment is on its face, hands, and clothing.*

---

* Mumbavut, lewd and evil spirit,
Wheresoever thou roamest, hear me.
** By (or through) Thasaidon's power
Arise from the death-time-dominion.
*** The spell (or mantra) is finished by the necromancer.
**** Yes, master: the *vongh* (corpse animated by a demon) will do the rest. (These words are from Umlengha, an ancient language of Zothique, used by scholars and wizards.)

*It shambles forward and presses close to the outer circle, in a menacing attitude. Natanasna raises the staff, and Kalguth the arthame, used to control rebellious spirits. The Lich shrinks back.*)

*The Lich* (*in a thick, unhuman voice*):
You have summoned me,
And I must minister
To your desire.

*Natanasna:*
Heed closely these instructions:
By alleys palled and posterns long disused,
Well-hidden from the moon and from men's eyes,
You shall find ingress to the palace. There,
Through stairways only known to mummied kings
And halls forgotten save by ghosts, you must
Seek out the chamber of the queen Somelis,
And woo her lover-wise till that be done
Which incubi and lovers burn to do.

*The Lich:*
You have commanded, and I must obey.
(*Exit the Lich. When it has gone from sight, Natanasna steps from the circles, and Kalguth extinguishes the censers and repacks them in the bag.*)

*Kalguth:*
Where go we now?

*Natanasna:*
Whither the first road leads
Beyond the boundary of Yoros. We'll
Not wait the sprouting of the crop we've sowed
But leave it to lesson him, who would have crimped
My well-loved minion and my acolyte
For the toothed beds of his dark torture-chambers.

(*Exeunt Natanasna and Kalguth, singing:*)
The fresh fat traveler whom the ghouls
Waylaid in the lonesome woodland gloom,
He got away, and they'll go now
For gamy meat in a mouldy tomb.
(*Curtain*)

## SCENE IV

The queen's bed-chamber. Somelis half-sits, half-reclines on a cushioned couch. Enter Baltea, bearing a steaming cup.

*Baltea:*
With wine that stores the warmth of suns departed,
And fable-breathing spices brought from isles
Far as the morn, I have made this hippocras
Slow-mulled and powerful. Please to drink it now
That you may sleep.

*Somelis* (*waving the cup away*):
Ah, would that I might drink
The self-same draft that Galeor drank, and leave
This palace where my feet forever pace
From shades of evil to a baleful sun.
Too slow, too slow the poison that consumes me—
Compounded of a love for him that's dead
And loathing for the king.

*Baltea:*
I'll play for you
And sing, though not as gallant Galeor sang.
(*She takes up a dulcimer, and sings*):
Lone upon the roseate gloom
Shone the golden star anew,
Calling like a distant bell,
Falling, dimming into death.

Came my lover with the night,
Flame and darkness in his eyes—
Drawn by love from out the grave—
Gone through all the loveless day—
(*She pauses, for steps are heard approaching along the hall.*)

*Somelis:*
Whose footsteps come? I fear it is the king.
(*The door is flung open violently, and the fiend-animated Lich of Galeor enters.*)

*Baltea:*
What thing is this, begot by hell on death?
Oh! How it leers and slobbers! It doth look
Like Galeor, and yet it cannot be.
(*The Lich sidles forward, grinning, mewing and gibbering.*)

*Somelis:*
If you be Galeor, speak and answer me
Who was your friend, wishing you only well
In a bitter world unfriendly to us both.
(*Baltea darts past the apparition, which does not seem to have perceived her presence, and runs from the room.*)
But if you be some fiend in Galeor's form,
I now adjure you by the holy name
Of the goddess Ililot to go at once.
(*The features, limbs, and body of the Lich are convulsed as if by some dreadful struggle with an unseen antagonist. Then, by degrees, the convulsions slacken, the lurid flame dies down in the dead man's eyes, and his face assumes a look of gentle and piteous bewilderment.*)

*Galeor:*
How came I here? Meseems that I was dead
And men had heaped the hard dry earth on me.

*Somelis:*
There is much mystery here, and little time

In which to moot the wherefores. But I see
That you are Galeor and none other now,
The dear sweet Galeor that I thought had died
With all the love between us unavowed,
And this contents me.

*Galeor:*
I must still be dead,
Though I behold and hear and answer you,
And love leaps up to course along my veins
Where death had set his sullen winter.

*Somelis:*
What
Can you recall?

*Galeor:*
Little but night-black silence
That seemed too vast for Time, wherein I was
Both bounded and diffused; and then a voice
Most arrogant and magisterial, bidding
Me, or another in my place, to do
A deed that I cannot remember now.
These things were doubtful; but I feel as one
Who in deep darkness struggled with a fiend
And cast him forth because another voice
Had bade the fiend begone.

*Somelis:*
Truly, I think
There is both magic here and necromancy,
Though he that called you up and sent you forth
Did so with ill intent. It matters not,
For I am glad to have you, whether dead
Or living as men reckon bootless things.
'Tis a small problem now: Baltea has gone
For Smaragad, and he'll be here full soon,

Mammering for twofold murder. (*She goes to the door, closes it, and draws the ponderous metal bars in their massive sockets. Then, with a broidered kerchief and water from a pitcher, she washes the grave-mould from Galeor's face and hands, and tidies his garments. They embrace. He kisses her, and caresses her cheeks and hair.*)

Ah, your touch
Is tenderer than I have known before....
And yet, alas, your lips, your hands....
Poor Galeor, the grave has left you cold:
I'll warm you in my bed and in my arms
For those short moments ere the falling sword
Shatter the fragile bolts of mystery
And open what's beyond.

*(Heavy footsteps approach in the hall outside and there is a babbling of loud, confused voices, followed by a metallic clang like that of a sword-hilt hammering on the door.)*

(*Curtain*)

## SCENE V

The king's pavilion in the palace-gardens. Smaragad sits at the head of a long table littered with goblets, wine-jars and liquor-flasks, some empty or overturned, others still half-full. Sargo and Boranga are seated on a bench near the table's foot. A dozen fellow-revelers, laid low by their potations, lie sprawled about the floor or on benches and couches. Sargo and Boranga are singing:

A ghoul there was in the days of old,
And he drank the wine-dark blood
Without a goblet, with never a flagon,
Fresh from the deep throat-veins of the dead.
But we instead, but we instead,
Will drink from goblets of beryl and gold
A blood-dark wine that was made by the dead
In the days of old.

(*A silence ensues, while the singers wet their husky throats. Smaragad fills and empties his flagon, then fills it again.*)

*Boranga* (*in a lowered voice*):
Something has ired or vexed
The king: he drinks
Like one stung by the dipsas, whose dread bite
Induces lethal thirst.

*Sargo:*
He's laid the most
Of our tun-gutted guzzlers 'neath the board,
And I'm not long above it.... This forenoon
He held much parley with the necromancer
Whose stygian torts outreek the ripened charnel.
Mayhap it has left him thirsty. 'Twas enough
For me when Natanasna passed to windward.
I'm told the king called for incensories
To fume the audience-hall, and fan-bearers
To waft the nard-born vapors round and round
And ventilate with moa-plumes his presence
When the foul mage was gone.

*Boranga:*
They say that Natanasna
And his asphalt-colored ingle have both vanished,
Though none knows whither. Faraad will lose
One bone for gossip's gnawing. I would not give you
A fig-bird's tooth or an aspic's tail-end feather
For all your conjurers. Let's bawl a catch. (*They sing:*)
—There's a thief in the house, there's a thief in the house,
My master, what shall we do?
The fuzzled bowser, he called for Towser,
But Towser was barking the moon.
(*Enter Baltea, breathless and disheveled.*)

*Baltea:*
Your Majesty, there's madness loose from hell.

*Smaragad:*
What's wrong? Has someone raped you without leave?

*Baltea:*
No, 'tis about the queen, from whose bed-chamber
I have come post-haste.

*Smaragad:*
Well, what about her? Why
Have you left her? Is she alone?

*Baltea:*
She's not alone
But has for company a nameless thing
Vomited forth by death.

*Smaragad* (*half-starting from his seat*):
What's all this coil?
A nameless thing, you say? There's nothing nameless.
I'd have a word for what has sent you here,
Panting, with undone hair.

*Baltea:*
Well, then 'tis Galeor.

*Smaragad:*
Hell's privy-fumes!
He's cooling underground, if my grave-diggers
Shirked not their office.

*Baltea:*
And yet he has returned
To visit Queen Somelis, with dark stains
Of earth upon his brow, and goblin torches
Lighting his torrid gaze.

*Smaragad* (*standing up*):
Tell me about it,
Though I cannot believe you. Though he be
Quick or dead, by Thasaidon's dark horns
What does he in the chamber of the queen?

*Baltea:*
I wot not how he came nor why. But she
Was parleying with him, speaking gentle words
When I ran forth to seek you.

*Smaragad:*
Sargo, Boranga, hear you this? Attend me,
And we'll inquire into this nightmare's nest
And find what's at the bottom. (*He starts toward the door, followed by the others.*) By all the plagues
Afflicting the five senses, there's too much
That stinks amid these walls tonight.... Where were
The guards? I'll prune their ears with a blunt sickle
And douche their eyes with boiling camel-stale
For such delinquency as lets
Goblin or man or lich go by them.
(*Curtain*)

## SCENE VI

The hall before Somelis' bed-chamber. Enter Smaragad, Sargo, Boranga and Baltea, followed by two chamberlains. Smaragad tries the queen's door. Finding that it will not open, he beats upon it with the hilt of his drawn sword, but without response.

*Smaragad:*
Who has barred this door? Was it the queen? I vow
That she shall never close another door
When this is broken down. I'll bolt the next one for her,

And it will be the tomb's. Boranga, Sargo,
Give here your shoulders, side by side with mine. (*All three apply their weight to the door but cannot budge it. Sargo, more intoxicated than the others, loses his balance and falls. Boranga helps him to his feet.*)
Truly, my stout forefathers built this palace
And all its portals to withstand a siege.

*Boranga:*
There are siege-engines in the arsenal,
Great rams, that have thrown down broad-builded towers
And torn the gates of cities from their hinges.
With your permission, Sire, I'll call for one
Together with men to wield it.

*Smaragad:*
I'll not have
A legion here to witness what lies couched
In the queen's chamber. Nor am I accustomed
To beat on closen doors that open not.
In all my kingdom, or in Thasaidon's
Deep tortuous maze of torments multi-circled,
There is no darker gulf than this shut room
Which reason cannot fathom, being shunted
From the blank walls to madness.

*Sargo:*
Your Majesty,
If this indeed be Galeor, it smells
Of Natanasna, who has called up others
From tomb or trench, inspiriting with demons
Malign or lewd their corpses. There'll be need
Of exorcism. I would have the priests
Brought in, and rites performed.

*Smaragad:*
I hardly doubt
That the curst necromancer is the getter

Of this graveyard fetus. But I will not have it
Either your way or Boranga's. (*Turning to the chamberlains*) Bring to me
Fagots of pitch-veined terebinth, and naphtha.

*Boranga:*
Sire, what is your purpose?

*Smaragad:*
You will see full soon.

*Baltea:*
Your Majesty, bethink you, there are windows
To which armed men could climb by ladders, finding
Ingress to the queen's room. It may be she's
In peril from this intruder, who had about him
The air of an incubus.

*Smaragad:*
Truly, I think
That he is no intruder to the queen
Who has barred these portals. Nor am I a thief
To enter in by a window.
(*The chamberlains return, bearing armfuls of fagots and jars of oil.*)
Pile the wood
Before the door, and drench it with the naphtha. (*The chamberlains obey. Smaragad seizes a cresset from one of the sconces along the hall, and applies it to the fagots. Flames leap up immediately and lick the cedarn door.*)
I'll warm the bed of this black lechery
That lairs within my walls.

*Boranga:*
Have you gone mad?
You'll fire the palace!

*Smaragad:*
Fire's the one pure thing
To cleanse it. And for fuel we lack only

The necromancer and his swart catamite.

(*The fire spreads quickly to the curtains of the hallway, from which flaming patches begin to fall. Baltea and the chamberlains flee. A section of the burning arras descends upon Sargo. He reels, and falls. Unable to rise, he crawl away, screaming, with his raiment ignited. A loosened splotch sets fire to the king's mantle. He flings the garment from him with an agile gesture. The flames eat steadily into the door, and assail its heavy wooden framework. The heat and smoke compel Boranga and Smaragad to stand back.*)

*Boranga:*
Your Majesty, the palace burns about us.
There's little time for our escape.

*Smaragad:*
You tell me
A thing that's patent. Ah! the goodly flames!
They will lay bare the secret of this chamber
Whose mystery maddens me.... And at the last
There will be only ashes
For the summoning of any sorcerer.

*Boranga:*
Sire, we must go.

*Smaragad:* Be still. It is too late for any words,
And only deeds remain.

(*After some minutes the charred door collapses inward with its red-hot bars, Boranga seizes the king's arm and tries to drag him away. Smaragad wrenches himself loose and beats at Boranga with the flat of his sword.*)

Leave me, Boranga.
I'll go and carve the lechers while they roast
Into small collops for the ghouls to eat.

(*Brandishing his sword, he leaps over the fallen door into the flaming chamber beyond.*)

(*Curtain*)

# The Hashish-Eater; or, The Apocalypse of Evil

Bow down: I am the emperor of dreams;
I crown me with the million-coloured sun
Of secret worlds incredible, and take
Their trailing skies for vestment, when I soar,
Throned on the mounting zenith, and illume
The spaceward-flown horizons infinite.
Like rampant monsters roaring for their glut,
The fiery-crested oceans rise and rise,
By jealous moons maleficently urged
To follow me forever; mountains horned
With peaks of sharpest adamant, and mawed
With sulphur-lit volcanoes lava-langued,
Usurp the skies with thunder, but in vain;
And continents of serpent-shapen trees,
With slimy trunks that lengthen league by league,
Pursue my flight through ages spurned to fire
By that supreme ascendance. Sorcerers,
And evil kings predominantly armed
With scrolls of fulvous dragon-skin, whereon
Are worm-like runes of ever-twisting flame,
Would stay me; and the sirens of the stars,
With foam-light songs from silver fragrance wrought,
Would lure me to their crystal reefs; and moons
Where viper-eyed, senescent devils dwell,

With antic gnomes abominably wise,
Heave up their icy horns across my way:
But naught deters me from the goal ordained
By suns, and aeons, and immortal wars,
And sung by moons and motes; the goal whose name
Is all the secret of forgotten glyphs,
By sinful gods in torrid rubies writ
For ending of a brazen book; the goal
Whereat my soaring ecstasy may stand,
In amplest heavens multiplied to hold
My hordes of thunder-vested avatars,
And Promethèan armies of my thought,
That brandish claspèd levins. There I call
My memories, intolerably clad
In light the peaks of paradise may wear,
And lead the Armageddon of my dreams,
Whose instant shout of triumph is become
Immensity's own music: For their feet
Are founded on innumerable worlds,
Remote in alien epochs, and their arms
Upraised, are columns potent to exalt
With ease ineffable the countless thrones
Of all the gods that are and gods to be,
And bear the seats of Asmadai and Set
Above the seventh paradise.

Supreme
In culminant omniscience manifold,
And served by senses multitudinous,
Far-posted on the shifting walls of time,
With eyes that roam the star-unwinnowed fields
Of utter night and chaos, I convoke
The Babel of their visions, and attend
At once their myriad witness: I behold,
In Ombos, where the fallen Titans dwell,
With mountain-builded walls, and gulfs for moat,
The secret cleft that cunning dwarves have dug

Beneath an alp-like buttress; and I list,
Too late, the clang of adamantine gongs,
Dinned by their drowsy guardians, whose feet
Have felt the wasp-like sting of little knives,
Embrued with slobber of the basilisk,
Or juice of wounded upas. And I see,
In gardens of a crimson-litten world
The sacred flow'r with lips of purple flesh,
And silver-lashed, vermilion-lidded eyes
Of torpid azure; whom his furtive priests
At moonless eve in terror seek to slay,
With bubbling grails of sacrificial blood
That hide a hueless poison. And I read,
Upon the tongue of a forgotten sphinx,
The annuling word a spiteful demon wrote
With gall of slain chimeras; and I know
What pentacles the lunar wizards use,
That once allured the gulf-returning roc,
With ten great wings of furlèd storm, to pause
Midmost an alabaster mount; and there,
With boulder-weighted webs of dragons'-gut,
Uplift by cranes a captive giant built,
They wound the monstrous, moonquake-throbbing bird,
And plucked, from off his sabre-taloned feet,
Uranian sapphires fast in frozen blood,
With amethysts from Mars. I lean to read,
With slant-lipped mages, in an evil star,
The monstrous archives of a war that ran
Through wasted aeons, and the prophecy
Of wars renewed, that shall commemorate
Some enmity of wivern-headed kings,
Even to the brink of time. I know the blooms
Of bluish fungus, freaked with mercury,
That bloat within the craters of the moon,
And in one still, selenic hour have shrunk
To pools of slime and fetor; and I know
What clammy blossoms, blanched and cavern-grown,

Are proffered in Uranus to their gods
By mole-eyed peoples; and the livid seed
Of some black fruit a king in Saturn ate,
Which, cast upon his tinkling palace-floor,
Took root between the burnished flags, and now
Hath mounted, and become a hellish tree,
Whose lithe and hairy branches, lined with mouths,
Net like a hundred ropes his lurching throne,
And strain at starting pillars. I behold
The slowly-thronging corals, that usurp
Some harbour of a million-masted sea,
And sun them on the league-long wharves of gold—
Bulks of enormous crimson, kraken-limbed
And kraken-headed, lifting up as crowns
The octiremes of perished emperors,
And galleys fraught with royal gems, that sailed
From a sea-deserted haven.

Swifter grow
The visions: Now a mighty city looms,
Hewn from a hill of purest cinnabar,
To domes and turrets like a sunrise thronged
With tier on tier of captive moons, half-drowned
In shifting erubescence. But whose hands
Were sculptors of its doors, and columns wrought
To semblance of prodigious blooms of old,
No eremite hath lingered there to say,
And no man comes to learn: For long ago
A prophet came, warning its timid king
Against the plague of lichens that had crept
Across subverted empires, and the sand
Of wastes that Cyclopean mountains ward;
Which, slow and ineluctable, would come,
To take his fiery bastions and his fanes,
And quench his domes with greenish tetter. Now
I see a host of naked giants, armed
With horns of behemoth and unicorn,

Who wander, blinded by the clinging spells
Of hostile wizardry, and stagger on
To forests where the very leaves have eyes,
And ebonies, like wrathful dragons roar
To teaks a-chuckle in the loathly gloom;
Where coiled lianas lean, with serried fangs,
From writhing palms with swollen boles that moan;
Where leeches of a scarlet moss have sucked
The eyes of some dead monster, and have crawled
To bask upon his azure-spotted spine;
Where hydra-throated blossoms hiss and sing,
Or yawn with mouths that drip a sluggish dew,
Whose touch is death and slow corrosion. Then,
I watch a war of pygmies, met by night,
With pitter of their drums of parrot's hide,
On plains with no horizon, where a god
Might lose his way for centuries; and there,
In wreathèd light, and fulgors all convolved,
A rout of green, enormous moons ascend,
With rays that like a shivering venom run
On inch-long swords of lizard-fang.

Surveyed
From this my throne, as from a central sun,
The pageantries of worlds and cycles pass;
Forgotten splendours, dream by dream unfold,
Like tapestry, and vanish; violet suns,
Or suns of changeful iridescence, bring
Their rays about me, like the coloured lights
Imploring priests might lift to glorify
The face of some averted god; the songs
Of mystic poets in a purple world,
Ascend to me in music that is made
From unconceivèd perfumes, and the pulse
Of love ineffable; the lute-players
Whose lutes are strung with gold of the utmost moon,
Call forth delicious languors, never known

Save to their golden kings; the sorcerers
Of hooded stars inscrutable to God,
Surrender me their demon-wrested scrolls,
Inscribed with lore of monstrous alchemies
And awful transformations.

If I will,
I am at once the vision and the seer,
And mingle with my ever-streaming pomps,
And still abide their suzerain: I am
The neophyte who serves a nameless god,
Within whose fane the fanes of Hecatompylos
Were arks the Titan worshippers might bear,
Or flags to pave the threshold; or I am
The god himself, who calls the fleeing clouds
Into the nave where suns might congregate,
And veils the darkling mountain of his face
With fold on solemn fold; for whom the priests
Amass their monthly hecatomb of gems—
Opals that are a camel-cumbering load,
And monstrous alabraundines, won from war
With realms of hostile serpents; which arise,
Combustible, in vapours many-hued,
And myrrh-excelling perfumes. It is I,
The king, who holds with scepter-dropping hand
The helm of some great barge of chrysolite,
Sailing upon an amethystine sea
To isles of timeless summer: For the snows
Of hyperborean winter, and their winds,
Sleep in his jewel-builded capital,
Nor any charm of flame-wrought wizardry,
Nor conjured suns may rout them; so he flees,
With captive kings to urge his serried oars,
Hopeful of dales where amaranthine dawn
Hath never left the faintly sighing lote
And fields of lisping moly. Or I fare
Impanoplied with azure diamond,

As hero of a quest Achernar lights,
To deserts filled with ever-wandering flames,
That feed upon the sullen marl, and soar
To wrap the slopes of mountains, and to leap
With tongues intolerably lengthening,
That lick the blenchèd heavens. But there lives
(Secure as in a garden walled from wind)
A lonely flower by a placid well,
Midmost the flaring tumult of the flames,
That roar as roars a storm-possessèd sea,
Impacable forever: And within
That simple grail the blossom lifts, there lies
One drop of an incomparable dew,
Which heals the parchèd weariness of kings,
And cures the wound of wisdom. I am page
To an emperor who reigns ten thousand years,
And through his labyrinthine palace-rooms,
Through courts and colonnades and balconies
Wherein immensity itself is mazed,
I seek the golden gorget he hath lost,
On which the names of his conniving stars
Are writ in little sapphires; and I roam
For centuries, and hear the brazen clocks
Innumerably clang with such a sound
As brazen hammers make, by devils dinned
On tombs of all the dead; and nevermore
I find the gorget, but at length I find
A sealèd room whose nameless prisoner
Moans with a nameless torture, and would turn
To hell's red rack as to a lilied couch
From that whereon they stretched him; and I find,
Prostrate upon a lotus-painted floor,
The loveliest of all beloved slaves
My emperor hath, and from her pulseless side
A serpent rises, whiter than the root
Of some venefic bloom in darkness grown,
And gazes up with green-lit eyes that seem

Like drops of cold, congealing poison.

Hark!
What word was whispered in a tongue unknown,
In crypts of some impenetrable world?
Whose is the dark, dethroning secrecy
I cannot share, though I am king of suns
And king therewith of strong eternity,
Whose gnomons with their swords of shadow guard
My gates, and slay the intruder? Silence loads
The wind of ether, and the worlds are still
To hear the word that flees me. All my dreams
Fall like a rack of fuming vapours raised
To semblance by a necromant, and leave
Spirit and sense unthinkably alone,
Above a universe of shrouded stars,
And suns that wander, cowled with sullen gloom,
Like witches to a Sabbath.

Fear is born
In crypts below the nadir, and hath crawled
Reaching the floor of space and waits for wings
To lift it upward, like a hellish worm
Fain for the flesh of seraphs. Eyes that gleam,
But are not eyes of suns or galaxies,
Gather and throng to the base of darkness; flame
Behind some black, abysmal curtain burns,
Implacable, and fanned to whitest wrath
By raisèd wings that flail the whiffled gloom,
And make a brief and broken wind that moans,
As one who rides a throbbing rack. There is
A Thing that crouches, worlds and years remote,
Whose horns a demon sharpens, rasping forth
A note to shatter the donjon-keeps of time,
And crack the sphere of crystal.

All is dark
For ages, and my tolling heart suspends
Its clamour, as within the clutch of death,
Tightening with tense, hermetic rigours. Then,
In one enormous, million-flashing flame,
The stars unveil, the suns remove their cowls,
And beam to their responding planets; time
Is mine once more, and armies of its dreams
Rally to that insuperable throne,
Firmed on the central zenith.

Now I seek
The meads of shining moly I had found
In some remoter vision, by a stream
No cloud hath ever tarnished; where the sun,
A gold Narcissus, loiters evermore
Above his golden image: But I find
A corpse the ebbing water will not keep,
With eyes like sapphires that have lain in hell,
And felt the hissing embers; and the flow'rs
About me turn to hooded serpents, swayed
By flutes of devils in a hellish dance
Meet for the nod of Satan, when he reigns
Above the raging Sabbath, and is wooed
By sarabands of witches. But I turn
To mountains guarding with their horns of snow
The source of that befoulèd rill, and seek
A pinnacle where none but eagles climb,
And they with failing pennons. But in vain
I flee, for on that pylon of the sky,
Some curse hath turned the unprinted snow to flame—
Red fires that curl and cluster to my tread,
Trying the summit's narrow cirque. And now,
I see a silver python far beneath—
Vast as a river that a fiend hath witched,
And forced to flow remèant in its course
To fountains whence it issued. Rapidly

It winds from slope to crumbling slope, and fills
Ravines and chasmal gorges, till the crags
Totter with coil on coil incumbent. Soon
It hath entwined the pinnacle I keep,
And gapes with a fanged, unfathomable maw,
Wherein great Typhon, and Enceladus,
Were orts of daily glut. But I am gone,
For at my call a hippogriff hath come,
And firm between his thunder-beating wings,
I mount the sheer cerulean walls of noon,
And see the earth, a spurnèd pebble, fall
Lost in the fields of nether stars—and seek
A planet where the outwearied wings of time
Might pause and furl for respite, or the plumes
Of death be stayed, and loiter in reprieve
Above some deathless lily: For therein,
Beauty hath found an avatar of flow'rs—
Blossoms that clothe it as a coloured flame,
From peak to peak, from pole to sullen pole,
And turn the skies to perfume. There I find
A lonely castle, calm and unbeset,
Save by the purple spears of amaranth,
And tender-sworded iris. Walls upbuilt
Of flushèd marble, wonderful with rose,
And domes like golden bubbles, and minarets
That take the clouds as coronal—these are mine,
For voiceless looms the peaceful barbican,
And the heavy-teethed portcullis hangs aloft
As if to smile a welcome. So I leave
My hippogriff to crop the magic meads,
And pass into a court the lilies hold,
And tread them to a fragrance that pursues
To win the portico, whose columns, carved
Of lazuli and amber, mock the palms
Of bright, Aidennic forests—capitalled
With fronds of stone fretted to airy lace,
Enfolding drupes that seem as tawny clusters

Of breasts of unknown houris; and convolved
With vines of shut and shadowy-leavèd flow'rs,
Like the dropt lids of women that endure
Some loin-dissolving rapture. Through a door
Enlaid with lilies twined luxuriously,
I enter, dazed and blinded with the sun,
And hear, in gloom that changing colours cloud,
A chuckle sharp as crepitating ice,
Upheaved and cloven by shoulders of the damned
Who strive in Antenora. When my eyes
Undazzle, and the cloud of colour fades,
I find me in a monster-guarded room,
Where marble apes with wings of griffins crowd
On walls an evil sculptor wrought, and beasts
Wherein the sloth and vampire-bat unite,
Pendulous by their toes of tarnished bronze,
Usurp the shadowy interval of lamps
That hang from ebon arches. Like a ripple,
Borne by the wind from pool to sluggish pool
In fields where wide Cocytus flows his bound,
A crackling smile around that circle runs,
And all the stone-wrought gibbons stare at me
With eyes that turn to glowing coals. A fear
That found no name in Babel, flings me on,
Breathless and faint with horror, to a hall
Within whose weary, self-reverting round,
The languid curtains, heavier than palls,
Unnumerably depict a weary king,
Who fain would cool his jewel-crusted hands
In lakes of emerald evening, or the fields
Of dreamless poppies pure with rain. I flee
Onward, and all the shadowy curtains shake
With tremors of a silken-sighing mirth,
And whispers of the innumerable king,
Breathing a tale of ancient pestilence,
Whose very words are vile contagion. Then
I reach a room where caryatides,

Carved in the form of tall, voluptuous Titan women,
Surround a throne of flowering ebony
Where creeps a vine of crystal. On the throne,
There lolls a wan, enormous Worm, whose bulk,
Tumid with all the rottenness of kings,
O'erflows its arms with fold on creasèd fold
Of fat obscenely bloating. Open-mouthed
He leans, and from his throat a score of tongues,
Depending like to wreaths of torpid vipers,
Drivel with phosphorescent slime, that runs
Down all his length of soft and monstrous folds,
And creeping among the flow'rs of ebony,
Lends them the life of tiny serpents. Now,
Ere the Horror ope those red and lashless slits
Of eyes that draw the gnat and midge, I turn,
And follow down a dusty hall, whose gloom,
Lined by the statues with their mighty limbs,
Ends in golden-roofèd balcony
Sphering the flowered horizon.

Ere my heart
Hath hushed the panic tumult of its pulses,
I listen, from beyond the horizon's rim,
A mutter faint as when the far simoon,
Mounting from unknown deserts, opens forth,
Wide as the waste, those wings of torrid night
That fling the doom of cities from their folds,
And musters in its van a thousand winds
That with disrooted palms for besoms, rise
And sweep the sands to fury. As the storm,
Approaching, mounts and loudens to the ears
Of them that toil in fields of sesame,
So grows the mutter, and a shadow creeps
Above the gold horizon, like a dawn
Of darkness climbing sunward. Now they come,
A Sabbath of abominable shapes,
Led by the fiends and lamiae of worlds

That owned my sway aforetime! Cockatrice,
Python, tragelaphus, leviathan,
Chimera, martichoras, behemoth,
Geryon and sphinx, and hydra, on my ken
Arise as might some Afrite-builded city,
Consummate in the lifting of a lash,
With thunderous domes and sounding obelisks,
And towers of night and fire alternate! Wings
Of white-hot stone along the hissing wind,
Bear up the huge and furnace-hearted beasts
Of hells beyond Rutilicus; and things
Whose lightless length would mete the gyre of moons—
Born from the caverns of a dying sun,
Uncoil to the very zenith, half disclosed
From gulfs below the horizon; octopi
Like blazing moons with countless arms of fire,
Climb from the seas of ever-surging flame
That roll and roar through planets unconsumed,
Beating on coasts of unknown metals; beasts
That range the mighty worlds of Alioth, rise,
Aforesting the heavens with multitudinous horns,
Within whose maze the winds are lost; and borne
On cliff-like brows of plunging scolopendras,
The shell-wrought tow'rs of ocean-witches loom,
And griffin-mounted gods, and demons throned
On sable dragons, and the cockodrills
That bear the spleenful pygmies on their backs;
And blue-faced wizards from the worlds of Saiph,
On whom Titanic scorpions fawn; and armies
That move with fronts reverted from the foe,
And strike athwart their shoulders at the shapes
Their shields reflect in crystal; and eidola
Fashioned within unfathomable caves
By hands of eyeless peoples; and the blind
And worm-shaped monsters of a sunless world,
With krakens from the ultimate abyss,
And Demogorgons of the outer dark,

Arising, shout with multitudinous thunders,
And threatening me with dooms ineffable
In words whereat the heavens leap to flame,
Advance on the magic palace! Thrown before,
For league on league, their blasting shadows blight
And eat like fire the amaranthine meads,
Leaving an ashen desert! In the palace,
I hear the apes of marble shriek and howl,
And all the women-shapen columns moan,
Babbling with unknown terror. In my fear,
A monstrous dread unnamed in any hell,
I rise, and flee with the fleeing wind for wings,
And in a trice the magic palace reels,
And spiring to a single tow'r of flame,
Goes out, and leaves nor shard nor ember! Flown
Beyond the world, upon that fleeing wind,
I reach the gulf's irrespirable verge,
Where fails the strongest storm for breath and fall,
Supportless, through the nadir-plungèd gloom,
Beyond the scope and vision of the sun,
To other skies and systems. In a world
Deep-wooded with the multi-coloured fungi,
That soar to semblance of fantastic palms,
I fall as falls the meteor-stone, and break
A score of trunks to powder. All unhurt,
I rise, and through the illimitable woods,
Among the trees of flimsy opal, roam,
And see their tops that clamber, hour by hour,
To touch the suns of iris. Things unseen,
Whose charnel breath informs the tideless air
With spreading pools of fetor, follow me
Elusive past the ever-changing palms;
And pittering moths, with wide and ashen wings,
Flit on before, and insects ember-hued,
Descending, hurtle through the gorgeous gloom,
And quench themselves in crumbling thickets. Heard
Far-off, the gong-like roar of beasts unknown

Resounds at measured intervals of time,
Shaking the riper trees to dust, that falls
In clouds of acrid perfume, stifling me
Beneath a pall of iris.

Now the palms
Grow far apart and lessen momently
To shrubs a dwarf might topple. Over them
I see an empty desert, all ablaze
With amethysts and rubies, and the dust
Of garnets or carnelians. On I roam,
Treading the gorgeous grit, that dazzles me
With leaping waves of endless rutilance,
Whereby the air is turned to a crimson gloom,
Through which I wander, blind as any Kobold;
Till underfoot the grinding sands give place
To stone or metal, with a massive ring
More welcome to mine ears than golden bells,
Or tinkle of silver fountains. When the gloom
Of crimson lifts, I stand upon the edge
Of a broad black plain of adamant, that reaches,
Level as windless water, to the verge
Of all the world; and through the sable plain,
A hundred streams of shattered marble run,
And streams of broken steel, and streams of bronze,
Like to the ruin of all the wars of time,
To plunge, with clangour of timeless cataracts
Adown the gulfs eternal.

So I follow,
Between a river of steel and a river of bronze,
With ripples loud and tuneless as the clash
Of a million lutes; and come to the precipice
From which they fall, and make the mighty sound
Of a million swords that meet a million shields,
Or din of spears and armour in the wars
Of all the worlds and aeons: Far beneath,

They fall, through gulfs and cycles of the void,
And vanish like a stream of broken stars,
Into the nether darkness; nor the gods
Of any sun, nor demons of the gulf,
Will dare to know what everlasting sea
Is fed thereby, and mounts forevermore
With mighty tides unebbing.

Lo, what cloud,
Or night of sudden and supreme eclipse,
Is on the suns of opal? At my side,
The rivers run with a wan and ghostly gleam,
Through darkness falling as the night that falls
From mighty spheres extinguished! Turning now,
I see, betwixt the desert and the suns,
The poisèd wings of all the dragon-rout,
Far-flown in black occlusion thousand-fold
Through stars, and deeps, and devastated worlds,
Upon my trail of terror! Griffins, rocs,
And sluggish, dark chimeras, heavy-winged
After the ravin of dispeopled lands,
With harpies, and the vulture-birds of hell—
Hot from abominable feasts and fain
To cool their beaks and talons in my blood—
All, all have gathered, and the wingless rear,
With rank on rank of foul, colossal Worms,
Like pillars of embattled night and flame,
Looms on the wide horizon! From the van,
I hear the shriek of wyvers, loud and shrill
As tempests in a broken fane, and roar
Of sphinxes, like the unrelenting toll
Of bells from tow'rs infernal. Cloud on cloud,
They arch the zenith, and a dreadful wind
Falls from them like the wind before the storm.
And in the wind my cloven garment streams,
And flutters in the face of all the void,
Even as flows a flaffing spirit, lost

On the Pit's undying tempest! Louder grows
The thunder of the streams of stone and bronze—
Redoubled with the roar of torrent wings,
Inseparably mingled. Scarce I keep
My footing, in the gulfward winds of fear,
And mighty thunders, beating to the void
In sea-like waves incessant; and would flee
With them, and prove the nadir-founded night
Where fall the streams of ruin; but when I reach
The verge, and seek through sun-defeating gloom,
To measure with my gaze the dread descent,
I see a tiny star within the depths—
A light that stays me, while the wings of doom
Convene their thickening thousands: For the star
Increases, taking to its hueless orb,
With all the speed of horror-changèd dreams
The light as of a million million moons;
And floating up through gulfs and glooms eclipsed,
It grows and grows, a huge white eyeless Face,
That fills the void and fills the universe,
And bloats against the limits of the world
With lips of flame that open.

# Bibliography


"The Animated Sword" is published here for the first time.

"The Red Turban" is published here for the first time.

"Prince Alcouz and the Magician." First published as a chapbook limited to 190 numbered copies printed on letter press by Roy A. Squires, Glendale, California, in 1977.

"The Malay Krise." *The Overland Monthly* 51, No. 4 (October 1910): 354–55. In *Other Dimensions* (Sauk City, WI: Arkham House, 1970).

"The Ghost of Mohammed Din." *The Overland Monthly* 51, No. 5 (November 1910): 519–22. In *Other Dimensions* (Sauk City, WI: Arkham House, 1970).

"The Mahout." *The Black Cat* 16, No. 11 (August 1911): 25–30. In *Other Dimensions* (Sauk City, WI: Arkham House, 1970).

"The Raja and the Tiger." *Black Cat* 17, No. 5 (February 1912): __-__. In *Other Dimensions* (Sauk City, WI: Arkham House, 1970).

"Something New." *10 Story Book* 23, No. 9 (August 1924): 36–37. *10 Story Book* 25, No. 9 (September 1927): 40–41.

"The Flirt." *Live Stories* 36, No. 1 (March 1923): 98. In *Strange Shadows: The Uncollected Fiction and Essays of Clark Ashton Smith.* Ed. Steve Behrends with Donald Sidney-Fryer and Rah Hoffman (Westport, CT: Greenwood Press, 1989).

"The Perfect Woman," "A Platonic Entanglement," "The Expert Lover," "The Parrot," "A Copy of Burns," "Checkmate," and "The Infernal Star" were all first published in *Strange Shadows: The Uncollected Fiction and Essays of Clark Ashton Smith.* Ed. Steve Behrends with Donald Sidney-Fryer and Rah Hoffman (Westport, CT: Greenwood Press, 1989).

"Dawn of Discord." *Spicy Mystery Stories* 9, no. 4 (October 1940): 30–41, 106–114 (as by E. Hoffmann Price).

"House of the Monoceros." *Spicy Mystery Stories* 10, no. 1 (February 1941): __ (as "The Old Gods Eat" by E. Hoffmann Price). Reprinted in *Far Lands, Other Days* by E. Hoffmann Price (Chapel Hill, NC: Carcosa, 1975).

"The Dead Will Cuckold You." First published in *In Memoriam: Clark Ashton Smith.* Ed. Jack L. Chalker (Baltimore: Anthem, 1963). In *Strange Shadows: The Uncollected Fiction and Essays of Clark Ashton Smith.* Ed. Steve Behrends with Donald Sidney-Fryer and Rah Hoffman (Westport, CT: Greenwood Press, 1989).

"The Hashish-Eater; or, the Apocalypse of Evil." This version was originally published in *Ebony and Crystal: Poems in Verse and Prose* (Auburn Journal, 1922). Smith would later revise the poem for inclusion in *Selected Poems* (Sauk City, WI: Arkham House, 1971).

# O Amor Atque Realitas!

## Clark Ashton Smith's First Adult Fiction
## by Donald Sidney-Fryer

When *Strange Shadows: The Uncollected Fiction and Essays of Clark Ashton Smith,* as compiled and edited by Steve Behrends (together with two associate editors), was published by Greenwood Press in April of 1989, the volume brought to the attention of Smith cognoscenti for the first time what appears to be almost all of his first adult fiction, the major part of it from the first half of the 1920s, among other hitherto ungathered materials. However, in the book itself there is only one reference to this fiction, but not (we hasten to add) in the terms that we have just set forth immediately above. This one reference occurs in the first paragraph on page xxi of *A Note on the Contents,* as follows: "The reader will also find Smith's ironic fiction, composed for the most part before the 1930s". Possibly the term "ironic-romantic fiction" is more inclusive, and so this is the one that we shall use by preference throughout the present article, in addition to that of "his first adult fiction." Thus, while the fact that this ironic-romantic fiction is also his first adult fiction is not exactly obscured, neither is it exactly highlighted. It should also be pointed out that apart from this one editorial reference on the part of Steve Behrends, there is no other information on these stories in the book, whether preceding them in the section *Non-Fantastic Fiction* in which they are included, or in the excellent and extensive section *Notes to the Text* immediately following the main (i.e., Smithian) text.

The present article seeks to add to whatever other little information that we possess on these stories. The quotations that we proffer in the course of this article are taken exclusively from Smith's letters to George Sterling for the first half of the 1920s. The principal compiler and editor of *Strange Shadows* has thoughtfully included, wherever known, the extant dates of composition, or (rather) of completion of composition, for at least a few of the pieces, which with one exception (as noted below) also stem exclusively from the first half of the 1920s. The stories and their dates, as presently known, are as follows, arranged more or less chronologically:

| | |
|---|---|
| "The Flirt" | (December 22,1921.)* |
| "The Perfect Woman" | (February 28,1923.)* |
| "Gossip" | (possibly Winter-Spring, 1923.) |
| "A Platonic Entanglement" | (ditto.) |
| "Something New" | (probably Spring, 1924.) |
| "The Expert Lover" | (possibly Winter, 1924-1925.) |
| "Checkmate" | (November 7,1930.)* |

*Dates furnished by Steve Behrends

Certain additional observations should be made at once. Although not included in *Strange Shadows,* but previously collected into *Other Dimensions* (published by Arkham House, Sauk City, Wisconsin, in April of 1970), "Something New" belongs to the above group of stories.[1] "The Perfect Woman", as extant, is much more of a plot-sketch than it is a finished short story. "Gossip" is but a fragment, and "A Platonic Entanglement" may possibly be just the beginning of a longer story, and hence, as extant, also a fragment. "The Flirt" and "Something New" are perfect examples of a "short short" story, and only "The Perfect Lover" and "Checkmate", as extant, are typical short stories of the usual length.

As far as our present information allows us to state, only two of these tales were apparently published in magazines during Smith's lifetime, again exclusively during the first half of the 1920s, as follows:

"The Flirt", in *Snappy Stories,* sometime probably either late 1922 or early 1923.

"Something New," in *10 Story Book,* August 1924.

It is doubtful that Smith would have mentioned these stories or prose-sketches of an ironic-romantic nature to most of his correspondents, who were never numerous even in the best of circumstances. It is possible that he might have mentioned them to fellow poet Samuel Loveman, in addition to his great friend and mentor George Sterling. During the period for 1911/1912 through 1925/1926 Smith's chief correspondents were Sterling, Loveman, and (from 1922 onward) H. P. Lovecraft. While admittedly no great masterpieces—they are frankly experimental—these tales are much more than "trite tearjerkers" as one reviewer of *Strange Shadows* has characterized them. In fact, the term is a complete misnomer. Love, death, loss, and irony are among the principal themes or elements in Smith's oeuvre, whether in verse or in prose. What gives his ironic-romantic fiction its characteristic and amusing tone, distinguishing it from his other and later fiction (written for the most part during the 1930s), is the complete absence of death. Smith wrote these stories quite frankly in the hope that he might sell them to such characteristic magazines of the early 1920s as *Snappy Stories, 10 Story Book,* and other periodicals of a similar nature, and that he might thus add to his perennially meagre income. He intended them apparently as no more than deft and lightweight stories, to beguile an idle moment or two. Moreover, it becomes obvious to anyone reading Smith's letters to Sterling just for the period 1918 to 1926 that he wrote them drawing directly upon much of his own life's experiences for the same period. Next to the epigrams, apothegms, and pensees that he contributed to *The Auburn Journal* for 1923–1926 (and in addition to his private letters, of course), his ironic-romantic stories are almost unique in his oeuvre for the fact that they do something that his verse and prose almost never do—these tales deliberately reflect or cultivate something of the spirit of the times, the Jazz Age and the period of Prohibition that went into effect in the U.S.A. after the Great War (i.e., World War I), with their then chic, clever, and up-to-date qualities characteristic of the then modernism and avant-gardism.

We herewith present the relevant passages from Smith's letters to Sterling. The reader should be cautioned that, in considering his own work, Ashton Smith typically often complained of its deficiencies and inadequacies to himself and to his correspondents. If the description "trite tearjerkers" might seem a complete misnomer, then it might strike us as equally anomalous that both Sterling and Smith should have considered such relatively innocent fiction to be so much "literary whore-mongering." Such magazines as *10 Story Book, Snappy Stories,* and others of a similar class were in fact the "girlie" publications of the time, but in content and by nature they were never directly erotic. They featured a typical mixture of light and lighthearted fiction combined with rather charming but certainly not directly sexually provocative photographs of attractive young women usually in a state of semidress. These periodicals were as far removed from *Playboy* magazine as they were from frankly pornographic stories and pictures. Any eroticism that such periodicals possessed was always implicit and never explicit.

> November 23rd, 1922:
> "Snappy Stories" has accepted a little prose-sketch of mine, entitled "The Flirt." They pay 2 cents a word for prose. Maybe I'll do some more whore-mongering, at that price.
>
> March 7th, 1923:
> As for me, I'm trying to write verse and prose-fillers, in the hope that some of them, at least, will sell. I'm doing it absolutely without inspiration, with lacerated nerves and a sodden brain.
>
> July 21st, 1924:
> Hope you received the *Ten Story Book* containing a storiette of mine. I received $6.00 for it—on publication! But the story was rotten, anyhow—except for the spanking—which was what I *ought* to have administered, some time back, to a certain badly spoiled female person.
>
> August 25th, 1924:
> I'll tackle some more fiction when the wet weather comes. Literary whore-mongering is distasteful to me; but I don't want to break my back, if I can help it—or tie myself down to a {regular} job, either. I'd rather starve than be a wage-slave for anyone in Auburn.

Collating the data in these excerpts from Smith's letters with the list of extant ironic-romantic stories, we are able to reach a number of conclusions and to make a number of statements about their composition. According to the first excerpt, "The Flirt" was thus published about a year or so after its composition. Then, according to the second excerpt,

"The Perfect Woman" was one of the prose-fillers that Smith was trying to write during the winter of 1922–1923; and "Gossip" and "A Platonic Entanglement" could also very well be the others. According to the third excerpt, *10 Story Book* like other periodicals both before and since was antedated; thus the issue for August 1924, which carried "Something New," was probably produced and printed in June so as to appear on the stands in July. Even though "Checkmate" bears the date of composition, or of completion of composition, as November 7,1930, both "The Expert Lover" and "Checkmate" could then quite likely stem from the winter of 1924–1925, according to one possible interpretation of the fourth and last excerpt presented just above.

In assessing and interpreting properly the autobiographical quotient in the make-up of these ironic-romantic stories, however, we still need to consider (at least) not only two further excerpts from Smith's letters to Sterling for the early 1920s but also certain general conditions of Smith's life during the period from 1911/1912 through 1925/1926, especially between 1918 and 1926. We should recall that, after the publication of his first volume *The Star-Treader* in late 1912, and lasting into the latter part of the 1910s, Ashton Smith suffered from generally poor health, and was consequently unable to do much mundane work in order to earn some necessary funds. Therefore his great and good friend George Sterling did all he could, either by taking from his own small store of money, or by soliciting a wide range of wealthy people in Northern California, to supplement the collective income of the Smith family.

By virtue of his unique position as the unofficial poet laureate of San Francisco and hence, by extension, of the entire West Coast as constituted at that time, Sterling had access to many persons of genuine wealth, whether as friends or as acquaintances, and he did manage to convince less than a handful of millionaires or persons close to being millionaires, who could thus well afford it, to send the young Smith a monthly or quarterly stipend, and over a period of at least a few years. Since the Smith family's needs were comparatively simple and few, the total money thus donated sufficed to take care of them. Most of these stipends would last until the latter 1910s when some of them ceased, and when circumstances thus forced Smith to return to mundane labor at least on a part-time basis. Consequently, the early to middle 1920s witnessed not only the publication of *Ebony and Crystal* in late 1922 and of *Sandalwood* in late 1925, but also the performance by Ashton Smith of such likely work as he could obtain. However, it was almost never regular jobs of a permanent nature but almost always either odd jobs or regular jobs of limited duration. Temperamentally the latter type of mundane labor suited Ashton Smith much better because he could then continue with his own creative work during those times when he was not earning money by working for other people.

Between 1918 and 1926, Ashton Smith not only underwent a variety of physical maladies and mishaps, but also, when he was well, he performed a variety of odd jobs for some dozen or more local people principally located in and around Auburn and Long Valley. Some of this work in particular consisted in fact of quite hard labor of a physically demanding type. Recovering from "incipient tuberculosis" and a "nervous breakdown" (Smith's own terms) that he suffered c. 1918, this hard physical labor, which included woodcutting, at which he became quite expert, appears to have helped the convalescent to become physiologically stronger and psychologically more self-reliant in a variety of ways.

The two further excerpts from Smith's letters to Sterling from the early 1920s which we still need to consider are unusually revealing, not only for the light that they throw on his ironic-romantic fiction but just as much for what they tell us of his life for that period, as well as before and after. In his letter of December 27th, 1920, Ashton Smith had mentioned that he might visit George Sterling in San Francisco with the clear implication that this would be soon. However, writing again on January 31st, 1921, he has now decided, after all, not to visit his friend and mentor at the latter's place in the celebrated "Monkey" or Montgomery Block situated in the downtown area of the City. (The reference below to Bologna is to the Cafe Bologna in San Francisco, a well-known haunt of creative people and their friends.) Smith continues:

> I doubt if I'll visit San Francisco, I don't feel that I can afford the trip; anyway, there wouldn't be much pleasure in it for me. I've sworn off prohibition-booze, and have no time to bother with semi-virgins of the Bologna variety. Anyway, I never make love to girls. Only married women need apply.

Later that same year Smith expatiates a little on this rule of behavior. From the context of this letter and others, as well as from the known circumstances of his life, especially during the over-all period from 1910 until 1930, this rule appears to be one which he reached after careful deliberation, and to which he more or less adhered until his last decade. When he did finally marry, it would be to a woman more or less his own age, and past the capacity to conceive and bear any further children. The next letter in which he mentions the topic again is dated September 5th, 1921:

> Marriage is an error I was never tempted to commit: I have not been in love with an unmarried woman since I was fifteen!

The reader should keep in mind that Ashton Smith had been fifteen during 1909. It is probably safe to say that, if his very first complete sexual experience with a human female did not occur precisely when he was fifteen, then it must have happened sometime between his eleventh and fifteenth years. The advantages of such a stance—i.e., making love only to married women—for a man of limited income are perfectly obvious. At best it represents a sensible and responsible compromise between his own erotic drive and the human world outside his own person. It must be recalled and emphasized that the modes of controlling human conception, even early in the first half of the twentieth century, were still relatively limited and crude, apart from actual sterilization. However, apart from the threat of conception and unwanted children, the principal problem was to avoid arousing the suspicions not only, and primarily, of the husband involved but also, and in its way just as importantly, of such of the local citizenry as were given to gossiping.

We must not forget that Ashton Smith was living if not right inside, then certainly not far from, a small town already celebrated for its gossipmongers when Ambrose Bierce was residing there, off and on, during the 1880s, just before Smith would be born in January of 1893. In such circumstances as these, a discreet young man would not go out of his way to advertise his amorous and sexual preferences and proclivities—even when they were of the accepted heterosexual variety—if he could help it! Such a stance or attitude on the part of Ashton Smith does not by any means indicate that the noncorporeal aspects of love did not have considerable importance for him. Rather, he had clearly chosen a method whereby he could enjoy those aspects of a mature loving relationship which possessed the greatest value for him, and also whereby he could minimize, biologically and socially, those potentially negative possibilities of such a regular relationship with a woman.

For anyone who can read between the lines of Smith's letters to Sterling for the first half of the 1920s—and who can correlate his behavior *vis-à-vis* his women friends with the amorous duplicity or two-timing on the one hand, as well as with the discreet cuckoldry on the other, such as he describes in his ironic-romantic fiction—it is quite obvious that Smith was directly writing out of his own life, or was directly and strictly extrapolating therefrom, when he was writing these particular stories. In other words, these richly ironical tales can make perfectly decent claims on our attention as examples of oldest but genuine realism. It is therefore appropriately ironical that, when they were finally published as a group, they should have been greeted as, inter alia, "trite tearjerkers." Making love to married women continued to claim Smith's creative attention to some degree even after he had turned his principal energies to writing prose fantasies sometime between the middle and latter 1920s. Why otherwise would he have composed, or completed, such a tale as "Checkmate" in late 1930 when such a type of comparatively realistic fiction had become much less salable for him than the type of prose fantasies that he was creating for and selling to *Weird Tales*, and by then with undoubted popular and artistic success? While it is extremely dubious that he would have gone on to become a major realist of any type—if we may judge at least by such marginal prose—yet Smith's ironic-romantic fiction will probably remain as a fascinating and not unfruitful byroad that marketing circumstances alone caused him to pursue no further than he did.

For permission to quote excerpts from the letters of Clark Ashton Smith to George Sterling, cordial acknowledgement is hereby made to the Henry W. and Albert A. Berg Collection / The New York Public Library / Astor, Lenox and Tilden Foundations. The New York Public

Library is the physical proprietor and custodian of the Sterling-Smith correspondence, together with related MSS. and art-work. For further permission to quote these same excerpts, grateful acknowledgement is likewise made to "CASiana Literary Enterprises," representing the literary Estate of Clark Ashton Smith.

*Note*

1. Additional non-fantastic fiction includes "The Parrot" (1930) and "A Copy of Burns" (1930), both collected in *Strange Shadows*. Both are "ironic" rather than "ironic-romantic" —Ed.